OLIVIA HAYLE

To my parents,
neither of whom will ever be allowed to read my romances, but who
are nonetheless my biggest fans.

1

FREDDIE

I'm sorting through junk mail when my fingers gloss over a thick golden envelope. My address is handwritten on the front in sprawling black letters, but there's no name. Mentally, I run through all my friends who might be getting married… no, no and no.

Golden envelope in hand, I sink onto my kitchen chair and flip it over. It has a black wax seal. Stamped into it is a mask, the kind people wear to fancy masquerades in movies. I've never received anything like this.

If this is junk mail, it's gotten very classy.

Can it be to the previous tenant? I've only lived in this studio for a month. Best to make sure… I tear the envelope open with a kitchen knife and pull out a card-stock invitation with gold, printed lettering.

Dear Rebecca Hartford,

It's a new month, and that means new sins to explore. Join us at the Halycon Hotel at ten p.m. the following Saturday and wear the accompanying mask as proof of invitation.

Don't forget that secrecy is fun, phones are not (no one likes a tattle-

tale), and everyone looks better in lace. Or disrobed. But we're getting ahead of ourselves...

Yours in pleasure,
The Gilded Room

Oh God.

I read the invitation twice to sort through all the innuendos.

The Gilded Room? Everyone looks better disrobed? Rebecca Hartford, you minx!

This might be the most elaborate practical joke I've ever been on the receiving end of. Peering into the envelope, I find a mask lined in delicate black silk, two feathers curling above the cut-out eyes like eyebrows. Black jewels crust the bottom half, and three words are written in gold cursive along the edge. *United in pleasure.*

Okay.

Maybe not a practical joke.

I open my laptop and type the Gilded Room in the search bar. A bunch of newspaper articles have been written about the organization, but not a single one of them features pictures. I click open the one entitled *A night in the elite's world of pleasure.*

What I read makes my eyes widen. The Gilded Room is one of New York's best kept secrets, primarily because those in it don't want to be known. They don't want to be seen, heard, and especially not pictured. The Gilded Room guarantees anonymity to its high-flying members, many of whom pay over twenty thousand dollars for their yearly memberships.

I scroll down, my eyes scanning paragraph after incredible paragraph.

Rules are simple. No one is invited that isn't rich, beautiful, or both. Anyone caught with a phone is immediately expelled... and women have all the power at these parties.

There are whispers of politicians attending Gilded Room parties, football players, billionaires and media tycoons... but if they have, the journalist couldn't find anyone willing to talk. It seems this is the only venue among New York's upper echelons where name-dropping *isn't* the norm.

I close my laptop and stare down at the mask and invitation, now lying on my sofa table. Who had Rebecca Hartford been, to be invited to a party like this? I know for a fact that the previous tenant had left the country, my landlord telling me she'd been offered a job in Hong Kong. Contacting her about this feels out of the question.

What if I go myself?

The idea makes me smile. Secret sex parties for the rich? I'm not rich, nor a partier. I am sex-interested, though. It's been a long time since I last...

What am I thinking? Of course I'm not going.

I toss the invitation and the mask in the paper-basket and the lid closes decisively behind them. Besides, I have things to do, like preparing for the internship of a lifetime. I'd worked too hard to get accepted into Exciteur Global's Junior Professionals program, and my first day as a trainee is on Monday.

I have things to do before then.

Get three new pairs of stockings to go with my professional outfits. Unpack the last of the moving boxes. Schedule a time at the DMV to update my driver's license to New York instead of Pennsylvania.

Attend secret sex party is nowhere on that list.

I make it almost an hour and another moving box unpacked before I fish the invitation and mask back out of the paper-basket. Standing in front of the bathroom mirror, I put on the black, feather-adorned mask.

I look moderately pretty. Thick, dark hair, and more than my fair share of it, thanks to my Italian mother. Quite short, but I like to think I'm just petite. Eyes that are a muddy sort of green. It did say you had to be rich or beautiful to get in...

I tug at my ratty old T-shirt to make a V-shaped neckline.

Courtesy of an unusually large chest, I never wear anything that revealing. But I had just unpacked the black dress I got on sale last year. The one that showed a lot of cleavage... Could I pass for Rebecca Hartford? Or at least beautiful enough to gain admission?

"An adventure before the real one starts on Monday," I tell my masked reflection.

———

I once heard it said that women have three forms of showers. The first, a quick body wash. The second, a quick hair and body wash. The third? That's the date-shower, where things get scrubbed and shaven and deep-conditioned.

As it turns out, I've discovered a fourth shower, the help-I'm-going-to-an-elite-sex-party shower. It has a lot of elements from shower number three, like shaving and scrubbing, but includes a few minutes of panicking on the shower floor.

My mind clings to the words I'd read online, that women have all the power. If I don't like it, I'll leave. The Halycon Hotel is one of the nicest in the city, so it's not like I'm walking into an organized crime syndicate.

At least I tell myself that.

It's nearly ten-thirty when I arrive at the hotel. My high heels click on the floor as I walk to the reception. My invitation and mask are both safe and secure in my clutch, ready to be whipped out in lieu of an ID.

"Good evening, miss," a hotel attendant says. His eyes dip to the deep V of my black dress before returning to my eyes.

And *that's* why I usually wear high necklines.

A flush rises on his neck. "You're here for the private party?"

I tug my coat shut. "Yes."

"The elevator to your left," he says, "and straight up to the thirty-second floor. Have fun, miss."

4

"Thank you." And because I can't resist, I add, "I plan to."

I ride alone in the elevator, my eyes tracking the ever-increasing number of floors on the display. It's become a sure-fire way to keep my fear of heights at bay. Focus on the floors I'm passing and soon enough, it's over. I still breathe a sigh of relief as I step out.

Showtime, Freddie.

I put the mask on and tie the silken strings together, ignoring the way my heart runs amok in my chest with nerves. The scene that awaits me is exceedingly normal. An empty corridor and an open doorway with a pretty, dark-clad woman in front, her face radiating calm professionalism.

She tucks an iPad under her arm. "Welcome, miss."

"Thank you."

"One performance has already concluded, but the next one should be starting just now."

I nod, like I understand what she's referring to. "Terrific, thank you."

She holds her hand out with an expectant look in her eyes. "Right," I say, digging through my clutch to hand her my invitation card. *Don't ask for ID, don't ask for ID...*

But she just looks it over and gives me another smile, this one more friend-to-friend. "Welcome, Miss Hartford. Don't forget to check your phone in on the right, after you enter."

"Of course."

She pushes aside the curtain blocking the door. The contrast is sharp from the bright corridor outside to the dimly lit, smoke-filled rooms beyond. A scent hangs in the air... something thick, like magnolia and incense.

A man dressed only in a pair of black slacks and a tie, no shirt to cover up the broad chest on display, welcomes me. "I'll check your coat, miss."

"Yes, thank you," I say, shrugging out of it. He hangs it up and returns, a hand extended. "Oh! Right." I hand him my phone.

His answering smile makes me think I'm not masking my

nerves as well as I thought. "I'll put your phone right here," he says, opening one of a hundred identical security boxes. "The code is automatically generated, and you'll get a printed receipt with it... here you go. Only you know this. Don't lose it."

"All right," I murmur. "Awesome."

He gives me another encouraging smile, this time tinged with humor. "Enjoy yourself, and remember that we're here at any time if you need help or you have any questions."

"Thank you."

Gripping my clutch tight, I walk into the main space. The first impressions strike me in flashes. White lace and high heels. Drapes of black silk from the ceiling. Men in impeccably fitted suits and dark masks.

People mingle, some standing, some reclining on sofas. A beautiful woman strolls past me in lingerie. It's the imposing kind, with garters and thigh-highs.

"Champagne, miss?" a waiter asks, holding out a tray of flutes. Just like the man working the coat check, he's shirtless.

"Yes, thank you," I murmur. Walking through the throngs of people in a dazed sort of wonder, I think I see people I recognize. It's difficult to tell with the masks, but not impossible, and a few have discarded theirs entirely. One woman is a news anchor and I've seen her on TV dozens of times. A tall, broad-shouldered man has the face of a football player. If I'd been more sports interested, his name would have come to me, but as it is I settle on furtive glances his way. Bottles of champagne with golden labels line an entire wall.

This is wealth like I've never seen it before. It's a rich person's playground, a study in how the wealthy amuse themselves.

Then I see it.

The performance.

There's a raised stage in the middle of the room, and what's taking place on it makes my high school drama club's rendition of *Macbeth* look like child's play. Two lingerie-clad women circle a man on a chair, his hands in cuffs behind him. One runs proprietary nails over the man's sculpted chest, the other sliding her hand up his bare thigh.

My eyes are glued to the scene.

And yet all around me, guests of the Gilded Room continue to mingle in varying states of undress as if three people aren't currently engaged in *very* public foreplay in front of us.

A masked woman in her mid-forties walks past me, pulling a man along behind her by his tie. She shoots me a triumphant look. "The next performance should have pyrotechnics," she says.

I give her a weak smile. "Just what this party needs. Fire."

"I like you!" she calls over her shoulder. "Feel free to join us later!"

Join them, wow. I smile into my champagne and look across the room, hoping to spot more famous people. There is no way my friends will believe me, but I still want to make sure this night turns into the best anecdote possible.

My gaze lingers on a man on the other side of the room. Like most men here, he's in a suit, but he's one of the few not wearing a mask. Not speaking to anyone, either. He just leans against the wall and watches the performance with arms crossed over his chest.

Looks like he's sitting this one out.

I turn in my empty glass of champagne for a full one and lean against the wall opposite him. There's nothing familiar about him, and yet I can't seem to look away.

His gaze snaps to mine, and the laser-focus makes it clear he's well aware of my staring. He raises an eyebrow.

My lips curve into the universal sign of *hi, there.* It's the smile you give a man in a bar to let him know you want him to come over. It's brazen.

A group of guests stop in the middle of the room and it sunders our eye contact. I look down into my champagne with a heart that's suddenly pounding. I'd come here to observe, without any plans of participating…

But a girl can flirt, can't she?

When I see him again, he's no longer alone. A woman runs her hand down his arm in a manner that would be easy to read even if we *weren't* at an elite sex party.

I push off the wall and take a lap of the room. There's a steady, pounding beat emanating from the speakers, heady in its power. More than a few of the mingling guests have moved on from simple conversation, and I pass by a man taking off his partner's bra while discussing New York real estate.

I find a dark corner of the space to retreat to, far away from the couples in varying states of undress. I've never watched other people… well. Perhaps it's time for me to declare this little adventure finished.

That's when he appears by my side, a crystal tumbler in hand.

Brown hair rises over a strong forehead and the square of his jaw covered in two days' worth of stubble. Up close, it's even harder to look away from him.

He raises that eyebrow at me again, but says nothing. He just leans against the wall beside me and we gaze at the crowd in silence.

I take another sip of my champagne to keep my nerves at bay. Who is he? A media mogul? A celebrity I don't recognize? The scion of a political family? For the night, he's a stranger, just like me.

"So?" I ask, watching him through the slitted eyes of my mask. "Are you planning on introducing yourself?"

2

FREDDIE

His lips quirk like I've made a joke. "Eventually," he admits. "Though talking is often one of the less enjoyable pastimes at these events, comparatively speaking."

I wet my lips. "Not if it's done well."

"Which pastime?" he asks, amusement an undercurrent in the rich baritone of his voice. "Doing things well is one of my favorite hobbies."

"Being modest is not, I'm guessing?"

He turns, and I have to look up to meet his dark gaze. "Modesty is forbidden at the Gilded Room."

"Is that in the rulebook?" I ask. "I think I missed that point."

His lips curve into a crooked smile. "I don't think you've read the rulebook at all, considering it's your first time here."

"What makes you think that?"

"You asked me if I was planning on introducing myself."

"And that gave me away?"

His smile widens. "There are only two iron-clad rules at these parties. The first is complete anonymity. The second? Women initiate. Men can't speak unless spoken to."

Oh. Women wield all the power. *Right.*

Groaning, I lean back against the wall. "I gave myself away that easily, did I?"

"Not yet, you haven't," he says, amusement glittering in his eyes. "What are your thoughts so far?"

"Of the Gilded Room?"

He inclines his head in a yes.

I look out over the mingling guests. People are shifting into separate corridors and rooms, and on the stage, one of the women is now—oh. Wow.

She's going down on the man tied to the chair. His head is thrown back in pleasure as hers moves in a practiced rhythm.

"I had no idea what to expect when I came here tonight. Didn't know how… controlled the hedonism would be." I tear my eyes away from the choreographed performance. "I've also come to the sad realization that I probably think I'm more open-minded than I actually am."

He raises an eyebrow, faint crow's-feet fanning out around his eyes. Thirty, perhaps, or thirty-five. No more than a decade older than me. "Not used to seeing other people have sex?"

"Not in person," I admit.

He smiles at my words. "There are no musts here. You could spend your first time just admiring the scenery. Enjoying a few drinks. Making conversation."

My expression of dismay must have been clear, because he raises an eyebrow. "That doesn't interest you?"

"Well, I don't think I like the idea of being a voyeur. It seems intrusive, somehow."

He turns his face, but I catch the smile. "Most people here *enjoy* being watched. A closed door means off-limits, but open ones mean anyone is free to watch or join."

"Another one of the rules I don't know," I say, taking a sip of my champagne. Now that I'm here, now that I'm talking to this man… I'm not nervous anymore. It's like an out-of-body experience, and the Frederica Bilson who should be nervous doesn't even know she's here. I left her out in the corridor.

"There aren't many rules."

"Enlighten me?" I ask. "I'd hate to embarrass myself further."

He smiles, a slow and wide thing that makes my stomach tighten. The dim lighting casts shadows over his face. "It would be my pleasure," he says. "You already know the first one, and the most important one."

"Women initiate conversation?"

"Yes, as well as sex," he says. "Men can suggest it, if they've been spoken to, but it's considered more proper for the woman to speak the words."

I swallow against the dryness in my throat. "The Gilded Room is big on consent, then."

"It is, not to mention security. You won't see them, but there are guards stationed throughout the party."

"There are?"

Slowly, giving me time to react, he reaches over and puts his hands on my shoulders. They're warm and steady as he turns me toward the opposite corner. "The man in the back. Masked, wearing a leather loincloth?"

"*That's* security?"

"Yes. See the earpiece?"

I narrow my eyes. His hands are still on me, hot through the thin fabric of my dress. "No. He's too far away."

"Well, it's there. And you should get your eyesight checked."

"Hey, that's not nice."

His chuckle is hoarse as he turns me toward the bar. "One of the men sitting down, nursing a scotch. He's wearing a suit."

"They drink on the job?"

His hands slip from my shoulders. "It's likely apple juice. No one here wants to *feel* guarded, so they blend in. All part of the illusion."

"The illusion?"

"That we all just happened to be here tonight, that this is a real party, that we're not vetted and screened."

There's truth to that, I suppose. Security guards in uniform would ruin the mood. "So they step in if anyone gets too rowdy?"

"Yes, but that rarely happens. Few pay to get in here only to tempt a lifetime ban." He lifts his crystal tumbler and drinks, the long column of his throat moving.

"You're not wearing a mask. Wasn't that one of the rules?"

He shoots me a look. "Some rules can be broken."

"By the right people?"

He lifts a shoulder in an elegant shrug. Not denying it, not confirming it. A suspicion grows in my mind, and I narrow my eyes at him. "You're not the owner of the Gilded Room, are you? The operator?"

"Christ, no."

"You know a lot about how it works."

"It's not my first party," he counters. A second later and I feel the warmth of his hand on my arm. "Care to sit down?"

He nods to an empty couch nearby, further concealed in shadow. A pounding of nerves explodes beneath my breastbone. His hand falls away. "Women have all the power," he reminds me. "You say the word and I'll leave you alone for the rest of the night."

"What's the word?"

"'Go away' usually works, but that's two words."

I laugh. "I'll stick with that, then. Though it's not very polite."

"You can add please to it, if you like."

"How kind of you." We sink down on the couch, the leather cold under my legs. I cross them and clasp the champagne to my chest like a weapon. "So you're a regular?"

"I suppose you could call me that." He drapes his arm along the back of the couch, hand resting somewhere behind my head. We both look out over the crowd of people. What had seemed so orderly when I first arrived is now broken up, people divided into pairs or smaller groups. And dear God, a woman is completely naked on a couch across the room. Completely, one hundred percent nude. She's draped over a man's lap, his hands on her breasts. Another is working between her splayed legs.

I swallow at the sight. "Performers, too?"

"I doubt it," he murmurs. "They just got inspired."

Perhaps my silence says it all, because he laughs quietly, stretching out long legs in front of him. "I have to say, gorgeous, that you have me curious."

"Curious?"

"Yes. How did a woman like you end up with an invite to the Gilded Room."

I frown. "A woman like me?"

"So clearly strait-laced," he says, meeting my gaze with one of his own. "Someone who loves being in control. Who fears letting go."

"I don't fear letting go."

He raises an eyebrow, and I blow out a breath. "All right, I do, but I'm sure everyone does to some degree. Do you think it's holding me back here tonight?"

"I don't know. Do you think it is?"

"I'm not sure," I say. "So far I'm watching a performance of live sex… well, almost-sex, while having a conversation with a perfect stranger. I'd say I'm letting go already."

His smile flashes. "It's not almost-sex anymore."

I look at the stage and then quickly away, my gaze settling back on his face. His smile widens at my expression. "I'm not shocked," I protest.

"Sure you're not."

"Not strait-laced at all."

"Then look," he challenges.

So I do. I turn full toward the stage, to where one of the women is riding the man handcuffed to the chair. The look of pleasure on his face makes it clear he bears the weight of restraint gladly. The pounding of my blood rises as I watch them, the silky movement of her hips and the glaze in his eyes. The way they revel in us observing them.

"Okay," I murmur. "I get it."

"The appeal?"

"Yes."

His deep laughter rolls over my skin like soft thunder. "Not so opposed to being a voyeur after all."

"I suppose it has its appeals." I wet my lips and drag my gaze from the stage to him. "You know, I think anonymity does too."

"It certainly does," he agrees. "Even if you know someone inside of here, you're not allowed to acknowledge it."

My eyebrows rise. "Let's say I knew your name. I wouldn't be allowed to call you by it?"

"No. Some people do break that, though."

"The couples who come here must."

"They're the worst offenders." He tips his head back and drains the last amber liquid in his glass, a thick watch on his wrist. It looks expensive.

"But you're not here with someone?"

"I'm not," he confirms, reaching past me to set down his glass. The movement brings with it the scent of whiskey and sandalwood. "Nor are you."

"How are you so sure?"

"I doubt a partner of yours would leave you alone this long."

"Well, I doubt I'd have a partner who put so little faith in me that he had to watch me constantly."

His eyes spark. "Oh, that's not what I meant. No, he wouldn't be able to stay away from the trouble you might be getting into."

I glance down into my champagne glass and away from the force of his gaze. "You're good at this."

"At complimenting a woman?" He snorts, but I think it's more at himself than at me. "I try my best."

I tilt my head and observe him. Here in the dark alcove,

with the incense of the party mixing with heady intimacy, it feels like I could ask him anything. "What do *you* usually do at these parties?"

"Searching for inspiration?"

"Perhaps I want to know who I'm dealing with," I murmur.

He leans back on the sofa, pulling his shoulders back. "What happens at these parties doesn't leave them."

"Well, we're at a Gilded Room party," I say. "So talking about past exploits wouldn't break that rule."

His lip curves, an acknowledgment of the loophole. "You know, I keep trying to figure out if you got into the Gilded Room because of your brains or your beauty, and it's damn difficult to decide."

"It has to be one or the other?"

He sweeps an arm at the party. "Most people here pay for membership, men more often than women, after they've been approved by the selection committee. But there are always a few women who don't, and who are granted membership solely from their looks."

"Well, that seems sexist."

He laughs, the hand behind me brushing the bare skin of my shoulder. "So you're not one of those women. You could be, though."

I frown at him, which only makes him grin wider. "So I'm one of the women who could have benefitted from a loophole that is in and of itself pretty sexist?"

"I never claimed my compliments were politically correct."

"No, you didn't." Ignoring the nerves resurfacing, I slip out of my heels and pull my legs up on the sofa. His fingers don't leave my shoulder. "I saw you speaking to a woman earlier. You'd been approached by someone?"

"Several someones," he acknowledges. "But you'd already smiled at me from across the room. I told them I was called for."

The nerves ranch up a notch. "Oh. Was I that intriguing?"

"I'd never seen you here before."

I make my voice teasing. "And you saw someone who looked like she needed guidance? How kind of you to reach out."

"I'm a saint."

"I told you I liked this anonymity thing," I say, "and I do. The idea that we have no idea what the other person does during the days. Perhaps you spent the whole day working as a surgeon at a children's hospital."

He raises an eyebrow. "I wasn't honest when I said I was a saint."

"Then perhaps you spent the whole day evading the New York Police Department, because you're the head of an organized crime ring."

I turn toward him on the couch, and he responds in kind, his free hand landing on my thigh. The touch is casual, but the racing of my heart it sets off isn't. "You think I'm about to make you an offer you can't refuse?"

"You're welcome to try. But it's exciting not knowing, don't you think?"

"It is. Do I have a European princess beside me? A young Hollywood actress? A surgeon who works at a children's hospital?"

"We'll never know."

"A complete mystery," he agrees.

"I like it. Although it does feel odd not to have a name to call you, or even refer to you in my head."

His eyes flash with heated amusement. "There are a ton of things you can call me."

I shift closer, leaning against the back of the sofa. "You know, you came over to talk to me. Even though you weren't allowed to."

He raises an eyebrow. "I did. But I waited for you to speak first." His voice grows deeper, something I should hear from a Jumbotron, narrating a movie, reading me my favorite audiobook. It slides over my skin like a dark caress.

"Despite all the women who approached you. Despite the… fascinating performance currently on display."

His hand slides an inch higher on my thigh, the only place we're touching. A thumb brushes across the hem of my black dress. "Is there a question here somewhere?"

"I'm not sure if I'm ready to ask it."

"I'm perfectly comfortable where I am," he murmurs. "So no need to ask me anything."

"I could rephrase it, actually. So it's more like a hypothetical."

His lips quirk again. "A hypothetical? Sure."

"Considering you approached me, and considering what you usually do at these parties, I—"

"What *you* think I usually do at these parties," he interjects. "I have the feeling a lot of it is conjecture."

"You're telling me you don't participate?"

His smile turns wolfish, an eyebrow raised. "I participate."

Nerves mixed with heady, dizzying want sweep through my stomach. What would his hand feel like higher up my leg? His lips on mine?

Am I brave enough to do this?

"Of course you do," I say. "You're probably in high demand."

He reaches up with a free hand to run it through short, dark hair, thick through his fingers. "I'm rarely complimented by women."

"Do you enjoy it?"

Shaking his head in disbelief, he takes my champagne glass out of my hand and lifts it to his lips. There's amusement in his eyes as he takes a large sip.

"Stealing my drink?"

"I think I need it more than you do."

"I'm that challenging?"

"No," he says, his thumb moving in a circle on my knee. "And yes. This conversation isn't anything like the ones I've had at the Gilded Room before."

"Oh." I narrow my eyes at him. Are they all discussions about sex, then? Although I suppose that's what we're talking about as well, but not very directly.

"I can see you thinking again," he says. "Strait-laced."

I frown. "That can't be the nickname you're giving me."

"Oh? What would you like me to call you?" Seeing my expression, he chuckles again. It's just as dark as the other times. "I'll surprise you, then."

I clear my throat. "I still haven't asked you my hypothetical question."

"You were wondering if I wanted to sleep with you," he says. "And the answer is yes."

My throat goes dry, but I don't look away from his steady gaze on mine. "Oh. Right. Okay."

"I saw you across the room, the way you smiled at me, and I knew I wanted you beneath me."

I wet my lips. "Is this more similar to how your conversations with women usually go here?"

He shakes his head. "No, they're far more clinical."

"Well, I suppose you rarely have to seduce anyone here," I murmur, still reeling from his earlier words. His hand slides higher, settling around the curve of my outer thigh.

"I'm finding it enjoyable."

"So that's what we're doing, then." I trace my finger along the edge of the champagne glass, and his eyes track the movement. "Seducing one another."

"Isn't all conversation a form of seduction?"

"Definitely a mafia boss," I breathe.

His surprised chuckle feels hot against my skin. "You're welcome to think whatever you like about me."

I put a hand on his broad chest and watch it there, my fingers flat against the strength beneath his shirt. He's more tangibly male than the men I usually interact with, as if he's been baked and hardened into steel. If this is what men in their thirties are like, I've been missing out. Or maybe it's just the kind of men who frequent places like the Gilded Room?

"I don't know if I'm daring enough for this," I admit.

His smile is reassuring. "We'll just have to try and see. Another rule of the Gilded Room is that there are no expectations."

I slide my hand up to his neck, tentatively running my fingers across the rough, five-o'clock shadow that coats his square jaw. "There are some things we can try from the comfort of this couch."

"I agree. But let's get rid of this first…" He reaches up slowly, giving me time to object. I don't, holding still as he unties the mask and slips it off my face. "There," he murmurs. "Much better."

We hover, nearly touching, as the sweet sensation of closeness washes over me. My eyes flutter closed as he braves the distance between us and presses his lips to mine. The kiss is competent and warm, and my body reacts to it like a flower to the sun. Heat spreads through my limbs and my mouth opens to him on a soft exhale.

His tongue sweeps across my lower lip, his hand curving around my thigh in a tight grip. My nerves melt away in the face of this, no match at all against his skill, his heat, the way my body warms.

This is the easiest thing in the world.

He lifts his head, just enough to speak. "I don't think kissing will be an issue," he murmurs.

I reply by kissing him again, capturing his answering chuckle against my lips. My hand slides up into his hair, the thick strands silky through my fingers. He growls into my mouth as I tug.

This is a risk worth taking. There's no telling when I'll have a man like this touch me again, a handsome man who exudes power and competence and dark, sly wit.

"I'm not this girl," I tell him.

His hands grip my hips, pulling me tight against him. "I know," he says, voice hoarse. "It only makes me want you more."

The words send delicious shivers over my skin. High on him, on my own bravery, I sling one leg over his lap and straddle him. We might be concealed in this dark alcove, but we're still at a party, and there are people milling about.

His hands run up the sides of my dress, ghosting past my breasts. "Kiss me again, Strait-laced."

"*Not* my nickname," I tell him, and he grins. I cover it with my lips and we're lost once more to the chemistry between us, to whatever magic happens when his lips and mine meet. My desire pounds in tune to the beat of the music, hypnotic and sensual. Beneath me, the hard length of him is evidence of his own. The surprise makes me break away.

He doesn't skip a beat, shifting to my neck instead. A large hand cups my breast and smooths a thumb through the fabric, finding the tight point of my nipple without effort. "I want you," he says, lips against my skin. "Do you want to find an unoccupied room?"

I swallow against the dryness in my throat. "There's still a third performance. I heard there will be pyrotechnics."

"I think," he murmurs, "that we have all the fire we need right here."

3

FREDDIE

His arm is strong around my waist as we walk through the party. We pass the naked woman on the couch kept busy by the two men pleasuring her. She catches me watching and gives me a wide, smug smile. *Look what I caught.*

I lean into the stranger at my side. "Not for you?" he murmurs.

I shake my head. "I think that requires more hedonism than I have in me."

"You know what they say," he says. "Under the right circumstances, anyone will do anything."

"See, it's you saying things like that that chalks you up in the mafia column." Turning the corner to a dark corridor, we pass the open door to a hotel room... only it's not unoccupied. I avert my eyes immediately from the naked bodies writhing on the bed. "Oh my God."

I can make out his smile in the dim lighting. "Not everyone enjoys it like that. A lot of the doors here are closed, after all."

"That's good."

"But this one isn't," he says, stopping at a door that's slightly ajar. The bedroom inside is bland and tastefully decorated. But most importantly? It's empty.

I walk past him into the room. The bed looks massive behind me, decked in innocuous-looking hotel linens. "I wonder what the Gilded Room tell the hotels they rent. Do they know what's going on?"

He has a hand on the half-open door, a wry smile to his lips. "Oh, they know. What do you think, Strait-laced? Door open or closed?"

I sink down onto the bed. "Just us, I think."

He shuts it with a decisive click, but the smile on his face lets me know he hadn't expected another answer. "Absolutely fine by me, gorgeous."

We stare at each other for a few long breaths. No words, just eyes, and with each passing moment the nerves and desire in my stomach grows sharper.

"Do you need to get used to me again?" he asks.

I lean back on my hands and give a simple nod. Lips quirked in wry humor, he shrugs out of his suit jacket and tosses it back. Large hands reach up to undo the buttons of his shirt. I watch as inch after inch of broad, olive-skinned chest comes on display, muscular and smattered with hair.

He stops when the shirt hangs off him. "Keep looking at me like that."

"Not difficult to," I breathe.

His shirt joins the jacket behind him, and my eyes follow the grooves of his abs down to the leather belt. His wide chest rises with every breath. I feel like I've accidentally wandered into one of my deepest, darkest fantasies. Because everything about him, from the dark, commanding eyes to the square jaw and broad shoulders, conveys power. He might not be mafia, but he is *something*, this man, and here he is with me, looking like he can't wait to have me. But waiting he is, because for as much power as he usually commands, in here women are the ones calling the shots.

I've never felt so empowered in my life. The thrill of it runs like a second pulse beneath my skin. "You're too far away," I tell him. "I want to touch you."

"Then touch me."

His words are soft and silky, but the challenge underneath them is unmistakable. I close the distance between us and reach out, my fingers trailing across his chest. He sucks in a breath as I trace the faint V of his hipbones. Strong grooves of muscle move beneath the skin.

"You still haven't asked the question," he murmurs.

My hands come to rest on the leather belt, my eyes finding his. "Will you sleep with me?"

"Not hypothetically?"

I shake my head in mute response.

His answer isn't in words, either. Not as he takes my hair in his hands, the heavy, dark weight of it, and pushes it to the side. I turn for him and he finds the zipper of my dress, pulling it down in one smooth motion. The black sheath releases me from its grasp.

His eyes darken as they travel over my body, my underwear, the matching lace bra and panties. Perhaps I'd told myself I would just watch, not play, but... a small part of me had made sure I'd be ready. Just in case.

"So gorgeous," he murmurs, hands closing around my waist. The competitive streak in me roars to life. I want to rise to this challenge, to him, to please him like I know he'll please me.

I want to be the best sex this man has ever had.

I kiss him with the strength of that conviction, and he responds in kind, pulling me tight against him. One kiss flows into the next, each of them tightening the ache inside. We break apart when his hands find the buckle of my bra.

I hold my arms out as he slides it off, eyes watching as the cups release my breasts. He sucks in a dark breath and reaches out, hands replacing the fabric. They might be a pain when I'm shopping for sports bras, but they know how to dazzle.

"So fucking gorgeous," he repeats and bends to suck a nipple into his mouth. I inhale at the sensation, but it quickly turns into a moan as he adds his teeth. "I've wanted to see these uncovered all night."

"That's why you wanted to talk to me, huh?" My hand tangles in his hair and my eyes close at the sensations. Men never pay enough attention to my nipples, but he does.

I take the moment to undo the buckle of his belt, but he pushes my hands away when I reach for the zipper. "Lie back on the bed," he tells me.

So I do, stretching out on the luxurious linen, and tuck my elbows beneath me to watch as he undoes the zipper. My throat goes dry at the sight.

He's hard and thick in his grip, and bigger than I'd antici-pated. I watch as he strokes himself slowly once, twice, three times. "I'm so hard because of you, Strait-laced," he says. "Have been since you kissed me out there like you wanted me more than your next breath."

Our eyes lock.

I turn, crawling toward the edge of the bed. Pleasure and power and this man all make my head swim, giving rise to confidence I didn't know I had in the bedroom.

He steps closer to the bed, groaning as I take him into my mouth. "Christ," he mutters. "Just like that…"

I give it my all, like this is a sport and I'm aiming for the gold medal. My hand is fisted at the base of him, my tongue swirling over the swollen head. There's so *much* of him, my insides aching at the thought of taking all of him inside.

And he tastes good, like man and desire and need. His hand threads through the length of my hair, a curse escaping him as I hollow my cheeks and suck the length of him into my mouth.

"You," he growls. "I need to taste you."

His hands are on my shoulders, and then I'm flipped over, my legs dragged to the edge of the bed. The dark in his eyes is burning, his gaze on mine one no woman would ever mistake. I don't know if I've ever been looked at like that before.

He grips my panties and gives a single command. "Up."

I raise my hips and watch as he pulls the underwear down my legs and throws them away, discarded, leaving me fully naked with a man whose name I don't even know.

And it's the most empowering thing I've ever done.

There's no hesitation in his sure movements, the way his lips trace my body from my breast to my hipbone. He pushes my legs apart, settling between them like a ravenous man to a meal.

A muffled word against me, one I can barely make out. *Gorgeous.*

But then his lips are otherwise occupied, his tongue and mouth trailing blazing fire across my sensitive skin. I gasp as he adds his fingers, circling and spreading.

He closes his lips over the sensitive bud at the apex and I buck against his head, the touch too much, but he doesn't relent. No, he uses his tongue instead and slides a finger inside of me.

The sweet intrusion is everything. I can't think around his touch, can't form words. Everything centers on him, starts and ends with this man between my legs, dedicating himself to the task like *I'm* the one doing *him* a favor.

The pleasure starts deep inside me, stoked by his tongue. By the time it reaches my limbs it's too late. My orgasm washes over me like a tidal wave. It makes my legs clamp down against his back, my hips rising. He keeps going through it all, his tongue turning languorous and slow.

I'm still blinking up at the ceiling when he slides my legs off his shoulders, his hand lazily stroking between my legs. "Wow," I breathe. "And here I was, planning to rock *your* world."

His low, masculine laughter rolls across my skin like silk. "Feeling you come against my lips just did, Strait-laced."

"I don't think I'm strait-laced anymore."

"Well, you're not wearing anything lacy anymore." He stands at the foot of the bed and pulls me along with him, until I'm lying right by the edge. I watch as he grabs a condom from his back pocket.

"Another rule," he says, biting through the packet. "Condoms on, always."

I swallow at the sight of his length, looking painfully hard. He rolls the condom on in a sure movement. A flash of nerves pass through me. He's big and it's been a while.

Large hands stroke my inner thighs apart. "I think…"

"What, gorgeous?" His thumb brushes over my clit and I shiver.

"We'll have to go slow, I think."

He cups my head in his hands and kisses me deeply, his tongue soft, stroking perfection against mine. My legs relax on their own, the heavy weight of his erection against my thigh. "Slow it is," he tells me. "Trust me, sweetheart."

Sweetheart?

The endearment is so much better than strait-laced, soaking through my defenses. "I do."

"Good." He grips himself, stroking up and down along the seam between my legs. We both watch as he pushes in, a breath escaping through his clenched teeth. The sweet burn of his intrusion is real. I hiss out a gasp, turning my head to the side.

"Look at me," he tells me, gripping my legs so they're flat against his chest.

I do, biting my lip against the feeling of inch after inch filling me up. He goes slow, until the burn of his length morphs into a different kind of fire.

"That's it," he murmurs, buried to the hilt. He closes his eyes. "Fuck, you feel good."

I open my mouth to respond, but my words turn into a gasp as he starts to move. One thrust. Two thrusts. I fist the comforter and try to hold on as he rolls his hips in deep movements.

I don't think I've ever been fucked this deeply before.

"Do you know how good you feel inside me?" I ask him,

reaching up to cup one of my breasts in a hand. His hooded eyes trace the movement, a growl falling from his lips as I flick my own nipple.

Give him the best sex of his life, Freddie, I remind myself. Everything about this man demands that others around him rise to his level, and I'm no different.

His hips slam into mine, and I know the training wheels are off now. "Yes," I moan, arching my back. "Please… give it to me."

His breath hisses out and then I'm half-lifted off the bed, his hands supporting my hips. I gasp at the intensity of the new angle. He's so deep, so deep, and I tell him that.

His answering chuckle is dark with pleasure and pride. "So you'll feel me," he groans. "So you'll remember me."

The idea that I wouldn't is ridiculous, that this won't become a glorified memory in my mind. He looks down at me with eyes hooded with pleasure, my ankles on either side of his face.

He's glorious.

"I can feel every inch of you inside me," I murmur. "Fuck me just like this, don't stop. Please don't stop."

He speeds up, the muscles in his neck straining. He likes dirty talk, then. He does something with his hips, changes the angle… and oh God. It hits a spot inside of me I didn't know I had, pleasure rising like a storm through me once again. This is a man who knows his way around a woman's body.

I'm going to come again.

Closing my eyes, I devolve into a gasping, moaning mess. "Please," I beg him. "I need you, I need this… I'm so close."

His hips speed up until he's hammering into me, the speed too much, the pressure too much. His thumb grazes over my clit and I explode around him.

I'm vaguely aware of moaning, but his voice cuts through all of it.

"Fuck yes, sweetheart, just like that. Just like that." A growl of pleasure from him and I open my eyes, having to see this. His handsome, masculine features are relaxed in plea-sure, hips slamming into me with desperate thrusts. It might be the most erotic thing I've ever seen.

I feel the pulse of his length inside me as he reaches his peak, buried deep inside. My eyes never leave his face as he enjoys the sensations.

I know I'll never forget that expression.

When he opens his eyes, they're swimming with satisfac-tion and pleasure. He turns his head and presses a soft kiss to my ankle. "Your pussy damn near cut off my blood circula-tion when you came around me."

My laughter is wheezy, tired. He lowers my legs to the bed and pulls out of me, disappearing to throw away the condom. Seconds later he stretches out beside me on the bed and I turn to him on instinct, my head on his shoulder. A moment later his arm comes around me.

"I don't think I'm strait-laced anymore," I murmur. "You'll have to think of a new nickname for me now."

He laughs, the sound rumbling through the chest beneath my hand. "I think it'll take more than one night of this to properly undo your laces."

I run my fingernails through the smattering of hair on his chest, wondering how long this'll last. Do we have the room all night? By the hour?

What's the protocol at parties like this? I'm not sure if cuddling on the bed is part of it, but he makes no effort to move, his arm keeping my body tight against his.

And it does feel wonderful, skin against skin, his body warm and firm to the touch.

"It feels very odd not to know your name," I comment, rising up on an elbow.

He raises an eyebrow. "You're not trying to bend a rule here, are you?"

"Me? I'm a rule-follower through and through," I say, resting my head in my hand. "It's just, now I've slept with another man, and I have nothing to refer to him by in my head."

His smile widens into something wickedly thoughtful. He reaches out and drags his fingers through my long hair, the ends tickling my bare breasts.

"Best you've ever had," he suggests. "Lover of the year. A sex god."

"A sex god?"

He gives a faint grimace. "Yeah, not that one."

"You're pretty full of yourself, you know."

He snorts, fingers closing around one of my nipples. He plays with it idly, dark eyes meeting mine. They're bottomless now, the same man I'd sparred with on the couch an hour ago.

Who is this man?

"There's a difference," he says, "between being full of yourself and knowing your worth."

Right. "And your worth is measured in gold?"

A quirk of his lips. "Diamonds, sweetheart."

Groaning, I stretch out next to him. He laughs as he rises up on an elbow, hand smoothing across my stomach. "I'm drifting away from mafia boss."

"Oh?" His hand drifts lower, teasing between my legs with sure fingers. "How so?"

"You fuck like a man who does his own dirty business."

The fingers pause, and an eyebrow quirks. Our eyes meet and lock for a moment that stretches into eternity, into something that's real and scary and tender.

I want to get to know this man.

I know it down to my very toes, despite the artificial nature of this meeting, the no-names clause, the doubtless fact that our lives couldn't be more different.

His lips twitch, the spell broken. "And you're too observant for your own good."

"Is there such a thing?"

And then, pain of all pains, he glances down at the thick

watch on his arm. I recognize the small logo on the watch face.

Yes, definitely different worlds.

"Somewhere you have to be?"

"Unfortunately, yes." His fingers give me a final, lazy stroke, and to my eternal surprise, he bends his head to kiss me once between my legs in farewell.

He reaches for his clothing as I watch, turning onto my stomach. "I was just about to ask you when parties like these end, but you beat me to it."

"I'm more of an instructor than a teacher." He looks at me from a height that is no less than six feet, perhaps six-two, buckling the belt in his pants. "You look fucking fantastic lying like that, by the way."

"Thank you." I rise up on an elbow, knowing my breasts look great like this. The whole purpose of these parties is great, amazing, uncomplicated sex.

Sex that doesn't have strings.

Sex that doesn't come with expectations.

"Will you instruct me on one final point?"

He nods, doing up the buttons to his shirt. "I'm feeling generous."

"Are you allowed to have sex with the same guest at another party?"

"Ah." His grin flashes crookedly. "And this is a hypothetical?"

"Of course."

"It's allowed," he says, and the heat in his eyes makes it clear that I'm not the only one thinking it.

It seems like I'm not done being Rebecca Hartford after all.

Scooping my mask up from the floor, he approaches me on the bed. He's fully dressed now.

"My unmasked beauty," he murmurs, tying the mask back on silken strings around my head. "Fucking you has been the highlight of my month."

"How quaint," I say. "It was only the highlight of my week."

He barks out a surprised laugh, his fingers beneath my chin. He lifts my face to his and gives me a final, lingering kiss, one that speaks not of goodbyes but of unspoken promises. "See you around, Strait-laced."

I stop him when he has one hand on the door, my words rushing out of me. "Tell me one true thing about you."

He pauses, his gaze traveling across my nude body with unmistakable admiration. "If you hadn't spoken to me tonight, I would have broken the rules and done so first," he says. He gives me a crooked grin and shuts the door behind him.

4

FREDDIE

My first day at Exciteur Consulting starts with a presentation that is at least fifteen minutes too long. I glance left and right to my fellow Junior Professionals, the company's fancy euphemism for *paid trainee*, and see them diligently taking notes.

So I resume taking my own.

Exciteur Consulting recruits three trainees for this one-year program every year, one of the most prestigious in the industry. Exciteur Consulting might not be a household name, but they're *everywhere*. Advising a large medical company on advertising? Exciteur Consulting. Hired to oversee the strategic overhaul of a failing conglomerate? Exciteur Consulting. Come an alien invasion or the apocalypse, I have no doubt they'd be hired on the spot for their crisis management expertise.

The presentation wraps up with a flourish, and we're sent off to our different departments. The woman who calls my name is blonde, short-haired, and in her mid-forties. "Frederica Bilson?"

"Yes."

"You're with me."

I grab my handbag and notepad, following her neat steps through a glass-covered hallway.

"Eleanor Rose," she informs me over her shoulder. "I'll be your supervisor while you're working with us in the Strategy Department."

"A pleasure to meet you."

"Yes, I'm sure." She punches in the code to a door, and we step into a lobby with elevators. "Strategy is on floor eighteen. We're a closed loop system, Miss Bilson. We advise management and all the different consulting teams, but we never talk to outsiders."

"Got it."

"And because I know how people talk, I want to ensure you hear it from me first. You were not my first choice for this position, but I've read your resume, and believe you'll do well here."

Ouch.

But I have no doubt that I will either, regardless of her preferences. I'd gone through three rounds of interviews to be hired here and I'd nailed every last one. So I meet her brisk, businesslike tone with one of my own. "I understand, and I appreciate your honesty."

There's approval in her gaze. "I figured you would. I'll introduce you to the team and your workspace, and set you up with your first task."

"I'm ready," I say and mean it, practically chomping at the bit. From my straightened hair to the heels I'd worn inside my apartment for a week to break in, I've never been this prepared in my life.

Eleanor leads me through a second set of doors, using her key card to get in. "You'll get yours by the end of the day."

"Excellent."

She pauses with a hand on a divider, looking over a spacious office landscape with a handful of desks. Individual glass offices line the back wall. "This is your home for the coming twelve months. The Corporate Strategy division."

"Home sweet home," I say.

Snorting, she leads me to an empty desk, throwing out names as we pass. "That's Toby, you'll work closely with him. Here's Quentin, he's in charge of strategic implementation."

Quentin gives me a sour nod and turns back to his computer. "Another fresh-faced MBA," he comments. It's clear it's not a compliment.

"Exciteur only hires the best," I quip back.

Both Eleanor and Toby chuckle at that. "Here's your password," she tells me. "Get settled in, get acquainted with your computer, and I'll be back to give you your first assignment in an hour."

And that's it.

I sink into my new office chair and watch as she retreats to an office in the corner, the glass door shutting behind her.

"The ice queen," Toby says beside me. I jump at his sudden nearness and he rolls back, a sheepish smile on his lips. "Sorry," he says, reaching up to adjust bright-orange glasses. "Unlike Eleanor, scaring you wasn't my intention."

"She meant to scare me?"

"Intimidation is the name of the game on first days around here." He shrugs, unfazed. "Quentin and I aren't like that, though."

"Don't bring me into this," Quentin retorts. With his ill-fitting suit and mop of ink-black hair, he reminds me of a certain perpetually sad donkey in a children's cartoon.

Toby rolls his eyes. "He'll warm up."

"I won't," Quentin says.

"You always do," Toby responds. "Don't fight the inevitable. Anyway, welcome! What's your name?"

I extend my hand. "Freddie."

"Freddie?"

"Short for Frederica, but I never go by that."

"Freddie it is," he confirms, leaning back in his chair. A slim build, a shirt that's designer, and an eager smile. "You can't imagine how happy I am to get a new deskmate."

"Was the last one bad?"

"He wasn't *bad*, exactly, he just…"

"Kept stealing your pens," Quentin says. "I told you to tell him off about it, Toby."

My new deskmate shrugs. "Anyway, he's gone now, and you're here. Exciteur's shiny new acquisition."

I chuckle, crossing my legs. "Acquisition?"

"The company is aiming high. Every new hire is highly educated, young and hungry." Toby winks at me. "Just like you and me."

"All thanks to our new fearless leader," Quentin mutters.

I type my password into the sleek new computer I get to call mine. "New fearless leader?"

"Oh, this is too good. Quentin, we have to give her all the details."

"I'm not paid to gossip," is his response.

Toby rolls his eyes and turns to me. "About a year ago Exciteur was purchased by a group of venture capitalists, Acture Capital."

I nod. "I've read about this."

"Right. Well, they put one of their own in charge of the company. I'm not saying the next bit to gossip, by the way. But we're in Strategy, and that means we interact a lot with upper management."

"Right." It was one of the reasons I'd wanted this department.

"Well, the new CEO has… high standards."

"He's a demanding asshole," Quentin adds, finally turning around in his office chair.

Toby looks over his shoulder, but the office landscape is unchanged.

Quentin snorts. "He's not here. He's *never* here."

"That's not true. I saw him speaking to Eleanor in her office once."

"No, you didn't."

Toby shakes his head. "I don't know why you don't believe me about that. He has been here, at least once."

"I believe you *think* you saw him speaking to Eleanor in her office once."

"Why would that be so unthinkable?" I ask. I know the new leadership by name from my research, but I had no idea they were such characters. Clearly I have more to learn.

"He wouldn't come down here in person," Quentin tells me. "He'd send one of his minions, and they'd summon us to the thirty-fourth floor."

"Just so I'm clear, we're talking about Tristan Conway here?"

Toby glances over his shoulder again and Quentin shakes his head at the paranoia. "The very one, in all his venture capitalist glory. Since they bought Exciteur, he's been slashing unprofitable departments and promoting others. There's been a lot of personnel turnover."

I nod, leaning back in my chair. "And we meet him in meetings a lot?"

"No," Quentin says.

"We don't *meet* Tristan Conway," Toby continues, his arms moving as he gesticulates. "We get orders *by* Tristan Conway and the COO or the department head."

"We don't talk to him, we don't look at him, we don't exist to him," Quentin continues.

I can't help smiling. "Is this a hazing thing? Are you exacerbating this for shock value? Because you can consider me shocked."

Toby chuckles. "I like your attitude, Freddie, but we're not."

"Dead serious," Quentin adds.

"All right, noted. I'll stay well clear of him." Silently, I vow never to *not look at him*, though. That sounds like more respect than a CEO should be awarded. He's not royalty.

Toby turns to Quentin. "Did you see the Thanksgiving email they sent out?"

The other man snorts. "Yes. Pathetic."

"What email?"

"Management is planning a Thanksgiving lunch for the company next month."

"The entire company?"

"New York office," he clarifies. "Headquarters. Anyway, apparently management *itself* will be the ones to serve the food, as a gesture of thanks for all of our hard work."

Quentin snorts. "I can't wait to see Clive Wheeler or Tristan Conway serving mashed potatoes to two hundred and fifty people."

"That sounds like a terrible idea," I agree, opening the email software on my computer. There's a pre-registered email address waiting for me.

f.bilson@exciteur.com.

The words make me smile. My name, next to Exciteur, the company that's cutting-edge right now. I'd fought with over ten of my old classmates from Wharton to get this spot, not to mention all the other applicants.

I play around with it for a bit, changing the pre-written sign-off phrase that gets added to the bottom of every email. *Frederica Bilson, Junior Professional Trainee, Strategy Department.*

Smiling, I change Frederica to Freddie. No one in this world calls me Frederica, with the exception of my grandparents, but to the best of my knowledge neither one of them works at Exciteur.

Over the coming hours, Toby shows me the ropes, and even Quentin helps out. They introduce me to the projects we're working on and it doesn't take me long to learn that the two of them work great together, despite their banter. Or perhaps because of it?

I'm sure I'll find out.

Eleanor shows me around and briefs me on the first of several projects I'm to assist on. When I fall back into my office chair that afternoon, my inbox is filled to the brim with emails.

Most of them are automated and company-wide. Others are from Quentin, Toby or Eleanor, all with "Good to know" or "Information for you to read through" in the subject line.

That's my evening reading sorted for tonight.

My gaze snags on a corporate send-out, an email titled "A Thank You to the Troops." It's sent from t.conway@exciteur.com, the devil CEO himself, apparently.

My smile widens as I read through the letter. It's classic corporate fluff, probably not even something he wrote himself, thanking all employees for their hard work. *Under my leadership, the company has doubled its profits.* A humble brag there, Mr. Conway.

Grinning, I scan through to the last paragraph. *Don't forget to pencil in the Thanksgiving lunch next month, the company's treat for all the hard work and long hours you've put in. I know you won't want to miss it.*

I see my chance to get in with Toby and Quentin's banter. There's nothing like a well-timed jab at upper management to become one with co-workers, the lot of you in the trenches together.

So I hit forward and write a snarky comment.

Do you think management genuinely believes everyone has marked a giant, excited X on their calendar for the Thanksgiving lunch? Perhaps he should serve a side of humility with the mash...

A few minutes later, I peer around my desk to Toby's, but he's focused on his work and not responding. I can wait. An hour later, Quentin rises from his desk and announces he's going home. Eleanor soon does the same, telling me to leave.

Toby gives me a yawn. "Come on, Freddie. Everything will still be here tomorrow."

There's no acknowledgment of my snarky email. Ice-cold dread punches me in the stomach. "Just give me a minute, and we can walk out together."

I open the sent folder in my email and scroll down. Perhaps it had just not delivered? No, it had…

Then I see it.

The letter hasn't been delivered to Toby, because I hadn't forwarded it. No, I'd accidentally hit reply. On the recipient line is an email address that hurts to look at.

t.conway@exciteur.com

5

TRISTAN

The bastard that invented email should be hung and quartered, I decide, staring at the shiny icons on my screen. I have a secretary who sorts through my mailbox, marking the important emails as unread for me to take a look at. She's good at what she does.

But there's still one hundred and sixty three waiting for me?

At this rate, I'll need another espresso before it's nine o'clock. I'd only had half of my first, at any rate. Joshua had knocked it out of my hand as he reached across me for another croissant.

Yes, my kid eats croissants now. I don't know when he became so fancy, but he woke up one day and asked if we could switch from New York bagels to croissants, pronounced damn near perfectly. It took me two days to learn about a new girl in his class, recently moved here with her family from Paris. Her name is Danielle and my son had overheard her asking if the school cafeteria had croissants one day.

So now I'm stuck eating the flaky things every morning with my kid before I'm attacked en masse by tiny, electronic messages. For a consulting firm, most people at Exciteur

Global aren't particularly good at consulting their own judgement before emailing.

So I work my way through the list, replying as I go. *No. Yes. Schedule the meeting. I'll call you tomorrow.*

I'm frowning as I open one from f.bilson@exciteur.com. It's not an address I recognize.

RE: A Thank You to the Troops

Do you think management genuinely believes everyone has marked a giant, excited X on their calendar for the Thanksgiving lunch? Perhaps he should serve a side of humility with the mash...

Sincerely,

Freddie Bilson
Junior Professionals Trainee,
Strategy Department

My eyes re-read the letter once. Twice. Serve a side of humility?

Despite the insolence of the words, the turn of phrase makes me snort. This fucker thinks he knows better than me, does he? My hand hovers over the *forward* button, ready to let HR know what type of person we've hired as part of the yearly trainee program. Mr. Bilson would be let go on the spot.

But if I do, I'd be fulfilling the very reputation I'm trying to work against. The first months at this company, I'd had to slash things that weren't working and return to the core of what Exciteur does best. The previous leadership had lost its footing, and I'd had to course correct. But I'm well aware that a lot of people at the company don't see it that way.

I can't fire this young man for being insolent. Not even for being so incompetent as to not know the difference between the forward and reply button. Doesn't mean I can't teach him a lesson, though.

Hitting reply, I type a sarcastic response that should send him shaking in his newly bought Oxford shoes.

RE: A Thank You to the Troops

Freddie,

What a pleasure to hear directly from one of the most inexperienced members of our company. A person with as spirited opinions as yours is naturally inclined to share them, so please tell me what, besides humility, you'd like served with your mash?

Tristan Conway
CEO of Exciteur Global

Then I hit send and lean back in my chair, imagining the terror that just crept up my newest employee's spine as he saw my name in his inbox, realizing his mistake. He hadn't sent the commentary to a friend in the company.

I doubt I'll get a response. No, somewhere further down in the building, a brain is firing on all cylinders. *Will I be fired? Will I be reprimanded?*

And he'll never make the same mistake again. Shaking my head, I dive back into the pile of emails. They need to be finished before my daily meetings start.

But he responds—an hour later, the email is there, winking at me from the top of my email inbox.

RE: A Thank You to the Troops

Mr. Conway,

Thank you for your quick reply. While I may be a person of spirited opinions, I recognize that I don't have the experience you do, just as you pointed out. I think I've given all the unsolicited advice I should, at least for the time being.

Sincerely,

Freddie Bilson,
Junior Professionals Trainee,
Strategy Department

I stare at the email for a few seconds. He actually replied, and it wasn't in apology or abject fear. Despite myself, I have a begrudging respect for the arrogant trainee. I'd expected him to go silent and not toe-to-toe with me like this. Very few at this company consider telling me what they genuinely think, at least not to my face.

I don't have time to indulge in this, and Freddie is probably like all the other young guys Exciteur hires. They're a dime a dozen, the newly minted MBAs who think they've made it big for scoring a trainee position here, when in reality they know absolutely nothing and are on the bottom rung of the ladder.

My instinct is to dig down deeper into this one, though. Much as it pains me to admit, perhaps he'd been on to something with his first email.

RE: A Thank You to the Troops

Freddie,

A wise course of action, if I wasn't specifically asking you for your advice now. You seem to be under the impression that my employees are anything but excited about the Thanksgiving lunch. Tell me why you believe that.

Tristan Conway
CEO of Exciteur Global

I hit send and wonder if I'm being a heartless bastard, forcing it out of him. A nicer person would make it clear that he won't face any repercussions for speaking his mind. But I don't have the time to coddle employees, and he's the one who emailed me, mistake or not.

I forget all about Freddie Bilson for the coming hours. There are too many fires to put out and not enough time.

Never enough time.

My mind drifts back to the past weekend, finding the contours of that Saturday night effortlessly. A Gilded Room party had never been this difficult to move on from before. The image of her dark hair unbound around narrow shoulders, the tight black dress and beckoning curves beneath, feels seared into my brain.

I close my eyes and see her naked in front of me, stretched out on the hotel bed. All the curves I'd touched, the crook of her neck, the ample breasts. The way she'd moaned without artifice or pretense.

Not to mention the way she'd looked while we'd talked. The confidence in her eyes, so at odds with the sudden bursts of nerves or shyness. Guests to the Gilded Room change often, and rare are the times I've slept with the same guest twice. But she better be at the next party.

And she better be looking for me, too.

Leaving her after only a few hours together had been a hard call. But I never stayed long at those parties, not when Joshua was at home with the sitter. I know he adores her and doesn't miss me at all... but I can't justify being away from home longer than necessary.

But it had been a close call with her.

Running a hand over my face in frustration, I re-open my email server. In the hours since I've last dealt with it, don't you know, it's grown again?

I swear, they breed in my inbox.

And wouldn't you know, there's one from Freddie Bilson waiting there for me.

RE: A Thank You to the Troops

Mr. Conway,

I am a new hire at your company, but I'll give my best assessment of the situation, just as you asked. Your employees appear to be either intimidated or outright afraid of you. Whether this is due to your managerial style or your track record, I can't say.

Management's plan for a Thanksgiving lunch in the break room as a thank-you doesn't seem to resonate with the staff, although I'll admit I've only interacted with a limited sample. Perhaps they'd prefer a day off or a bonus, if the aim is truly to reward them for a year of hard work and anxiety?

That's my solicited advice, Mr. Conway, based on less than twenty-four hours' work experience at your company. I look forward to deepening my understanding of Exciteur and being of further use to the company. You won't hear unsolicited advice from me again.

Best,

Freddie Bilson,
Junior Professionals Trainee,
Strategy Department

I lean back in the chair, crossing my arms over my chest. Well, he has balls, I'll give him that. He'd responded to what

I'd asked of him, short and concise, without unnecessary niceties and platitudes.

Except the last two sentences, that is. I recognized a blatant appeal to be allowed to stay when I heard one.

But I'm not planning on firing Freddie. What he said about the company's employees rings true, even if I hadn't wanted to admit it to myself. The last year has been brutal to many of the people who still work in this building. They'd seen co-workers laid off and positions re-shuffled. A lot had been sacrificed on the altar of ever-increasing profit margins. I know they're intimidated and afraid.

I grin as I realize exactly what to do, reaching for my phone and dialing the familiar extension to Clive, the COO. Freddie is a trainee in Strategy, after all. If he wants to contribute to Exciteur... perhaps we'll put him in charge of Thanksgiving.

6

FREDDIE

It's been four days since the fiasco with a capital F. I think that's what I'll always remember it as. "The Fiasco," when I, Frederica Bilson, underestimated how easy it is to mix up the act of forwarding and replying to an email.

Every email I've sent since is triple- and quadruple-checked to ensure it reaches the right recipient. Toby had seen me do it once and laughed, calling me neurotic.

I hadn't told my co-workers about The Fiasco, but at any moment, I expected Eleanor to come out of the glass box that doubled as her office and inform me my internship was over. That it came from the very highest authority.

But she hadn't, and I haven't heard back from Tristan Conway either, not since I responded to the last email. This gives me two possible outcomes. One, I'd pulled off the right amount of insolence and contriteness to earn his respect. Or two, he's preparing to fire me and just hasn't gotten around to it yet.

Each passing hour I leaned more toward option one, but it didn't stop me from anxiously refreshing my emails. This week had been altogether too exciting for me already. New job. Accidentally email my boss's boss's boss with an insult.

Sleep with the most magnetic man I'd ever met. All of it in the span of less than seven days.

Really, that should earn me some sort of medal.

"Uh-oh," Toby murmurs at his desk. "Someone's on the war-path."

Both Quentin and I look up to see Eleanor advance on us, her heels clicking with professional ease on the floor.

"Freddie," she says. Quentin and Toby turn back to their work, and my stomach drops out beneath me. This is it.

"Yes?"

"I just got a call from management. They're pulling together all of the Junior Professionals for some cross-department project." She blows out a breath. "And it's still your first week. I tried explaining that you needed to settle into your department first, but they were adamant."

I clear my throat. "And this came from management?"

"Yes. They didn't tell me anything else." The look in her eyes makes it clear she considers this an oversight on their part.

"Where do you want me?"

"You're to go to conference room six on the thirty-fourth floor."

Thirty-fourth floor is the top floor. The management floor. The one where Quentin and Toby warned me we go for project descriptions, where we don't speak, talk or *look* at management.

"Right away?"

"Right away," she confirms. "I'd join you, but it seems like it's trainees only."

I grab my notepad, my handbag, and push my chair back. "I'll head up now, then. Thanks for letting me know."

"Of course," Eleanor says. "Let me know what it's all about when you return."

"Will do."

Toby shoots me a thumbs-up and a *good luck* as I walk toward the elevators. I give him a confident grin, ignoring the doomsday look in Quentin's eyes. I'm also ignoring the pit of nerves in my stomach, put there by words like *management.*

Will I come face to face with Tristan Conway?

I smooth my hands over my pencil skirt and fight the familiar nerves that comes with riding elevators, courtesy of my fear of heights. The mirror confirms what I already know. Hair in a neat, low ponytail. Simple makeup. Navy pencil skirt and lavender-colored blouse. Dress to impress, my mother always likes to say.

I stop outside of conference room six with my shoulders straight, ready for battle, and knock.

"Come on in." A man's voice.

I step inside the brightly lit space. On one end of a table is a man in his mid-forties, hair lightly graying at his temples, glasses on his nose.

"Hello, Ms...." he looks down at his list. "Frederica Bilson?"

"That's me."

"My name is Clive Wheeler and I'm the Chief Operating Officer at Exciteur. We're expecting your two colleagues here as well, and then I'll brief you all. It shouldn't take long." He glances down at his paper and mutters, "At least I hope not."

I take a seat on the other side of the table and make my voice professional. "Sounds great. This is for a cross-depart-mental project? My supervisor wasn't fully briefed."

"Yes, of a sorts. It was the CEO's idea, really." He's not saying it, but it's there in the pitch of his voice. He hadn't approved.

The pit of nerves in my stomach grows. "Sounds interesting."

"*Interesting* is the right way to describe it," he agrees, looking down at his phone. "'Create some holiday spirit.' Those were his exact words."

Shit. Holiday spirit?

The odds of this being about Thanksgiving and my emails spikes dramatically. The door by Clive opens and I turn my gaze to the notebook. If it's Tristan Conway, I'm not ready yet. Not if he'd really called a meeting about Thanksgiving and invited the trainees.

"I'll handle this meeting, Clive." The voice is smooth and dark, a baritone as suited to dark alcoves in parties as it is to boardrooms.

It's familiar.

"Are you sure?"

"Yes. It was my idea, after all."

I keep my eyes on the notebook. *It can't be.*

"Can't say I'm disappointed," Clive admits.

Glancing up, I catch sight of the COO disappearing out the adjoining door, leaving me alone with the man leaning against the opposite wall. He's tall and suit-clad, arms crossed over a broad chest.

But it's his eyes my gaze locks on.

Eyes I'd seen laugh and challenge me just a few days ago. Eyes I'd seen closed in pleasure. My anonymous stranger. The dark mafia boss.

The slight widening of his eyes is the only sign of surprise. "What are *you* doing here?"

My hand tightens into a fist on the table. If my stomach was a ball of nerves before, it's detonated into butterflies now. "I'm one of the junior professionals here. I was called up for a meeting."

"Impossible."

I shake my head. "I started this past Monday."

He braces his hands on the conference table, the room shrinking with his presence. He's just as striking under the bright light of day, when there's no denying the squareness of his jaw or the high cheekbones.

"The three trainees are all male," he tells me.

Hold up, handsome. "No, they're not."

"Who are you?"

"I'm Freddie."

He shakes his head. "Freddie is a man."

"Well, I'm not."

"Clearly," he mutters.

"Freddie is short for Frederica," I say. "Frederica Bilson."

He blows out a frustrated breath, leaning back from the table. "Why are you here? *How* are you here?"

I frown at him and find a sliver of courage amidst the confusion. "What do you mean? I applied for this job six months ago. I sat through interviews and tests. I was chosen and hired, and I started this week." There's suspicion in his gaze, barely concealed. It rankles something in me. "Why? Do you think I targeted you this past weekend?"

The brief pause makes it clear that he'd been suspecting just that.

I clasp my hands together on the table to keep them from trembling. "Well, I didn't. I had no idea who you were."

He raises an eyebrow, but I stare right back at him, still unable to believe it's actually him. Sitting here in front of me.

"Fine," he grinds out. "I suppose we could find a different department for you. Perhaps another of Exciteur Global's offices."

Meeting his gaze is the difficult part. I shake my head and look somewhere over his, ignoring the eyes that had so capti-vated me last weekend. "I've done nothing wrong, and I *chose* the Strategy Department. It's not fair for me to be relocated because of something that happened outside of work, not to mention before my employment began." I clear my throat and force myself to add, "With all due respect, sir. Because you are Tristan Conway?"

"Last time I checked, yes." He crosses his arms over his chest. "Fine. You'll stay, *Freddie.*"

"Excellent, and I won't say a word of what happened last weekend," I say. "I remember your instructions. Anonymity was rule number one, and I'll keep it."

Oh, saying that was a mistake.

Staring into his dark eyes, watching the memory rise and burn in them... it sparks the same in me. I shouldn't have brought words like *past weekend* and *instructions* into this conference room. The memory grows between us until it scalds my cheeks and forces me to look away.

"I'd appreciate it if you don't," he says finally.

"Great," I say. "And for the record… I didn't mean to send you that email."

He raises an eyebrow. "I figured."

"It won't happen again."

"Learned the difference between replying and forwarding?"

My blush burns. "I have, Mr. Conway."

A tense few seconds of silence pass, neither of us looking away. I'm the one who breaks first. "The other trainees should be here soon."

He nods. "In a few minutes. I gave instructions that *Freddie* should be the first one here."

The way he says my name makes it clear he hasn't forgiven me for the sin of not being a man. I want to roll my eyes at him, but the difference in power between us stops me. We're not strangers in the darkness anymore.

We never will be again.

Any faint hope I'd had that I'd receive another wrongly delivered invitation, that I'd sneak away to a party and meet him… it dies and withers in my chest.

"You asked for me to be here so you could tell me off?"

"Something along those lines." He pulls out one of the chairs and sits, stretching long legs out in front of him. The thick watch glitters at his wrist, the same one I'd felt against my skin as he ran his hands over me.

I swallow. "Go ahead, then. I'm ready."

His lips quirk in unexpected humor, fingers tapping against the table. "Well, since you disagreed with just about everything the company had planned for next month, I'm putting the trainees in charge of Exciteur's Thanksgiving celebration."

I stare at him.

He stares right back at me.

"I beg your pardon?"

"The three of you," he says, voice smooth, "will get a chance to practice your project management skills. You're to pitch your ideas to me and the event organizers. Consider us, consider *me*, a client. As the Strategy trainee, you'll naturally be the team leader."

"Naturally," I murmur.

"You'll report back to management in a week with your suggestions for how we should show some Thanksgiving appreciation to the employees. I want timelines, projected outcomes, budgets." His grin is wicked, the same one that had sent shivers over my skin just a few days ago. "You clearly think you know better than me, Freddie, and I know you like a challenge."

The bastard.

He stares at me like he's daring me to object, like he knows he's being tough, but letting me know he won't back down just because of last weekend. Nor should he. Then was then, and now is now, and I don't want Tristan Conway's special treatment.

I pitch my voice to professional curtness. "Thank you for this opportunity, Mr. Conway. I won't disappoint."

He raises an eyebrow. "I'm sure you won't, Miss Bilson."

7

TRISTAN

What are the odds?

Very fucking low, that's what. Not once had I met anyone at the Gilded Room at work, and only a few times had I done so in a private setting. But Frederica Bilson is my company's trainee, so off-limits she's practically wearing a neon traffic cone on her head. The perfect memory of Saturday night is tarnished forever now, knowing she's met *me,* the real me. And I'm not a mafia boss.

I lean back in my chair and press the heels of my hands against my eyes. The insolent young trainee writing those emails had been Strait-laced.

I can't get the two images of her to merge into one in my head.

The dark-haired vixen, coy and seductive on Saturday.

The proper, pencil-skirted young woman meeting my gaze across the conference table.

The whole point of going to the Gilded Room is to provide anonymity—to ensure I stay in control. I'd erected a ten-foot concrete fucking wall between my private and my professional life, and somehow she'd managed to claw her away across like a beautiful but deadly weed.

And of course she's in Strategy of all departments, the one

place I'm convinced is bleeding information to our competitors. Our business moves had been anticipated by other consulting firms too often for it to simply be a coincidence. I'd been keeping a close eye on the department for the past month… and now my view will involve a woman I know the taste of but who I can't go back to for seconds.

The phone on my desk buzzes, and I press down on the speaker button. "Yes?"

"Your son's school is on the line, Mr. Conway."

St. John's Prep is always calling me, and it's only about my son every third time. The others? Do you want to donate to the school bazaar? Chaperone a trip to the Bronx Zoo? Join in on the bake sale? It's as time-wasting as it is guilt-inducing.

"Put them through."

Static crackles, and then a professional voice on the other line. "Mr. Conway?"

"I'm here. Is Joshua all right?"

"He is, but he says he has a stomachache and wants to go home." Her tone of voice is apologetic. "He didn't want us to call you, sir."

I'm already reaching for my cell. "I'll be there in ten minutes."

"Oh, that's perfect. We'll be waiting for you."

I hang up and close down my work laptop, slipping it into my briefcase. Joshua rarely has stomachaches, and he never wants to go home from school early. A thousand different scenarios spin through my head. Had I forgotten something? A doctor's appointment, the anniversary of his mother's death… no and no.

I stop by my secretary's desk. She looks up from her screen, her face snapping into the professional mask she always wears. "We need to clear my afternoon," I say, "and move any meetings from three p.m. to telephone meetings instead. I'll be working from home."

She's already tapping away at the keyboard. "Of course, sir. Everything all right with Joshua?"

Cecilia knows everything about everything, and has since I took over Exciteur. She's invaluable. "Yes," I reply, already heading to the elevators. "See you tomorrow."

I find myself tapping my foot against the steel floor the entire way down, and I know I won't be able let go of my worry until I arrive at St. John's. Ryan stops the car in the drop-off zone and I shoot out of the car, striding up the stairs to the old brick building.

Joshua, Joshua, where are you...

He's waiting with Mrs. Kim inside the school's main doors, sitting on a bench and kicking his legs out in front of him. He shoots me a sheepish look under a head of dark curls.

"Thank you for coming," Mrs. Kim tells me. "I'm sorry about calling you during your working hours, but I'm afraid Joshua was really in pain."

He hunches over at her words, an arm curling around his stomach.

"You made the right call," I say. "Thanks for letting me know."

Her exhale is one of relief. Had she been worried I'd be angry? Perhaps I hadn't hidden my annoyance at the bake sale calls as well as I thought I had.

Joshua and I head out of school, and I reach out to run a hand through his hair.

"Hey, Dad."

"Hey, kid. A stomachache, huh?"

"Yes."

Hmm. "Is it too bad for ice cream in the park on the way home?"

He looks up at me, eyes serious behind his glasses. "I think ice cream might make it better."

I press my lips together to keep from smiling. "Then ice cream it is, kiddo."

Joshua leaves his backpack in the car and Ryan takes off, back to the apartment. We walk home instead, side by side and hands in our pockets. The tall oak trees of Central Park beckon at the end of the street. An oasis in this world of stone.

"Did you have Math and English this morning?"

He nods. The lapels of his uniform shirt are askew and I reach over and correct them for him, ignoring his huff of irritation. "And? How did it go?"

"Math was fine. English was fine, too. We had to recite a poem and then tell the class what we thought it meant."

My eyebrows rise. "One you wrote yourself?"

"No, from a book." His voice darkens. "We got one each and then we had to stand by our desks and read them out loud."

"How did it go?"

"All right, I guess. I got an easy one."

So that's not what he got a stomachache from, then. We enter the park and both watch as a dog runs in front of us, its leash trailing behind it on the darkened grass. A teenage boy comes running after it.

"See?" I say. "That's why we don't have a dog."

"I would hold on to the leash," Joshua protests. "And we don't have to get a big dog."

"We're not a small-dog family."

"We're a no-dog family," he mutters. "I'm getting strawberry."

"Good choice. I think I'll get mango."

He groans. "You always get mango."

"It's my favorite, kid." I run my hand through his thick head of curls again. He'll never get me to stop doing that, not even when he's as tall as me. His mother had those exact curls.

"If it's not broken, don't fix it," he quotes with a sigh. It's one of my favorite sayings.

"Exactly. Besides, you like mango, too."

"Yeah, but not *all* the time."

"I'm old and set in my ways."

"You're not *that* old," he frowns. "Mike's dad is in his fifties!"

I snort. At thirty-four, I suppose it's nice that my kid doesn't consider me *that* old. But at nine, I guess all adults are old. "Well, people have children at different ages."

"Or they *get* children at different ages, like you got me."

"Exactly like that, yes."

He doesn't sound upset about it. For Joshua, his parents' deaths aren't something he remembers. He only knows of my sister and her husband's airplane crash in the Rocky Mountains from what he's been told, even if he'd been alive in those terrible days when rescue teams searched after the chartered airplane. He'd been two years old.

I'd signed Joshua's adoption papers six days after his parents had been officially declared dead.

We stop by the ice cream stand on the east side of Central Park. It's only a stone's throw from our apartment, and it's a place we frequent. Some might call us regulars. Like Larry, for example.

"My regulars!" he calls, seeing us approach. "And look at you, handsome man. In a uniform like your dad."

Joshua looks up at Larry in the ice cream booth. "Dad's not in a uniform."

"A suit's almost like a uniform," I say.

"Yeah, well, it's not like a policeman or a firefighter. They save lives. And," he adds, "they have *dogs*!"

Larry shoots me a knowing look. He's heard Joshua's desire for a puppy for months, if not years. "Their dogs are working dogs, little man. They're part of the force. Chocolate again?"

"No, thank you. Strawberry for me."

"Strawberry it is." Larry doesn't ask me for mine, as it never changes. A minute later and I pay for both of our ice creams, one mango and one strawberry.

"See you next week, guys."

"Thanks, Larry," I say. Joshua turns around with a single-minded focus on his ice cream. We take the long way home, walk past the pond. Joshua looks up at me in surprise when I head to one of the park benches, but doesn't protest.

I stretch out my legs in front of me. It's a beautiful fall day, I'm in the park with my kid, and I've got ice cream in my hand.

Time to do a little investigative work.

"When did the stomachache start?"

Silence as he stops licking his ice cream. "Dad…"

"Yeah?"

He sighs. "I didn't really have a stomachache."

I bite my lip to keep from smiling. If there is one thing my son is terrible at, it's dishonesty. I hope he never grows up and learns. "Oh? What happened, then?"

He looks at the ground beneath us, stretching out a leg to kick an errant pebble. "I didn't mean for them to call you. I know you're busy."

"Never too busy for you."

"I thought they'd call the house, and Marianne could come get me."

"Marianne's not authorized to pick you up during school hours. Only family is." I'd had to sign waivers to the school to allow Marianne and Ryan pick-up rights for Joshua *after* school was over. St. John's Prep takes safety as seriously as they take education, one of the many reasons I'd chosen it.

Joshua's quiet, but it's a heavy sort of silence. He's working up to something, and whatever it is, it's big. I take a shot in the dark.

"Did it have something to do with the new girl? The French one?"

He groans, throwing his head back against the bench. "Dad, it's going terribly!"

Bingo. I sling my arm behind him on the bench, tugging him closer. "Tell me."

"She doesn't know I like her."

"Mhm."

"I've thought of telling her," he says seriously, "but what if she doesn't like me too?"

"Could happen," I admit. "That's always a risk."

"So I decided I should become her friend first, and get to know her, and *then* tell her when I know she at least likes me as a friend."

"Very smart," I comment.

"But I heard Dexter telling her today that *he* likes her. And she said she liked him too." His shoulders curve forward, and I watch as strawberry ice cream drips onto his hand, forgotten.

"Oh, kiddo. That sucks."

"It does," he says. "It really really really sucks."

I reach out and wipe his hand off. "But you know, you two are in the same class now. You'll know her for the entire school year, perhaps even next year. And she could change her mind."

"Dexter is *awful.*"

I know for a fact that Dexter had once been considered a friend in our household. As a matter of fact, I think he's been to our apartment to play, but I keep that comment to myself. "Danielle can change her mind. Girls do that sometimes. Boys too, you know."

He sighs the sigh of unrequited love. "But *when?*"

"I don't know, kid. It might never happen, but you can't lose hope. Try to be her friend regardless. You still want to get to know her, don't you?"

"I guess," he mutters.

"Because she's nice and funny?"

"The nicest."

"Then you'll be her friend, because that's still a great thing to be, and hope her feelings change."

Silence as he digests this. When he's done, he jumps off the bench. "Let's go home."

"Stomachache cured?"

He rolls his eyes. "I never had one, Dad."

"Right." Grinning, I toss our things in a nearby trash can and put a hand on his back, between the wings of his shoulder blades. "She'll come around."

But his mind has already moved on, it seems. "What are we doing for Thanksgiving?"

"For Thanksgiving?"

"Maria is going with her family to Canada. Turner is celebrating at his grandfather's house in Martha's… somewhere."

"Vineyard," I correct.

"Vineyard," he repeats. "What are we doing, Dad?"

His question stumps me. The previous years we've always celebrated with my mother, who flies up from Florida for the holidays. Food and a few games, watching the parade on TV. That had been enough before.

"Grandma isn't coming this year," I say. "She's going to New Orleans with a few friends from her retirement community." She'd felt guilty about it, but I'd heard in her voice that she wanted to go. I'd told her to do it, and that we'd see her for Christmas instead.

"I know that," Joshua says. He jumps up on a low ledge and starts to walk in a line, one foot in front of the other. "But what are *we* doing? We can do anything we want, Dad."

"I suppose we can. What do you want to do?"

He thinks, holding his arms out for balance. At nine, he's big enough to think he doesn't need to hold my hand anymore, but I walk next to him just in case. "Mike's dad is having a Family Company Day for Thanksgiving."

"A Family Company Day?"

"Yeah. It's like a big fair, and he said there will be cotton candy for all the employees and their kids."

"Where does Mike's dad work?"

"Coney Island."

That explains things. "Well, my company isn't really like that."

"I don't know what your company is like," he complains.

"I had to explain it in class a few weeks back and I made stuff up!"

"I buy companies, then I make sure they work, and then sell them on." I've explained this to him before, but I understand that it doesn't make much sense to a child.

Joshua jumps off the ledge and lands neatly, knees bent. "What are you doing for your company for Thanksgiving?"

How am I having this conversation with my kid, right after having it with Frederica Bilson? I'm not even a holiday person. But as I stare into my son's wide, bright gaze, I know it's time to become one. Joshua deserves nothing but the best, but he's stuck with me, and I'll just have to buck up.

"Not enough," I admit. "They've been working very hard for me, but I haven't told them that."

"Thanksgiving is the time of year to tell people stuff like that," Joshua lectures. "Last year we wrote thank-you notes to our classmates with things we like about them. Perhaps you should do the same at your company?"

"Perhaps I should," I murmur, putting a hand on the back of his head. "You're smart, kiddo."

He looks up at me. "That's why I faked a stomachache. I've never had one before, so I knew they'd take it seriously."

I smile back at him. "Clever, but in the future, we don't run when things get difficult."

"I know, Dad."

An hour later, when we're both safe and secure back in our apartment overlooking Central Park, I sit down in my home office and open my laptop.

Subject: Company Thanksgiving Celebration

Ms. Bilson,

Your budget for this project has just been significantly increased. So significantly, in fact, that there is no limit at all for your initial suggestions. Perhaps something that includes employees' families?

Think big, Strait-laced.

Tristan Conway,
CEO Exciteur Global

8

FREDDIE

I press the clicker to change the slides on the screen. Beside me, William and Luke shift to the side, looking at our audience. "So," I say, "here are all three options for easy comparison. Feel free to let us know what you think."

Tristan and Clive gaze back at us across the meeting room, flanked by two women from Exciteur's HR and event-planning team. Tristan taps his fingers against the table and studies the slide on display with an inscrutable expression.

The three options on display all have clear budgets, timelines, and concepts. A Thanksgiving lunch on the company, where we rent a nearby restaurant. The second option, a cash bonus in hand for all employees, on a sliding scale.

The third? Renting the Wilshire Gardens in Central Park for an evening, the amusement park that's set up for a few months every fall. Inviting everyone's friends and family... and booking a nearby bar for singles to go afterwards.

It's outrageously expensive, but Tristan's email had specifically asked for family friendly. It had also included that nickname. *Strait-laced.* Taken from the intimate setting where we'd agreed to leave it and into the workplace. I'd deleted that before I forwarded the email to Luke and William and told them we had to go big.

And now Tristan is saying nothing.

Just staring at the three options, his eyes narrowed in thought. The people on either side of him glance over. Once, twice. Waiting for his verdict.

I cross my arms over my chest, refusing to let any nerves show. "What do you think?"

"Is option three feasible within the time frame?" Tristan asks.

I nod. "Absolutely. We've already reached out to the amusement park to inquire about availability."

Clive frowns. "The cost is considerable."

"It's high in comparison to the other two," I admit, "but in terms of renting a venue, it's really quite affordable."

Tristan gives a slow nod, his gaze on mine. "Right. Well, we're going with option three. Thank you for an excellent presentation."

Eyes turn to him and there's a beat of stunned silence.

"Sir," one of the women hedges, "this will take a significant cut out of our personnel budget for the year."

Tristan waves a hand. "We'll replenish it with our fourth quarter returns. I'm well aware that the cuts we've made over the last year have taken a toll on morale. How many of you on my side of the table have kids?"

Clive joins the women in agreeing that they do, even if they don't follow the reasoning behind Tristan's question.

"And you've all spent a lot of evenings here," he continues. "No, we're going to rent Wilshire Gardens for an evening and have a Thanksgiving Family Day, all on the company."

I clear my throat. "Excellent choice, sir. Luke, William and I will begin planning immediately. We'll have the rental contracts for the company to sign ready by the end of the week."

"Right you are." Tristan pushes away from the conference table. The others scramble to do the same, arranging the notes. "We are done here, then. Miss Bilson, I'd like a word before you return to the Strategy Department."

I give a stiff nod, painfully aware of how his words cause widened eyes amongst the others. William and Luke cluster at my side as I unplug my work laptop.

"Can't believe he chose the fair," William mutters, rolling up the cord. "I thought that was a dead end."

"Shows what we know about management," Luke murmurs. Both of them glance over their shoulders before giving me a quiet *good luck*. The door shuts behind them, and after a curious-looking Clive leaves the room, it's just Tristan and me.

He gestures at a chair next to him. "Whose idea was Wilshire Gardens?"

I sit on the opposite side of the table. "Mine, sir."

"And how did you think of it?"

"You mentioned family in your email. There aren't a lot of options around here that would interest kids, but still work for the employees who have none." A quick Google search of the area had given me very few options, and it was just our good luck that the amusement park was in town for the holiday season.

"As it so happens, it was an excellent suggestion."

"Thank you." The silence stretches out between us and I clear my throat. "Sorry, but why did you ask me to stay behind?"

"I wanted to ask you who first thought of the idea."

"I see. Although, without Luke or William here to correct me, I could simply be claiming credit for their ideas."

His eyebrow rises. "Are you?"

"No," I admit.

"I doubted you did."

"Still… in front of all those people, sir. They might start to think something untoward, or to… *suspect*."

Tristan runs a hand through his hair, his lips pressing into a tight line. It takes me a moment to recognize it's to keep from laughing. "Not a soul in this room knows of my membership to a certain room. They certainly don't know about *yours*. How on earth would they suspect?"

I press my hands flat on the table in front of me. "Reputations are precious things. I'm sure the other trainees will ask me later what you wanted to discuss in private, and if I don't have a good answer, rumors may spread."

The traces of amusement leave his face. "I don't like what you're implying."

"Well, neither do I, but it doesn't change the facts."

"They won't talk. They know better than that." He waves a large hand, and perhaps that works in his world. Power and prestige trumps everything.

It doesn't in mine.

"Why did you apply to this company?"

My eyebrows rise. "That's what you really wanted to know?"

"Yes. You were adamant last time that you'd worked hard to get here and that that you wanted the Strategy Department in particular. Tell me why."

I worry my lower lip between my teeth. Is he joking? Exciteur has one of the best reputations as far as consulting goes. It's a multi-national firm on the brink of joining the Big Five consultancy firms, turning them into the Big Six.

The answer should be obvious.

But the intensity in his gaze isn't the least bit joking. It's a side of him I'd sensed last weekend, but not until I'd met him here had I seen it in all its glory. Handsome might joke, but he's serious at heart.

"I was in the top of my class at Wharton," I say. "MBA. Working in consulting is a dream for a business grad. No other area allows you to get as much business exposure."

"Wharton?"

I nod. It hadn't been easy, not financing my studies or the classes themselves. "Both bachelor and MBA."

"So you're here to learn."

"Absolutely I am."

"Why Strategy?"

I meet his gaze. "My favorite courses in college were all on business strategy and strategic management. It's the art of connecting the past with the present, to create the future. The strategy department is where the real decisions are made. It's... well. There's no other area that interests me as much."

He gives a slow nod. "Strategy is the lifeblood of a company."

"Exactly. Firms live or die based on the soundness of it, and Exciteur has some of the best corporate strategists in the country."

"In the world," he corrects.

I smile, but I don't object. He's probably right.

He leans back in his chair and crosses his arms over his chest. For all that I know his name now, Tristan Conway is still as big of a mystery as he was in that darkened party. I don't know his background, his age. His interests and hobbies.

"What was this?" I ask. "A second interview?"

His lips quirk. "I never get to talk to the trainees. Figured I'd change that."

"Then why did Luke and William have to leave?"

"You know why they had to leave."

I break away from the magnetism of his eyes, nerves dancing down my spine. "This Thanksgiving Family Day may have started out as punishment," I say, "but I'd like to thank you. Since you chose the amusement park, this might become the biggest project I get to spearhead during my time here."

"Punishment?"

"For my first email," I say. Just the memory of is it is mortifying, but I don't look away from his gaze. "I realize it was perhaps more forthcoming than you're used to."

His eyebrows rise. "You don't think my staff tells me the truth?"

"Judging from what I saw today, every single one of your employees in the room were surprised when you picked the amusement park option, but only Clive really spoke about his misgivings… and only once."

"You don't seem to share their apprehension."

I blow out a breath. "I really want to work here, Mr. Conway. But I believe I've already given you cause to fire me with that initial email… yet you didn't. I'm hoping you won't in the future."

"That's a big bet," he comments, but a smile plays across his lips. "For the record, I didn't give you this project as punishment."

"No?"

"The Freddie who wrote back to my emails, who still hasn't apologized, by the way, refused to back down. I wanted to see what that person was capable of when given the opportunity."

Oh. "I won't disappoint you."

Tristan gives a single nod. "I don't expect you to."

Our eyes catch and hold, the eye contact anchoring me in place. Like it had at the party, where it cut through the throngs of mingling guests and throbbing music to sear me where I stood. This time, there's only a conference table between us, and it's quiet enough to hear a pin drop. My voice is faint when I find it again.

"Was that all, Mr. Conway?"

He clears his throat before responding. "Yes. And if asked, feel free to tell your colleagues the truth."

"The truth?"

"That I wanted to know who came up with the winning idea."

I stand, gathering my laptop and notebook, holding them like a shield against my body. "Thank you."

He taps his fingers against the table, too large for this conference room. It threatens to swallow me up whole. "And Miss Bilson?"

"Yes?"

"Despite the trouble it's caused, I'm glad you chose this company."

9

FREDDIE

"Eleanor is tough," Toby tells me, "but she's fair. Her bluntness is usually for the best. It makes it easier to do my job."

Quentin reaches for his beer. "You should be happy you weren't here during Conway's takeover, though."

"Was she bad then?"

"Everyone was bad back then." He shakes his head, eyes tracking my hand around the glass of whiskey in front of me. They'd both been surprised when I'd ordered it, as most men are. I love surprising them. As if they have a monopoly on drinks? Please.

"The takeover was that dramatic?" I ask.

Toby raises an eyebrow. "You've met Conway. Imagine him in front of the whole company, announcing that three departments would be slashed by the end of the month."

I grimace. It's not hard to picture the determined lines of Tristan's face, the sweep of his arm as he speaks the words without affect or equivocation. Telling people en masse that they'd have to find new employment.

"But it's made the company stronger," Quentin admits, running a hand through his overlong hair. "You can't fault the bastard that."

I nod, my fingers tightening on my glass. When I'd suggested grabbing drinks after work with my co-workers, I hadn't expected Tristan Conway to follow us. But here he is, the topic of choice.

Toby's smile widens. "Not to mention the entertainment factor. There's never a dull day when he's in the building. Employees scurrying about."

"You mean *you* scurry about," Quentin says. "I have never scurried in my life."

"I saw you scurry just last week, when Clive came down to speak to Eleanor."

Quentin crosses his arms. "You need to get new glasses."

"I got these just last month, thank you very much." Toby turns to me, winking. "Designer glasses at half-price."

"They look great," I say. The orange rims compliment his smart navy suit and match the colors in his tie. "Toby, did you say you had a date this weekend?"

"Yes. I'm just hoping this guy isn't as awful as the last one I matched with."

"Sock puppet guy," Quentin mutters.

"Sock puppet guy?" I ask.

Toby gives a grave nod. "Sock pocket guy," he confirms, pouring enough gravitas into the words that I hold up my hands in defeat.

"Say no more."

"I won't. Those details would haunt you."

I give a mock shudder. "Where are you going with the new guy?"

"We're going to walk the High Line. He's never been there."

"He's new to New York?" Quentin asks.

Toby nods. "Just moved in from out of state. The poor guy doesn't know his subway lines."

I take a sip of my whiskey. "Hey, I'm from out of the state. What's the High Line?"

"Oh dear," Toby says. Quentin shakes his head and

reaches for his beer, the too large sleeve flashing a glimpse of a digital watch.

I hold out placating hands. "It's that bad, is it?"

"The worst, I'm afraid." Toby puts a hand on mine. "Will you let me show you around the city? Please?"

"Don't say yes," Quentin warns.

"Quiet," Toby retorts. "He's just annoyed because I offered to go shopping with him and give a few constructive pointers. He declined."

"My clothes are perfectly fine."

"You're right," Toby agrees, a little too quickly. "They are."

I grin, looking between them. "You know the two of you are like an old married couple?"

"No, we're not," Quentin protests.

Toby shakes his head at me. "Very cute, but don't try to deflect. When did you move to the city?"

"A month and a half ago."

"And where do you live?"

"Upper West Side," I say, but seeing their widened eyes, I hasten to explain. "Oh, it's *tiny*. I'm practically renting a shoebox on the top floor. An old lady is renting it to me, and she thought I seemed trustworthy. Honestly, I know I'm lucky to have found it... even if it *is* the most expensive shoebox I've ever paid for."

"Another one in Manhattan," Toby tells Quentin. "See, that's why you should abandon Brooklyn and join us."

"No," Quentin says.

"Imagine how much shorter your commute will be."

"Brooklyn has soul. No offense," he adds to me.

"None taken," I say. "Should I have?"

But they've devolved into an argument, and I grin, watching it. The sparks are flying. I don't know if Quentin swings that way, but if he did... hmm.

My phone vibrates in my pocket. Once. Twice. Pulling it out, it's a New York number I don't recognize. It could be work, even if the odds of that are slim.

"Give me a minute, guys," I say, slipping out of the booth.

I hit answer. "This is Frederica Bilson."

"Freddie?"

"Yes, that's me." I sidestep a few students singing, their arms around one another, and make a beeline for the door.

"There is a lot of noise on your end."

"Yes, I'm sorry about that. Give me a moment…" I pull the door open and step out into the cool, New York air. "Who is this?"

"Tristan Conway," the deep voice replies.

"Mr. Conway?"

"The very one," he repeats, voice dry. "Am I interrupting your evening?"

"No. Well, I'm out for drinks with a few of my co-workers. I just stepped outside."

"Good," he says.

I can think of absolutely nothing to reply. How did he get my number? Why is he calling? We haven't spoken since the meeting in his office over a week ago.

"I'm calling about work," he says.

"Is it about the Thanksgiving Family Day? Because everything is in hand for the weekend."

"No, it's not about that." A beat of silence. "Perhaps it's better to speak about this when you're not surrounded by Exciteur employees."

"I'm not surrounded. I stepped outside."

"Still, I think it's better we have this conversation when you're in a place where no one can overhear. Call me when you get home."

"Call you, Mr. Conway?"

"Yes. This is work-related, Miss Bilson, but I think it's better we don't have this conversation in the workplace."

Curiosity gnaws at my insides. "I'll call you as soon as I get home. When is too late?"

"I'm up," is the curt reply. "Talk to you soon, Miss Bilson."

And then he hangs up.

I stare at my phone for a long few seconds. He can't be calling to fire me, can he? No. I thought I'd convinced him out of his suggestion of shifting my internship to a different company, too.

Work-related.

But I thought it was best to have the conversation outside of the office.

"Is everything all right?" Toby asks when I return inside. He's taken off his suit jacket, and it lies innocently between him and Quentin on their side of the booth.

"Absolutely," I lie.

The sky has darkened to a deep midnight black when I finally get home to my building, nodding hello to the doorman outside. I'm not sure when it will ever stop striking me as surreal that I live in a building with a doorman.

New York is my home now.

Correction, I think, as I unlock the door to my tiny studio on the top floor. This expensive shoebox is my home now. The single window offers a view of the opposite building's rooftops. Sometimes there's pigeons on them. It's riveting.

I sit down onto my bed and take out my phone. It's just past eleven, but he'd told me he'd be up.

Tristan answers after the first signal. "You were out late."

I bristle at the clear disapproval in his tone. "It's not midnight yet, but if I were, it would be my business."

"You could be performing at less than your usual standard tomorrow at work," he points out. "That would make it my business."

"I assure you, I always perform at the peak of my ability."

"Like when you confuse the forwarding and reply button on the email interface?"

A cheap shot, Mr. Conway. I push my hair back from my face and blow out a breath. "Perhaps that was a calculated move," I say, the whiskey I'd had speaking for me. "Perhaps I wanted to make an impact. Leave my mark. Most trainees are forgettable, you know. I don't want to be one of them."

The silence is brief and surprised. Then he chuckles darkly and I close my eyes as the sound washes over me. I picture him beside me on the couch at the Gilded Room, his features marked by shadow and desire.

"You're not forgettable, Freddie," he vows. "If avoiding that fate was your mission, consider it accomplished."

"I didn't expect to achieve success quite so soon."

"And yet you did." Another pause. "Where did you go out tonight?"

"A bar close to work."

"Did you take a cab home?"

"I walked," I say, digging my fingers into the thick comforter beneath me. How am I lying here, having this conversation with him?

"You walked? Do you live near the bar, then?"

"Yes, Upper West Side. We went to the bar next to work."

"Walking isn't necessarily safe."

"This neighborhood is one of the safest in the city. Besides, there were people out. Do you walk home alone?"

"Freddie…"

"Mr. Conway."

There's reluctant amusement in his voice. "I hope you find your co-workers to your satisfaction."

"They're lovely people," I say. "You said this was work-related, sir?"

"I did. You know, it's not necessary for you to call me sir."

"Your other employees do."

He sighs. "You're right. This is why I called you, by the way."

"To discuss what I should call you? I believe we've had that conversation before." The words are risky, reminding us both of the night we're not to speak of.

Tristan's voice darkens. "So we have," he says. "I don't believe we settled on anything then, either."

"You're difficult to pin down."

"Impossible," he says. "I've never let anyone try."

I take a deep breath. "Why did you call me *sir?*"

"Believe it or not, it is work-related."

"So you've said, yes."

"It's also sensitive."

"Classified information?"

"Of a sort. Tell me, Freddie, where do you see yourself at the end of this internship?"

"My ambition is the classified information?"

"Funny," he says, but the deep baritone of his voice sounds like he's smiling. "No. Do you see yourself with a permanent job here?"

"Potentially," I say. "I don't discount the possibility, and if I were offered, I'd most likely say yes."

"That's good to know."

"Where is this conversation headed?"

"I have a proposition for you," he says.

My brain short-circuits.

He can't be saying what I think he's saying, can he? I press a hand to my breastbone as the words flow out. "Tristan, I can't do that. You can't ask that of me. I'm not the type to—"

"Christ, Freddie, I'm not asking you for *that*. No."

I relax back onto the bed, my heart racing in my chest. "Okay."

"I should have worded it differently." A frustrated sound, and I can see him in front of me, running a hand through his thick hair. "No, I wouldn't ask that. This is about the Strategy Department."

"It is?"

"I believe we have a mole."

I frown. "Someone who leaks information?"

"Yes. Our competitors are learning about the business strategies we're proposing for our clients, and it's not just happened once, either."

"How do you know?"

"I have my sources," he says.

"And you're sure it's coming from Strategy?"

"I've eliminated the other possibilities. Strategy and management are the only people who deal with this information, and I know it's not management."

I turn over on my side. "You want me to keep my eyes and ears open?"

"Yes. You're new, you're a trainee. There might be many in your department who'd think to overlook you."

"Thanks." But I'm smiling.

"It's their loss," he says. "Not to mention that no one will suspect you to have the management's ear. To the best of their knowledge, you and I have never spoken outside of the Thanksgiving meeting."

The faces of my co-workers flash before me. Toby. Quentin. Eleanor. The three women working in our office who'd never given me more than a polite nod.

"It doesn't feel good, knowing one of the people I'm working with isn't on the same team."

Tristan's voice deepens. "I know. I'm *paying* one of them for the privilege of betraying my company."

"I'll do it. Of course I will."

"Good," he says. "I think it's for the best that this stays out of the company altogether."

"All right. What does that mean, exactly? I only report what I find to you over the phone?"

"Yes," is his swift reply. "We keep it off company email servers, we don't talk about it at work."

"Sounds like a plan."

"Excellent," he says. "Perhaps we'll finally catch this bastard."

I can't help but ask, "Why me?"

"Why not you?" he retorts.

"I mean, why do you trust me?"

There's a beat of silence, stretching out between us. Where is he in New York? Perhaps he only lives a few blocks away, and he's sitting alone in his apartment, just like me.

"I trust your ambition," he says finally, "because I recognize it."

The ground we're treading trembles beneath me. It's a compliment, but it's more than that. It's recognition. It seeps through my chest and warms me as it spreads. "Are you still in the office?"

"No," he says. "I'm at home."

"Did you walk home alone?"

His voice is amused. "No, I didn't. I don't give advice I don't follow myself."

"That's unusual."

"I'm looking out at the park, actually. They've started setting up the amusement fair."

His apartment overlooks Central Park. It shouldn't surprise me, but it does. I picture him standing in front of floor-to-ceiling windows, a hand in the pocket of his slacks and another gripping his phone.

"Does it look good?"

"It looks large," he says. "I'll send you the names of a few people tomorrow. They're not employees, but I want them granted access to the Thanksgiving Family Day."

"Of course. Business associates of yours?"

His voice is dry. "More like someone called in a favor."

"I'll have it done right away."

"Good."

Neither of us says anything, but his presence is a palpable thing on the other end of the line. I don't want to hang up.

And I don't think he wants to either.

Closing my eyes, I breathe out the admission. "Realizing I'd sent you the first email was mortifying."

His voice softens. "I figured."

"But do you know... I'm not sorry."

"Neither am I, Freddie," he murmurs. "Neither am I."

10

FREDDIE

The day has come.

Instead of a normal Friday afternoon at Exciteur, the office has moved to Central Park. I catch sight of Eleanor walking into the amusement fair with a blonde tween at her side, the girl's eyes lighting up when they spot a cotton candy stand.

Yes, this was a good idea.

"We have security at the entrance with the lists of names," Reece says at my side. Fifteen years my senior, Exciteur's event planner had been less than pleased at receiving instructions from three trainees. I'd given her as much power as I could to counteract that, and accepted every single one of her suggestions.

"That's excellent."

"Everything should go smoothly now," she says. Her phone dings, and she glances down. "Except someone forgot to put up the private hire sign by the exit, and now there's a line. Damn it…" She disappears down the path at a determined stride.

Luke rocks on his heels beside me. He's a trainee in the sales department, and his grin is as wide as he is tall. "I can't believe we pulled this off."

"I never thought they would go for it in the first place," William says. "Who knew all these people had kids?"

"How do they do it? I worked until nine every evening last week," Luke says. "The others in my department were right there along with me."

I re-tie the waistband of my coat, pulling it tighter around myself. There's no warmth in the late November air. "It's a good thing the company is doing this, then. Giving them time to have fun."

I scan the crowd, amazed at the number of people. Does Exciteur really employee this many people? When we're all stacked upon one another in the high-storied building on the Upper West Side, there's no telling.

My gaze snags on a tall figure. He's wearing a navy coat over his suit, a gray scarf around his neck. His thick hair is pushed back, the scruff of a few days of not shaving accentuating the square of his jaw.

I can still hear his deep voice in my ear. Feel the weight of his body against mine.

"Freddie?"

"Sorry?"

Luke grins at me. "You were completely lost there for a moment. Are you excited for the bar later?"

"Um, yeah. Absolutely." I tuck my hands into my coat pocket. "I'll make a lap, make sure everything's in order. Talk to you guys later."

I weave my way through the half-empty fair, trying to spot him again. Pass by Toby and Quentin bantering by the ring toss and smile to myself. Tristan's tall enough to stand out… should be here somewhere.

I turn the corner at a carnival game and there he is.

Tristan Conway, leaning against the counter of a game booth. He has his hand on the shoulder of a dark-haired boy. I blink, but the image doesn't go away.

"Can I try, Dad?" the boy asks.

Tristan hands him a set of darts. "Keep your elbow steady and aim for the balloons."

"I know," the boy says.

A smile flashes across Tristan's face. "Of course you do."

His son, because he has a *son,* takes aim and throws the first dart. That's when Tristan looks over his shoulder. Our eyes meet.

I'm busted.

"Hello," he says.

I swallow. "Hi. Didn't mean to ambush the two of you like this."

"That's not a problem." Tristan glances down at the boy, but he's deep in concentration. "Good job on the fair."

"Thank you. All I did was book it, though." I give a crooked smile, my mind still running on overdrive. Tristan Conway is a father.

"Take the credit," he advises me.

"Okay."

The boy turns around. "I didn't hit a single one."

"Try again," Tristan says, extending a new set of darts. "Really focus on aiming."

The boy pushes back a dark curl that's fallen over his brow. I'd peg him at nine, ten. "I'll get one this time."

"Of course you will, kid." Tristan must see my curiosity, but he doesn't say anything, just runs a hand over his neck. His jaw is tense.

His son sees me and gives me a little wave, darts clasped in his hand. "Hello."

"Hi there," I say.

Tristan gestures at me. "This is Frederica. She works for me."

"I'm Joshua," his son says politely. "It's very nice to meet you."

"It's nice to meet you too. Are you playing darts?"

"Yes. You're supposed to hit the balloons. If you hit three of them, you win a prize."

"What's the prize?"

He turns to the booth. The girl who runs it is off to the side, her eyes glued to her phone. But the ceiling is covered in stuffed animals dangling from ropes. "I'm not sure."

Tristan points at a sign on the wall. "Three hits and you get to choose any stuffed animal."

"Which one would you choose?" I ask, stepping up beside him. My hand goes to my wallet, looking for quarters. "I think I want the giant elephant."

Joshua gives me a smile, tinged with shyness and delight. "You like elephants?"

"They're one of my favorite animals," I say.

"I've seen them a couple of times," he offers. "Dad and I went to Thailand last year with Grandma for Christmas. We visited an elephant sanctuary." He pronounces *sanctuary* with great care, making me smile.

"That's amazing."

"It is." He pauses, looking back at his dad before returning his gaze to me. "Do you know they have the best memories of any animal?"

"Oh, I know, isn't that cool?"

"The coolest," he agrees. "Do you want to play darts too? Dad, can she get some darts?"

Tristan opens his mouth, but I beat him to it, fishing out two quarters from my wallet. "I'll play."

"Well, I suppose that means I have to as well," Tristan says. He waves over the teenager managing the booth. She accepts my quarters, but Tristan hands her a twenty. "Give us a bucket."

She grins but says nothing. A few seconds later and there's a near limitless supply of darts between us.

I raise my eyebrow at him. Tristan just shrugs, reaching for one. "This is good target practice."

Joshua takes aim, tongue clenched between his teeth. He narrowly misses. "Shoot," he says. "Dad, your turn. What are you going to choose if you win?"

Tristan weighs a dart in hand. My eyes track the strength of his jaw, the faint crow's-feet at the edges of his eyes. He can't be more than ten years older than me, and yet he has a son this old. It's hard to superimpose the image of him here, talking to his kid, with the man I'd met in the Gilded Room.

Tristan Conway, the enigma.

"I don't know." He aims, jaw tense, and throws. A balloon pops with a loud smack.

"Nice one!"

"Thanks, kid."

"If I win, I think I want an elephant too," Joshua tells me, reaching for a dart. "Although I think whales are cooler."

"Whales?"

"We've been watching a lot of *Blue Planet*," Tristan clarifies. His voice is deep, controlled... but is there a note of embarrassment there?

I can't picture him relaxing in front of the TV, period, but even less while watching a nature documentary with a kid. But even as I think it... an image emerges of him doing just that. My impression of the man shifts again, becoming even more attractive.

"I've seen *The Blue Planet*," I say. "It looks amazing. I really want to learn how to dive one day, and get my certificate."

"You do?" Joshua asks. "I really want to try too. *Allegedly* I'm too young."

"You *are* too young," Tristan says. "There's nothing alleged about it. But we'll go diving when you're older."

"Dad and I like to travel," Joshua tells me. "We go somewhere for every single one of my school holidays."

I grin at this chatty kid, looking from him to Tristan. The eyes are the same, but one pair is looking at me openly and excitedly, the others with something like wariness. "Your turn," Tristan tells me, nodding at the dart still in my hand. "Let's see what you got."

I throw and miss, but my second shot sends a balloon exploding. I make a victory gesture. "One down, two to go."

Joshua glances between us before fixing his gaze on the balloons in the distance. Tristan hands him a dart silently. He aims...

And a balloon pops.

"Yes!" He high-fives with Tristan. "That was awesome."

"It was," Tristan confirms. "You've really got the hang of it now."

Our eyes meet over Joshua's head. Perhaps he can see the questions in mine, but Tristan just gives me a single, elegant shrug. He turns back to the balloons.

Where's Joshua's mother? Is Tristan divorced? Widowed? Curiosity burns brighter in my stomach, the desire to unlock his secrets. Joshua hits another balloon. It pops with an audible snap, shaking me out of my thoughts.

"Nice one," Tristan says. "Just one more..."

It takes two more tries, but he hits a third one. He gives us both high fives after that, his curls shaking as he bounces. "Success!"

"Success," Tristan echoes. "Which stuffed animal do you want?"

Joshua scans the ceiling. There's no whale, but there's a dolphin. He points at the elephant. "That one."

"Really? Good choice," I say.

"I know," he says, with the supreme confidence of a child. He tucks it under his arm, and we turn from the booth, leaving the teenager to her social media scrolling.

Tristan puts a hand on Joshua's shoulder. "They're here," he says quietly.

Joshua goes still, his gaze scanning the crowd. I see nothing out of the ordinary. Just people milling about, a child holding cotton candy. In the distance, I can make out Toby and Quentin by a Whack-a-Mole.

"Oh," Joshua says weakly. "She came."

"Of course she did," Tristan says. "Go on, let's talk to them."

But they've already seen us, apparently, as a middle-aged

man and woman with a girl the same age as Joshua walk toward us. The girl is smiling, her wheat-blonde hair in a braid.

"Hello, Joshua," she says in an accented voice. French?

"Hi," he murmurs.

"This is your dad's place?"

He doesn't say anything. Tristan cuts in, extending a hand to the parents. "Tristan Conway, Joshua's father. Thank you for coming."

"Thanks for inviting us," the lady says, and she's definitely French. "We haven't met any parents from Danielle's school yet."

"No, people like to keep to themselves. But I'm sure there'll be a chance to meet others soon," he says. "There'll be a bake sale or walk-a-thon soon enough."

Okay, this is my cue to leave. Not only have I met his son, but now I'm trespassing on his socializing with other parents.

I take a careful step back. "I'll see you—"

"Do you want to go on the Ferris Wheel?" Joshua asks Danielle. His voice is high. "It's really tall."

"Oh, can I, Mama?"

"I'll go with them," Tristan says. "I'll be in the carriage behind theirs."

"Why not? We'll be by the hot dog stand, Danielle."

Joshua turns to me. "You and Dad can go in one carriage and Danielle and I in another."

"I'm not—"

"Sounds good," Tristan interjects.

"Will you take care of this?" Joshua hands me the stuffed elephant and I grip on to the plushy. The long trunk drapes down my arm. I open my mouth to protest, but the kids are already heading for the Ferris wheel. A light hand on my back and Tristan is directing me after them.

"Sorry about this," he murmurs.

"No, that's okay," I murmur back. The Ferris wheel isn't

that high, is it? It's in Central Park. We're not talking Six Flags here.

I should be able to do it.

I *can* do it.

"These were your special guests?"

"Yes," he says. "Danielle's a friend of Joshua's from school."

"I didn't know you had a son."

His breath is quiet, but audible. "I know."

"I'm sorry if I... intruded back there. I take it you don't like mixing business with your private life."

"No," he says, "I don't."

"Anonymity. I get it."

As he opens the latch for the Ferris wheel, he gives me a dark look that sends shivers down my spine. The guy manning the attraction motions for Danielle and Joshua to have a seat in their carriage, and the kids bundle in, chatting the whole way.

"I'll be right behind you," Tristan tells them. "Call out if you need anything at all and sit still in the car."

"I know, Dad," Joshua calls back.

Tristan extends an arm to our carriage. "After you."

My hands grip the elephant tight. It's just a Ferris wheel, Freddie. And I personally read the amusement fair's safety guidelines before I booked them. What can go wrong?

I step into the carriage, sitting down on the cold metal bench. It wobbles precariously as Tristan follows me in, folding his long legs into the space. His thigh presses against mine in the tight confines of the carriage.

The attendant closes the metal latch behind him, stepping back. "Everyone ready?"

No, I think. *How do I get off this?*

"Yes," Tristan calls back.

The mechanics churn into action and our carriage swings with the sudden jolt of movement. I grip the metal bar in front of us and focus on the heat of him next to me, evident even through the thick fabric of our coats.

"This turned out really well," he says. "You've done a great job."

"Thank you." We start our ascent, the people and stands beneath us shrinking with every inch we rise.

I close my eyes.

"Now you've met Joshua."

I nod, my words emerging through clenched teeth. "He's lovely."

Tristan clears his throat. "I don't talk about my family at work. Not at parties either."

"I understand. Anonymity, and all that."

"Yes." He shifts in the carriage and it rocks beneath us. I press my lips into a tight line.

There's no way I'm opening my eyes until we're safely back on the ground.

"Freddie? Are you all right?"

"Yeah, absolutely."

"You've gone completely white." His voice lowers, and when he speaks again, it's closer to my ear. "You don't like heights."

"Not a member of the fan club, no." One breath in, one breath out. That's all I have to do.

"Why on earth did you come up here with me?"

I give the stuffed animal in my grip a little shake. "Your son asked me to guard his elephant."

"Freddie…" His voice is frustrated, and so, so close. I have to open my eyes to peek.

He's only inches away, and watching me with a tiny furrow in his brow. I focus on his eyes. "It's okay," I murmur. "I just have to focus on not panicking."

"That's right." He's quiet for a beat, but then he tugs off a leather glove and pries one of my hands off the elephant. I grip his fingers tight and close my eyes again. His skin is warm and slightly rough against mine, my hand disappearing inside his completely. "It's only two laps."

"*Two?*"

"It'll be okay. Just breathe, okay?"

"I'm breathing." I lean my head back against the seat and tighten my grip on his hand. "Breathing is the only thing I can do right now."

"Then let's just focus on that," he murmurs, but I don't do what I'm told. I focus on his hand and his voice, too. It's deep and calming, like crushed velvet poured into a dark cup of espresso.

"Talk to me?"

"All right. So… elephants are your favorite animal. I can now chalk that up to the list of things I know about you."

"Must be a rather short list," I murmur.

"Not that short. I've made several observations."

Despite myself, my lips tug. "I'm sure I don't want to hear them all."

"Well, not all of them are fit for polite conversation. Doesn't mean they don't still make the list. It's a mental one. Don't worry."

"I won't."

"I'd say the view is amazing, but I don't think it's a good idea for you to open your eyes right now."

I screw them shut tighter. "I'm pretending we're on the ground."

"Keep pretending."

My hair lifts in the breeze and I lean into him, as if I can hide from the height. If it's windy, we must be at the very top.

Don't think about it don't think about it don't think about it.

I hear the rustle of another glove being removed, and then my hand is held in both of his. The sensation anchors me. "You're okay," he says. "I've got you."

A deep breath in. A deep breath out.

My fingers tighten around his. "Thank you. This is… mildly humiliating."

"It's not. Besides, you wouldn't be up here if it wasn't for me."

"That doesn't make it less embarrassing," I murmur. If anything, it makes it more so. Not only does he know how much I detest heights, but he also knows I braved them in order to spend more time with him. I should've just sent him another email with the words *I can't stop thinking about you* and be done with it.

"I don't know what you mean by that."

I give a tiny shake of my head. "Never mind."

His thumb moves over the back of my hand in a small, tight circle. "Joshua took to you quickly," he says. "I was... surprised."

A thousand questions I want to ask, and the only thing I can focus on is keeping my cool. "Oh?"

"Yes." A snort. "He doesn't understand what I do for a living, and I wonder if today will only confuse him more."

My lips tug. "Well, venture capitalism is a difficult concept to explain to a kid."

"It is." His voice darkens, close by my ear. "It wasn't one of your guesses, either, when you tried to think of what I worked with."

The memory of the Gilded Room washes over me, of us sitting just like this, me draped over him on a couch in a dark alcove.

My stomach tightens. "I wasn't imaginative enough."

"Or venture capitalist didn't sound sexy enough."

I swallow, my eyes still shut. "No, it's sexy."

Complete silence.

Damn it. I open an eye, only to see him regarding me with a raised eyebrow. The darkness in his eyes swirls with humor. "So you weren't disappointed I wasn't a mafia boss, then?"

"Honestly... I was disappointed when I found out you were the CEO of Exciteur."

His mouth opens. "You were?"

"Yes," I murmur. "Because it meant we could never meet at a Gilded Room party again."

His dark eyes bore into mine, quiet for a long time. I don't see the landscape moving behind him. I barely register the hitch in the carriage when we finally return from our second lap, stopping at the bottom.

I've said too much.

But then he murmurs something that slides across my skin like silk, his hands letting mine go. "So was I, Freddie."

11

FREDDIE

The Thanksgiving Family Day had gone off without a hitch. Luke, William and I had pulled it off, and even if it was more event management than project management, I'm still proud. Smiling to myself, I take a step back and survey the newly framed pictures on my dresser. The pictures I'd had enlarged had arrived in the mail just yesterday, one of my grandfather, another of my parents.

Three of the hardest-working people I know. Also the three people who believe in me the most. My parents had bought a bottle of champagne when I'd gotten the email telling me I'd been accepted into the junior professionals program at Exciteur.

Right next to their photos is my framed college diploma and a few books on business, completing the vignette.

It's my shrine to success.

One day, I think, looking around my tiny studio apartment, I won't live in a place without an oven again. All I have is a one-top stove, a microwave, and a miniature refrigerator.

Which is also empty.

I close the fridge door and glance at my watch. The deli down the street is open for another hour… it would make it my fourth time this week. Am I shameless enough?

Absolutely.

I've just pulled on my jacket when my phone rings, and the number is familiar, sending my heart racing. We haven't spoken since the Thanksgiving Family Day and I haven't even seen him at work. Not that I'd be able to talk to him there, even if I did.

I hit answer. "Hello?"

"Freddie."

"Tristan." My hand fumbles with the key. "How are you?"

Humor colors his voice, as if he's amused at my attempt at normalcy. "Good. How are you?"

"Excellent."

"Excellent? That's great to hear."

"What can I do for you?"

"I wanted to see how you're doing with your task, the one we spoke about on the phone a few weeks ago."

"The mole in the Strategy Department."

"The very one."

I pull out the lone chair at my table and sit down. "I haven't discovered anything yet. I'm keeping my eyes open, though. Perhaps once I'm invited to more senior meetings."

"Hmm. I wonder if we can fast-track that somehow."

I frown. "I'm not sure... that is, I want to prove myself by my work."

"I have no doubt you'll do just that, Freddie."

"Thank you." I reach down and pull on one of my boots. The weather has taken a turn for the worse, and the nip in the air has turned into a taste of winter. "I really am trying to overhear things, though. I'm not sure how much sneakier I can be. If I come into work in a trench coat and a newspaper with holes in it, they'll start to suspect something."

Tristan's deep laugh rumbles through the phone. "It's almost an idea worth considering."

"The mole might run, knowing we're on to him. You'd have to have security chase him."

"Or her," he adds. "My company is committed to gender equality."

"How noble of you."

"We all do what we can."

I bite my lip, smiling into the phone. We shouldn't be calling like this. Talking like this. And yet here we are.

"Thank you for last week," I say. "At the fair."

"Don't mention it," he says.

But I have to. "I'm sorry. I shouldn't have gotten on that ride in the first place."

"I shouldn't have assumed you wanted to," he retorts. "It's on me, not you."

It's absolutely on me, but I don't press the point. "Let's agree to split the blame, then. Gender equality and all that."

"All right. We're really taking a stand here, aren't we?"

"We'll be mentioned in the history books."

He clears his throat. "At least I didn't catch you out at a bar tonight. Are you in between social engagements for the evening?"

"I don't go to bars *every* night," I tease. "Only every other."

"Oh to live the careless life of a trainee."

I reach for my hat, stomach grumbling. "I worked pretty late, and then I *walked* back to my apartment."

"On the Upper West Side."

"Yes."

A brief pause, like he's considering his next words. But then they come. "You know I live on the Upper West Side too."

"I remember," I murmur. "We might be neighbors."

"We might be."

"I was just planning on heading out, actually."

"To a bar?"

"No, to a deli. The one down my street has the best pastrami sandwich."

"The best?"

"Yes. They also serve Chinese food, which is an interesting mix, but somehow they pull it off."

"Never heard of a place like that in this area."

"Well, it's pretty good," I say. And then, before I can stop myself, "Do you want to join?"

My question hangs in the air between us, and spoken out loud, it sounds ridiculous. He's busy. He has a son, a company, and probably a far more well-stocked fridge than me.

"All right," he says. "Text me the address."

"I will."

"See you soon," he says, hanging up.

I stare at my phone in half-horror, half-wonder. Tristan Conway is meeting me at the small, wildly unsophisticated deli on my street.

At nine p.m. on a Thursday.

I race into the bathroom and wipe at the faint mascara smudges beneath my eyes from a full day of wear. A quick pinch of blush, a brush through my dark hair… it'll have to do.

I'm halfway to the door when I realize I forgot mints. Finally ready to go. Nope, forgot perfume. It takes me a few minutes before I finally feel presentable enough to venture out.

He's waiting outside the deli when I arrive. Leaning against the brick wall, his hands in the pockets of his navy coat.

I swallow at the sight. There's no way he can possibly be here, waiting for me. But he is.

He nods when he sees me. "Freddie."

"Tristan."

"So this is your go-to place?"

I give him a crooked smile and push open the door to the deli. "Don't knock it till you try it."

He holds up a hand in surrender, a smile playing in his eyes. "I won't."

We order a pastrami sandwich each and a plate of fries to share. The familiar cashier with a beanie gives me a wide smile.

"Back again, eh?" he asks.

"I can't seem to stay away," I admit. "You guys save me most evenings."

"Well, it's our pleasure." He shoots Tristan a glance. "Glad to see you're bringing friends, too. Boosts our business."

"Anytime, Kyle."

Tristan and I have a seat in the plastic chairs by the shop window. There's a smile in the corners of his lips, one I remember from the teasing at the Gilded Room.

"What?" I ask.

The smile breaks into a grin. "I wasn't expecting this."

"Oh?"

"No. You're usually so… Proper. Self-contained." He raises an eyebrow. "Strait-laced. I wouldn't have thought you'd be a regular at a place like this."

"So a reformed goody two-shoes can't go to a hole-in-the-wall for food?" I shake my head at him and reach for a French fry. "Didn't expect someone who frequents… well, the places you frequent, to be so narrow-minded."

"Narrow-minded." Tristan reaches for a fry of his own, his fingers brushing mine. The small contact sends electricity racing up my arm. "I'm offended, Frederica."

"Frederica?"

"Your name is beautiful. I don't know why you insist on being called Freddie."

"I like Freddie."

He nods, leaning back. The plastic chair creaks ominously beneath his six-foot-two frame. "I do too, when it's not deceiving me into thinking you're a man."

"The deception was unintentional." I tear back the paper wrapping around my pastrami. "This, right here, is the best sandwich New York has to offer."

A glance up reveals Tristan, arms crossed over his chest, staring at me.

"Did I say something wrong?"

"How long did you say you'd lived in New York?"

"Um, a month and a half. No, almost two now."

"Then you're in no position to judge the city's best sandwich." He reaches for his own. "There's nearly as many restaurants as people in this city, and there's a shit ton of people, so that's saying a lot."

I take a bite of sandwich and flavors erupt in my mouth. Pastrami. Reuben dressing. Rye bread. Wiping at my mouth with my napkin, I shake my head at him.

"Don't tell me you're one of the snobby New Yorkers."

"*Snobby* New Yorkers?"

"Yes," I say. "Who disdain everything a tourist would like."

He takes a bite of his sandwich, his gaze not leaving mine. I wait as he chews. "Good, right?"

"It's good," he admits. "Not the best the city has to offer, though. And for the record, I don't disdain everything a tourist likes. I just… disdain that they are there too."

I laugh, leaning back in my chair. "That might be the most New York sentiment ever. Despite the money they bring the city, you'd rather will them away."

"Tourists and pigeons," he mutters, reaching for another French fry. "The bane of every big-city dweller."

I shake my head. "So you're cynical, too. You must have lived in the city for a long time?"

"All my life."

"Wow. A native New Yorker."

"Manhattanite," he corrects, but he's grinning as he says it. "We're very protective of the status."

"Oh, of course. My bad. I didn't mean to include the outer boroughs in my initial statement."

"I can overlook the mistake."

"Thank you, Mr. Conway. Very kind of you."

He puts down his sandwich. "Mr. Conway. A couple of days ago, I was Tristan."

I look away from the heaviness of his gaze, back down to my own sandwich. A stray pickle has escaped. "That was in a compromised position."

"Protecting my son's elephant," he says, "on a Ferris wheel from hell."

I reach for another French fry. "Exactly. Where's your son tonight?"

"At home."

I look over at him in surprise and he snorts. "He's not alone."

"Phew."

"I'm not that irresponsible of a parent." Tristan leans back in his plastic chair, crossing his arms over his chest, looking like he's never been irresponsible a day in his life.

I push an escaped tendril of hair back. "So, as a native New Yorker, what are your favorite spots?"

His smile is crooked. "You want insider tips?"

"I want to see the city. Tell me where I should go."

"There's a tiny deli on the end of 74th and West. It serves these great pastrami sandwiches," he deadpans, "but oddly enough, they also have Chinese food."

"Watch yourself," I warn him.

Tristan's smile is wide and uninhibited, leaving me dazed. "I'd never mock you, Freddie."

"Sure you wouldn't." But I'm smiling as I shake my head. "I should have known better than to ask advice from an Upper West Sider."

"There's something wrong with this area?"

"No one talks to one another," I say. "I don't know the name of a single person in my building, except the doorman and my super."

"That's New York." He raises an eyebrow. "I didn't know you were so sociable, Strait-laced."

I groan. "I really don't like that nickname."

"It's a shame, because I really do. It's what I called you in my head before I met the real you."

My fingers tighten around my sandwich. "So you thought about me after the party, huh?"

His eyes lock with mine. "You thought about me."

"You're so confident in that."

"Well?" he asks, an eyebrow rising. "Didn't you?"

"I did," I admit. The tension between us rises another notch, the air vibrating around me. "And when I met you, I couldn't help but wonder…"

"Yes?" he prompts.

"Wonder why you go to those parties."

Something sparks in his eyes. "They're fun."

"Yes, well, they certainly are." Heat rises to my cheeks, but I don't look away from his gaze. "That's it, then? It's a fun pastime."

His eyes darken. I hadn't meant for my words to sound judgmental, but hearing them back, it's there. And perhaps I do judge him. Not for going, no, I'd gone too. But for settling for that. He's in his mid-thirties, after all.

"They are what they are," he says gruffly. "No strings, no attachment, no commitments."

I bite my lip. "It's simple."

"It's simple," he agrees.

I think of his son, his job. The commitment to making Exciteur the best it could be. "So you don't have the time to date properly, then, and the Gilded Room is the second best option," I summarize.

"You have me all figured out, do you?"

My heart does a double-take, but I give him a confident grin. "I'm something of a people-reader."

"Is that so?"

"Yes."

"Then finding the mole in the Strategy Department should be a day's work for you. Tell me, Freddie," he says, reaching for the French fries, "why are you single?"

"Why am I single?"

"Yes. If you think you have my dating habits all figured out, it's only fair I get a look into yours."

"In that case, you should be guessing," I point out. "Since I guessed yours."

"Hmm, right."

"Equality and all that."

He braces his arms on the table. "God forbid we forget equality. Right, then. It's my turn to read you."

"I'm an open book."

"You just moved to the city, so you haven't had time to meet someone yet," he says. "That makes sense. But did you leave someone behind in Philadelphia?"

I cross my arms and meet his gaze with my own. "My lips are sealed."

"Unhelpful," he comments. "My guess is that you didn't."

"I didn't?"

Tristan leans back in his chair, mirroring my cross-armed stance. He pulls it off better. "I think you're afraid of men."

My mouth drops open at that. "I'm sorry?"

"Oh, not the kind of fear you have for heights. I mean the fear of being burned. You see, Freddie, I think you like to be in control."

"I do, do I?"

"Yes. You've kept your head down and focused on school, on internships, on your work. Told yourself there's no time for dating, but the truth is, you've never made the time... because it scares you. It's the one realm where you're not in control at all."

I stare at him, the half-eaten sandwich forgotten in front of me. Tristan stares gamely back at me with eyes that burn with triumph, and something else. Something that picks at my soul as surely as his words had. Recognition.

"Well," I breathe. "That was quite the analysis. Now it's my turn to wonder... do you tell yourself the same thing?"

His eyes narrow. "Do I tell myself what?"

"That you don't have time for dating. That the Gilded Room parties are all you have space for, putting the majority of your energy into your company and family instead."

"I don't have much time, that's true."

My next words are breathless. "And yet here you are, at a deli on a Thursday evening."

"And yet here I am," he murmurs. "Was I right, Freddie? In my analysis?"

"Was I?"

His lips curl ever so slightly, full in the five-o'clock shadow that darkens his lower face. "I got an envelope delivered today."

"Did you?"

"It was gold."

I bite my lip. "How exciting. Wonder what that can be."

"Wonder indeed," he agrees. "I'm assuming you got a similar one."

I hadn't. Moment of truth, moment of possibility...

"No," I admit. "I wouldn't be surprised if I don't get one at all this time."

He raises an eyebrow. "And why is that?"

"I might have done something that's slightly... against the rules."

"What's this, Strait-laced? Tell me."

"Well, *technically* speaking, the invitation I received last time was addressed to the former tenant."

A smile spreads across his lips. "Frederica Bilson."

"I went, I saw, I conquered."

"It's *came*," he corrects. "I came, I saw, I conquered. And you most certainly came."

I bury my head in my hands, unable to look at him. Thank God we're the only ones in the deli. "Christ, Tristan."

His laughter is unashamed. "So you snuck into a Gilded Room party. I have to say, this challenges my view of you."

"Terrific. Can we lose the nickname now?"

"No," he says. "I did wonder how you'd paid for

membership on a trainee's salary... so this solves that conundrum."

"I didn't pay at all."

"A beauty membership after all," he muses. "Well... let me phrase it this way. If you end up receiving an invitation, will you go?"

I look up at him. He's watching me with practiced casualness, like my answer is nothing but a curiosity. But there's a burning interest in his eyes that he can't entirely mask.

He's going.

And he's asking if I'm going too.

My stomach locks into a fist of anticipation as want floods me. We're playing with fire, and I've always been careful. Always done the right thing.

But now I want to be burned. "I think I will," I tell him. "If I get an invitation, that is."

"Good to know," he says, smiling. "Maybe I'll see you there."

"Maybe you will... Tristan."

12

FREDDIE

A thick, golden envelope is waiting for me when I get back from work a few days later. It's lying on my trodden doormat, innocuous. Like before, my address is written on it. Like before, my name isn't.

"Well, well... let's see what you have in store for me this time," I murmur, slicing it open with my finger. This is worth daring a paper cut for. I pull out an invitation printed on thick cardstock.

It's addressed to me.

Me, as in, Frederica Bilson. Not Rebecca Hartford.

I sink down onto my kitchen chair with the invitation still in hand. This has to be Tristan's doing—it *has* to be. Has he paid the fee for me? Pulled some strings with the selection committee?

My eyes scan the rest of the invitation.

Frederica Bilson,

It's December, and the holidays are just around the corner. You know what that means... a lot of gift-wrapping and bow-tying. Or untying. We know which one we prefer.

Join us at the Winter Hotel this coming Saturday. Leave your smartphone and inhibition at the door, and remember, anonymity is the currency that makes the world go round.

Yours in pleasure,
The Gilded Room

It feels like the invitation has a heartbeat of its own, and it's pounding just as fast as mine. Closing my eyes, I see Tristan's face in front of me, the way he'd looking sitting across from me in the dimly lit deli last week. Deep, blue eyes. Thick dark hair. Two-day-old beard along his square jaw. My stomach clenches at the idea of sleeping with him again. This time, we'll know each other. Who we are outside of the confines of the Gilded Room.

And we'd still be choosing one another.

I glance over at the dresser in my tiny room, at my shrine to success. My grandfather. My parents. My business books and my diploma.

Sleeping with a boss has *never* been the kind of move I want to make. I had once laughed at women who did that— I'd scorned it.

And yet here we are.

Tristan had been right, the arrogant bastard, when he said I'm afraid of dating. Somehow he'd found my weak spot and applied pressure to it, like he knew the ins and outs of me just by looking. It's the one realm of my life I've never managed to feel confident in. Where effort doesn't correlate to success, where I can't study my way to an A or work long hours to get a good performance review.

My fingers tighten around the invitation still in my hand. Perhaps I'm done being afraid.

Time to undo those laces.

When Saturday rolls around, I've repeated the same I'm-going-to-a-secret-elite-sex-club shower I did last time.

Shaved. Scrubbed. Contemplated my life decisions. Blow-dried my hair.

The dress I'm wearing isn't remotely as revealing as last time... but it is tighter. It clings to my skin like a second one, deep red in color. It's a dress I'd bought with friends in Philadelphia, the kind your girlfriends say *you have to get this!* but you have absolutely no business wearing to work or bars.

Turns out I have just the occasion for it now.

I arrive at the Winter Hotel just as it begins to snow. The flakes fall gently from the dark sky, whirling to the sidewalk like heaven-sent crystals. I pause outside to catch a few in my gloved hand. I've always loved the snow. Has to be a good sign.

The elevator to the thirteenth floor is smooth and uninterrupted. I keep my eyes trailed on the monitor for each passing floor. I've learned how to conquer elevators. Philadelphia taught me how, but it's still a small mental hurdle every time, and I breathe a sigh of relief when I step out.

"Welcome," a smartly dressed woman in a suit says. She's not wearing anything beneath her blazer, the open V neatly covering her breasts.

"Thank you," I say, extending my invitation. She smiles as she looks it over.

"Welcome, Frederica. Do you have your mask with you?"

I pull it out of my clutch. "I do."

"Then you're good to go. Enjoy yourself." She pulls back a draped curtain and I step into the Winter's grand ballroom and enter a world of decadence.

I hand my phone to the attendant, barely looking at him as I receive my numbers. Because there's a giant catwalk in the middle of the ballroom, and walking on it are women draped in silk and pearls... and nothing else. Guests mingle around the catwalk, applauding, whistling. As I watch, a guest is pulled up by a performer, and she joins them without breaking stride, pulling off her dress as she walks down the runway.

The same thick, pulsing beat resonates from the speakers, and my nostrils fill with the scent of incense.

"Champagne?"

"Yes, thank you," I murmur, accepting a flute from a waiter's tray. In a daze, I move through the party in search of a tall, broad-shouldered man I have no business talking to.

I don't see him.

A woman sitting on a couch sees my roving gaze. She gives me a grin and runs her hand over her partner's hair. His hand is moving between her legs.

"Join us, honey?"

"Thank you, but I'm here with someone."

"Bring him too," she purrs.

Christ. "Maybe later, thank you."

She smiles. "Enjoy yourself, then. Let loose."

Right. I nod at her and move on, weaving around draped compartments in search of the bar. A few people sit on the stools, but it's mostly empty.

Tristan's not here either.

Had he already disappeared into one of the private rooms? The party has barely begun.

I sit down by the bar and cross my legs, intimately aware of how the red fabric slides up. My gaze skims over people walking in various stages of undress, women in lingerie mixed with men in suits. An attendant in the corner in a silken loincloth gives me a cursory glance, and I smile. Security, just like Tristan had pointed out.

If only he was here.

Half an hour later, I motion the waiter for another glass of champagne. I repeat the motion forty minutes later.

Still no Tristan. And with no phone, there's nothing to do but watch the increasingly lascivious performance on stage. In a way, I can only applaud them, because there's no way I could do what they do. Being pleasured while suspended naked from the ceiling in silk, with dozens and dozens of people watching… Nope.

But no Tristan.

The shirtless bartender pushes a drink across the bar to me. He rests on his arms, giving me a grin. "Your first time here?"

I must look pathetic. "My second, actually."

There's a kind look in his eyes. "I see. You're hoping to see a special someone."

I frown. "That obvious?"

"Just because I've seen it before, darling. Second-timers are often set on repeating their first night. But guests change, and change changes the guests. Many come here in search of new partners... not to repeat the old ones."

"He said he would be here, though." But even as I say it, I hear the thinness of my words. I sound like someone who's been stood up at a bar. I'd assumed that Tristan had gotten me the invitation, that he'd been as excited to repeat this as me... but he's not here. Or if he is, he's already busy, distracted with someone else.

I glance down at my glass. "You're right," I tell the bartender. "I'm probably a textbook second-timer."

His smile widens. "Don't beat yourself up about it. There are plenty of people here who'd love to have fun."

"I'm sure there are," I say, thinking about the several interested looks I'd received from men already. None had come up to talk to me—the first rule of the Gilded Room in action. I slide off the high barstool. "Thanks for the pep talk."

"Anytime, gorgeous." He waves me away. "Have fun."

I give the room one last walk-around, tossing back the contents of the drink he'd given me. The gin and tonic burns as it goes down my throat. I discard it on a table, ignoring the couple furiously making out next to it, and head to the corridors beyond.

One open door reveals... oh God. No, no, why did I think I could do this? If Tristan is behind any of these, I don't want to see him. It would kill me. My painful high-heeled shoes steer me directly toward the exit. A few seconds later and I have my phone and my coat, hurrying to the elevator.

A pipe dream, that's what this was. Even if he was here… what then? He's still my boss. The CEO of Exciteur, older, more experienced, rich. A father. Someone who frequents a club like this. And I spent last night on my bed, watching old re-runs of *Gilmore Girls* and making s'mores by heating up chocolate and marshmallows in the microwave.

What was I thinking?

Arriving back in my tiny apartment feels like coming home for the first time since I'd moved in. Shutting out the city beyond, the temptations, the disappointments. I kick off my shoes and tug, tug, *tug* at the tight red dress. Slip into my sweatpants and old T-shirt. I've just sat down on my bed, my head in my hands, when my phone dings with a text.

There's just one thought in my head.

It's Tristan, asking where I was. Tristan, explaining that he couldn't come.

It's not.

Luke: Hey, team leader. Want to grab a coffee one of these days and let me show you New York?

My fingers tremble only slightly as I write back the response. I'm not afraid, I tell myself. I just know my lane. And it's with guys my age, perhaps a trainee in a different department, and not with the head of the company.

Freddie: I'd love to! How about tomorrow?

13

TRISTAN

The coffee is bitter and too hot, burning my throat. It does nothing to counteract the pit of jealousy in my stomach. It's a feeling I have no right to, not to mention no reason to feel, and I hate things that have no purpose.

But I hate things I can't control even more.

Yesterday's snow hadn't settled, but a light dusting of it remains on the trees in Central Park. Joshua and I spent an hour in the park earlier with an obligatory stop at Larry's. In our household, it's never too cold for ice cream. And the entire time I'd been debating the wisdom of calling Frederica.

Had she gone to the Gilded Room last night?

My hand tightens around the coffee cup. And what could I do about it if she had? I'd pulled a favor to get her a personal invite, and it hadn't been so she could get close and personal with some smarmy Wall Street banker. No, I'd planned on being there.

Joshua was supposed to spend the night at his godmother's. But one of her kids had gotten mono, so the playdate was cancelled. And with Linda scheduled, I'd already given both my housekeeper and the nanny the weekend off. Which meant there was no one left standing but me.

"Dad?"

I swallow the bitterness. I'd had an evening with my kid instead, ordering pizza and playing cards, and it had been great. "Yes?"

Joshua bounces past the grand piano and comes to stand beside me by the windows. The piano had been my sister's. Joshua doesn't like his weekly piano lessons, but I haven't let him quit yet. Jenny hated hers when she was his age too.

"Guess what?" he asks.

"What?"

"Marianne is making lasagna tonight."

I grin, ruffling his hair. "Did you ask her nicely?"

"I didn't have to ask." He does a little dance in his whale-print sweatpants, a gift from his grandmother. "She offered. I think she knows I have a test in school tomorrow."

"Your schedule is on the refrigerator, so she knows. And you're going to do great, kid."

"I know," he says, a little too quickly. "We've been practicing a lot."

"We sure have. Do you want to run through it again?"

"No."

"All right. We'll do it one final time after dinner, then." I follow him into his bedroom, glancing at the giant world map above his bed. That had been a birthday present from me. Together, we'd scratched out the places we've visited and circled the places that are still on the bucket list.

Between me and my sister, Jenny had been the worldly one. The one who jumped at the chance of an exchange year in Sydney, who went against our parents' wishes to backpack in Southeast Asia for five months. I'd had my head in numbers and school, and then, in business. No time for travel or frivolity.

That's changed. Joshua will have seen the world by the time he's eighteen, if I have a say in it, including the places his mother had loved.

"Have you spoken to Danielle since the Thanksgiving fair?" I ask him.

"Yes," he says, sitting down cross-legged by his latest Lego set. He's graduated to more complex builds and the pieces for each now number in the thousands.

"And?"

"She thought it was cool that we had the amusement fair to ourselves. She asked if it was *your* amusement fair," he says, laughing. "I told her no."

"I'm glad the two of you enjoyed yourselves."

He lies back on the carpet, staring up at the ceiling. "She said I was one of her favorite people in class the other day."

"Did she? Joshua, that's awesome."

"Yes," he says, kicking one of his legs up in the air. "But she also said Maria was one of her favorites. And Turner and Dexter."

I put my hand in front of my mouth to hide my grin. "Mhm."

"So I'm not the only one." He screws his eyes shut. "Dad, we can't talk about this right now. I have to prepare for my test."

"All right, all right. I was just curious."

"You're always curious," he accuses me, and now I have to laugh. That's what I've told him for years, right after he's asked me a string of fifteen increasingly impossible-to-answer questions.

"I'll leave you alone."

"Thank you," he says. "We'll talk at dinner."

It's such a teenage thing to say that I'm still chuckling to myself when I return to the living room. The smell of Marianne's lasagna drifts from the kitchen, meat and tomatoes and cheese.

My hand goes to my pocket. My phone. My musings. Without Joshua to distract me, my mind finds its way back to Freddie and the wound of last night. I know there's only one way to quell the jealousy simmering inside of me.

I shouldn't, of course. I could write a book about all the reasons why interacting with Frederica Bilson won't end well.

Not only is she a trainee, but she's a hungry one, with her eyes set on forging a career of her own. And I'm not the young man I was before Jenny and Michael's accident, when relationships were easy and fun.

And yet, the jealousy burns on.

When Joshua has gone to bed, I dial the now familiar number.

She picks up after four eternity-long signals. "Hello."

"Freddie."

"I don't have any more information on the mole in the Strategy Department," she informs me.

I blow out a breath, amused despite myself. "No, I didn't expect you would."

"All right, then." The question hangs in the abrasive silence. *What are you calling for, Mr. Conway?*

"How are you?"

"I'm good," she says. "I've had a relaxing weekend."

My teeth grit at the word relaxing. "Meet me at the deli down the street?"

"Sorry?"

"Turns out those sandwiches were some of the best in the city after all. I'm craving one."

"Why?"

"I'm hungry," I say. I'm not.

"Mr. Conway…"

"Meet me, Freddie."

"I just got back home and I've been out all day."

It's not a no, but it's not a yes, either. "Then you must be hungry. If I remember correctly, pastrami is your favorite."

She sighs. "I'll be there in five."

The tiny, reluctant yes soothes the flames in my stomach. I need to look her in the eyes when I ask her about yesterday. When I explain why I couldn't be there. Grabbing my coat from the rack, I pop my head into the kitchen where Marianne is prepping tomorrow's breakfast. "I'm heading out for a few hours, just down the street."

"All right, sir."

"If Joshua wakes up or needs anything, call me."

"Will do."

The deli is just as garishly lit by neon lighting as it had been a week ago. I must have walked by it a thousand times and never given it a passing thought, only two blocks from my apartment.

She'd said it was just down the street from her.

So it's not enough that Freddie infiltrates the club I frequent. It's not even enough that she starts working at my company. She also lives a ten-minute walk from my home, and now, it seems, she's occupying space in my mind rent-free.

Which means I'm pretty much doomed.

I'm there first, so I lean against the building and scan the surrounding streets. It doesn't take long before I see her. She has a beige coat wrapped tightly around her curvy figure, dark hair lifting in the wind. Red lips and sharp eyes that narrow as she sees me.

"You came," I say.

"You insisted," she says.

I push the door open to the near-empty deli. "After you."

She orders nothing but a soda, smiling at the guy behind the counter. He smiles back, smitten.

The expression disappears when it's my turn to order. "Coffee, if you have it. Black."

"Coming right up."

Freddie leads the way to the same table as before, right by the windows and the whirl of snowflakes in the air. I watch as she removes her black leather gloves, slim, long-fingered hands closing around her soda can. The sight brings other images to mind, memories I'd do better not to dwell on. Like her hand closing around me.

"Why did you call me?"

"I wanted to see you," I say. It's the truth.

Freddie glances out the window. "I didn't see you yesterday."

So she'd gone to the Gilded Room.

She'd gone, and she'd looked for me.

"I couldn't make it." Can she hear the burning regret in my voice?

"I figured as much, yeah."

I lean back in the plastic chair, my hand on the one next to me. "But you attended?"

"After you went through so much trouble to get me my own invite, how could I turn it down?"

My lips curve. "It wasn't too much trouble."

Her gaze returns to the can in front of her, and the question springs out of me, ill-advised and unstoppable. "Did you meet someone?"

"I met several someones," she murmurs.

Jealousy has a tight grip around my insides, squeezing until I feel nauseous. "Several someones, Strait-laced?"

Her eyes flicker up, widening as she registers the look in mine. "Oh, not like that, silly. I spoke to a few people. The bartender, mostly."

"You spoke to a few people."

"Yes." She crosses her arms. "Are you wondering if anything *more* happened? If I slept with someone?"

I meet her gaze baldly. "You know I am."

"And you should know better than to ask. What happens at the Gilded Room stays there. *You* were the one who taught me that."

"I know." Speaking through gritted teeth is difficult, but I manage. "I also know I have no right to ask."

"None," she says. "If you're so concerned, you should have showed up."

"Something came up."

"Yeah, you said that." She braces her hands on the table and leans forward. "As you've demonstrated tonight, you have my number. You could have texted me at any point before the party to warn me you weren't going to show."

The thought hadn't struck me. I'm not a texter, not to mention that *we've* never texted, her and I. But here she is, angry that I hadn't let her know.

Which means she'd waited for me.

She'd sat at that club, and she'd waited for me. Hell, she'd even resorted to talking to the bartender. The idea that a woman had waited for me...

"You didn't sleep with anyone," I say, sure now that I'm right. Freddie rolls her eyes, but I keep going. "I'm sorry. You're right, and I should have let you know."

Her palms fall flat on the table between us, her soda can untouched between them. "I would have appreciated that, yes."

"I never meant to leave you waiting. If anything, I spent the evening imagining all the things you were doing and growing more miserable by the minute."

She snorts, looking down at my hand on the plastic table. It's only inches away from her own. "That seems like a waste of energy."

"It was."

"Why didn't you come?"

I admit what must sound like a remote problem for her, unattached and young as she is. It's miles away from her own life. "My son was supposed to be at a sleepover, but it was cancelled. There was no time to get a sitter."

Freddie's eyes soften. "Oh. I understand."

"Damn annoying, though."

"There'll be more parties," she murmurs, and the acknowledgment makes my body tighten. The things I'd do to her, the things I'd let her do to me. My gaze strays to the dark red lipstick.

"What have you been up to today?"

Her gaze drifts back to the window, the whirling snow beyond. "I was out seeing the city with a friend."

And just when I thought I was beyond jealousy, it comes roaring back, an unwelcome friend. It's been years since I felt anything like this. "Where did you go?"

"The Met first, and then we had dinner at a place in Tribeca. There was a line. It's apparently very popular."

"Medusa?"

"That's the one, yes." In profile, her face is stunning. A nose that's lightly turned up, like she's judging everything around her, but with full lips that are quick to smile and laugh if you pass the test.

"I'm glad you're making friends in the city."

Her gaze returns to mine. There's no animosity there now, her brown eyes soft. "Actually, I think it might have been a date."

Is the woman trying to kill me? My scowl deepens without conscious thought. Of course she's dating. The woman is a fucking twenty on a scale of ten.

"Oh?" I ask, making my voice casual. *Behold, world, my acting abilities.* "How did it go?"

"I'm not sure I wanted it to have been a date in the first place." Shaking her head, she looks down at her hands. "I was a bit angry at you, and I was thinking about how you said I'm afraid of men. Of things I can't control. So I said yes when he asked me."

My eyes widen. I don't think she realizes it, but her honesty is breathtaking, and just as beautiful as she is. "You wanted to test yourself?"

"I suppose so, yes. Not to mention I don't know anyone in New York, and I want to make friends."

"You know me," I say. Her quirked eyebrow makes me smile, and I hold up a hand. "All right, all right. I suppose I don't really count?"

"Not really," she admits. "No offense, but I don't see myself calling you for help if my heater breaks down and my super doesn't respond."

"You could, you know. I'm only a few blocks away."

The look she shoots me makes it clear she thinks I'm ridiculous. "I live in a shoebox."

"So? That should make repairs easier, not more difficult," I say. She shakes her head, like I'm missing an obvious point. I brace my arms against the table. "We can be friends, Freddie."

"You're my boss. Well, technically my boss's boss."

"Sure, we're friends *outside* of the office. I thought that was a given."

Her smile widens. "Friends."

"Friends," I agree. "So if you need someone to show you around New York or take you to the Met, you can ask me. Not to mention I could get you past the line at Medusa." The improbable words fall from my lips, despite the fact that I have no free time, and what time I have I give to my son.

"Is this because I mentioned I had a date today?"

"The two are unrelated."

"Right." She laughs, shaking her head so the dark locks fly, tangled from the snow and the wind. "If I didn't know better, I'd say you're jealous, Tristan."

"I would never stoop so low," I say. "The emotion is beneath me."

"Oh, of course it is. Too common?"

"By far."

A smile plays across lips I can recall kissing all too well. "Now that we're unofficially friends, there are a ton of things I want to know about you," she says.

I groan, looking up at the neon lights in the ceiling. "I'm regretting this already."

"I'll start easy, don't worry. You're just fascinating to me." The sincerity in her voice is unexpected, seeping through my cracks. "Tell me why you go to the Gilded Room."

"I've already told you."

"I feel like it wasn't the entire truth."

I drag my gaze back to her, to eyes that are sparkling with humor and friendliness, and find myself actually considering answering the question. Even if the response isn't one that'll paint me in the best of lights.

A shadow next to our table stops me. "I'm sorry, guys, but we're closing in a few minutes."

"Oh," Freddie says with a frown, like she's disappointed she doesn't get to talk to me more.

We can't have that.

"Thanks for letting us know," I tell the employee. "We'll be out before then."

"Have a good night."

"You too," Freddie says.

When he's left, I reach over and lift up Freddie's soda can. It's full. "You haven't even had a taste."

"I was distracted."

I lift up my own cup of takeaway coffee, still full. "So was I."

She catches on immediately. "It would be a shame to throw these out."

"It would be wasteful, really. And I'm committed to eliminating all forms of waste."

Her smile widens. "You are famously committed to efficiency."

"So this can't stand." I push back my chair and grab my coffee cup, handing Freddie her gloves. "Show me your shoebox and we'll drink it on the way."

Her breathing hitches, despite the excitement in her eyes. "Show you where I live?"

"If I'm going to fix your heater one day, I'll need to know where it is, won't I?" I push open the door and a cold gust of wind sweeps in. "After you, Frederica."

14

TRISTAN

The coffee is cold and tastes like the bottom of a never-cleaned French press, but I drink it like the flimsy excuse of finishing our drinks is real. Snowflakes catch in Freddie's dark hair.

"This doesn't feel real," she says. "The two of us, walking to my shoebox apartment."

Damn her, for being ambitious and intelligent *as well* as sincere and shy. I can handle one or the other, but both? It's more than a man should have to face.

"We're friends, and this is a friendly thing to do. How'd you find the place?"

She takes a sip of her soda. "The lady who owns the apartment lives a few floors below. I think it used to be the place their au pairs lived in, and then the maid, when they had one. She's alone now, her husband dead and the children gone. A friend of mine from Wharton lived there while she studied for her undergraduate at Columbia."

I nod. "She put you in touch with the landlord?"

Freddie nods, smiling warmly. "Geraldine is lovely. She doesn't trust easily, you see, and so the fact that I was vouched for by someone she liked helped. Then we met, and she decided she liked me too."

"You do seem like the perfect candidate for impressing old women, Strait-laced," I say. "I trust she doesn't know anything about the Gilded Room?"

"God, no. And don't you dare mention anything about it while we're inside."

"Do you think she's spying on you?"

"Probably not, but I'm not willing to take any risks."

We stop in front of a gray-stoned building, looking much like any Upper West Side residential. Freddie nods to the doorman. He nods back, but gives me a look I know well. It's the you're-new-to-me look, coupled with a dose of watch-yourself.

So Freddie has managed to charm him too, on top of the guy who works at the deli place and her fellow trainees at Exciteur. I'm not surprised, because here I am, heading up to her apartment with cold coffee in hand that I'm apparently desperate to finish.

"I live on the top floor," she says, pausing by the elevators. "I have one window, but it doesn't overlook anything. Not if you don't count some rooftops, a solid brick wall and a few places where pigeons perch."

"They count," I say. "Brick is... interesting to look at."

"Liar," she says, stepping after me into the elevator and pressing the top button. Her hands clasp in front of her, and as I watch, she goes rigid. Her gaze is fixed on the floor numbers shifting on the monitor.

Ah. The fear of heights.

"I'm not going to judge where you live," I say, raising an eyebrow at her. "If that's what you're worried about."

Her gaze doesn't waver, but she smiles. "Sure you won't. Your apartment overlooks Central Park, right? I remember you saying that on the phone."

"It does," I admit. "But what's Central Park to a brick wall? Just a few trees. Nothing I haven't seen before."

That earns me a chuckle. "As opposed to brick."

"You know what they say, once you've seen one tree,

you've seen them all," I say, talking to keep her distracted as the elevator ascends at a snail's pace. "But bricks… there are endless nuances. Colors. Textures. Sizes."

She breaks her staring contest with the elevator panel to give me an amused look. "Is this some sort of fetish, Tristan?"

My smile is crooked. "Oh, if you want to talk about—"

The elevator groans and comes to a sudden stop. The lights flicker once, twice, before they give up. We're swallowed by pitch darkness.

Freddie doesn't scream, but the gasp coming from her direction is filled with such terror that I move toward her on instinct.

"It's okay," I say. "We're okay."

"This can't be happening." Her voice shakes with the effort to stay in control. My hand closes around her arm, her coat soft beneath my fingers.

"Breathe, Freddie. Breathe. We'll be okay."

She takes deep, shuddering breaths. I settle my hands on her shoulders and press inwards, as if I can anchor her by my touch alone.

"Are you breathing?"

"Yes," she whispers. "Tristan, I think I'm about to have a panic attack. At any second, a cord could snap, and we would plummet to—"

"No," I say firmly. "That's not going to happen. Do you know what will?"

"What?" she breathes.

"We're going to sit down, right here, and we're going to call maintenance as well as that doorman of yours. They'll have this fixed in no time." I reach for the steel wall, and then gently pull us both down to the floor. She follows in a fluid motion.

Then I do something I know I shouldn't, but it's just the two of us here, and judging by the shallowness of her breath, she's fracturing. So I pull her into my arms.

"Breathe, Freddie. Deeply in, deeply out."

She trembles but does what I say, following along to my own exaggerated breaths. I tighten an arm around her shoulders and her hair tickles my nose.

"We'll be okay," I say. "The elevator looks new. I'm sure an automatic alert has already been issued."

The panel in the elevator isn't lit up, though. Pressing the alarm button would likely do zilch. Perhaps a power outage? Freddie's hands tighten on the fastening of my coat, curling around the edges.

"Do you know the number to your doorman?"

She shakes her head, but after a few more breaths, she speaks. "I think it's in my phone."

"I'll call him."

"Okay. Just give me a minute."

I hold her, smoothing my hands over her arms, before she's composed enough to reach into her pocket and hand me her phone. There's a notification waiting for her on her phone. A message.

Luke: Had a great time today, Fred. I hope you'll let me show you around next weekend too.

I click the annoying message away—*now's not the time, Tristan*—although the name imprints itself in my mind. Scrolling through her contacts, I find the one titled *Doorman Tom* and hit call. Put him on speakerphone.

"This is Tom," a voice says. "What can I help you with?"

"This is Tristan Conway and Frederica Bilson. We entered the building just a few minutes ago, and we're now in the elevator. It stopped when we were roughly at the thirteenth floor. The lights are all out and the panel is unlit."

"Shit," Tom says, and despite the unprofessionalism, I can only agree with him. "I'll call for a technician right away. Don't worry, either of you. This has happened before."

Then it should have been fixed before, I think. "We'll wait. Please keep us updated of any developments."

"Of course, sir. We should have you out in no time." A brief pause. "Is everything all right with Ms. Bilson?"

Raising her head from my shoulder, Freddie clears her throat. "I'm fine, Tom."

"Good. All right, then. Sit tight," he says and hangs up.

A breathless, scared laughter bubbles out of Freddie. I can't see her face, but I don't need to to understand her reaction. "Sit tight," she wheezes.

I slide my arm down and circle her waist, evident even through the thickness of her coat. "You heard the man. Come here."

She sidles closer. "You don't think we'll die?"

"I don't," I say. "Not even a little bit. Let's breathe again, sweetheart."

We breathe in tandem for ten long, slow breaths, my hand moving over her lower back the entire time in languid strokes.

"Okay," she whispers. "I'm better."

"Good," I murmur back.

"I'm focusing on you and not on the hundred-feet drop beneath us."

My hand brushes the bottom of her hair, the thick strands tickling my skin. "Focus on me, then."

She clears her throat. "Can you talk for a bit?"

"Okay," I say, pitching my voice to soothe. "You said earlier that you wanted to get to know me. There are all kinds of things I could tell you, you know."

Her silence tells me to keep going, so I do, my hand rising to smooth over her hair. It's like silk beneath my palm. "I was born and raised in this neighborhood. Just a few blocks over, actually. There's no other place I'd want to live, not permanently. New York is my home."

"Despite the pigeons and tourists," she whispers.

"Despite them," I agree. "Perhaps it's all the brick in this city that appeals to me."

She snorts once in humor, a small victory. I stretch out my

legs in front of me and tighten my arms around her. "My favorite ice cream flavor is mango."

"Mango?"

"Yes. Mango sorbet, actually."

"That's unusual."

"Well, the way I see it, I'm leaving all the cookie dough and mint chocolate chip to the rest of you. It's a win-win situation. Let's see what more…" I cast my mind out for anything about myself, anything that would be interesting enough to keep her focus on me and away from the height we're currently sitting at. "You asked me why I attend the Gilded Room party, even though I'd already answered you."

"The real answer," she murmurs.

"Right. The real answer." Sighing, I lean my head against the steel wall behind us and bare my soul. "The last decade, I've become accustomed to a certain kind of woman approaching me. The one who expects designer handbags for birthdays, Valentine's days and Christmases, who shivers at the mention of a prenup."

Not that I'd dated many, not with Joshua and my job. There were none that I'd ever consider turning into a stepmom, and even fewer I think would actually relish the task. Joshua would be an unfortunate consequence of getting me, and my wealth, rather than a reason to stay.

But Joshua has never been an unfortunate consequence. He might not have come to me naturally, but over my dead body will he ever feel like he's a burden.

Freddie's caressing fingers makes me realize I've fallen silent. I cover her hand on my chest with my own, wrapping my fingers around hers. "Anyway. The women I meet at the Gilded Room don't know who I am, at least the majority of them. When one speaks to me, I know they don't want me for my money."

Freddie twists in my grip, like she's looking at my face. Perhaps she is, but it's too dark for either of us to see anything. "But they only want you for your body," she whispers. "Is that better?"

I walk my hand up her arm to cup her cheek in my palm. It's wet, and I use my thumb to brush away the panicked tears that have fallen in the darkness. "It is," I say. "Perhaps only marginally, but it's better. How are you doing, sweetheart?"

"Holding it together."

"Do you want us to breathe again for a bit?"

She nods, and we do another round of ten breaths. In and out, slowly and surely. I stroke my hand over her hair. "We'll be fine, Freddie. I don't think it'll be long now."

She doesn't call me on it, shivering instead. "Cold?" I ask.

"It's just the fear. God, I feel silly."

Fuck. I really don't want her to feel afraid, but there's nothing I can do but keep her distracted. "You're not silly," I tell her.

"But I know that I am, because there isn't any *real* danger. And now you're seeing me like this." Her breathing speeds up until it's in pants, her hands on my chest tightening into gripping claws.

"Hey, we're friends, aren't we? I'm here, and I won't go anywhere. Just focus on me."

"I'm trying," she whispers, but she's still trembling in my arms. In the darkness, I can't see her expression, but I can hear the increasing panic in her breathing.

So I tip her head back and stroke her full lips with my thumb, and do the only thing I can think of. I slant my mouth over hers.

Our lips meet in softness, fear meeting strength. I smooth my thumb over her cheek and try to convey comfort, stability. Try to tear her mind away from the panic.

She pulls me into it instead.

Her mouth opens on a gasp and slim fingers slide into my hair. They tug, sending shivers down my spine. Kissing her at the Gilded Room had been like drinking the sweetest wine. Here in the darkness she's whiskey, and she burns.

Her lips open and I take what's offered, sweeping my tongue over her lower lip. It's gentle.

She responds by climbing into my lap.

My hands shift to her thighs, gripping her as she straddles me. In the darkness, there's no telling where one of us ends and the other starts, and I kiss her like she's the only light available.

She kisses me back like she trusts me. Like she needs me as desperately in this moment as I need her. My fingers dig into her hips, craving the contact of her smooth skin instead of the fabric of her coat.

My entire body tightens in need.

She locks her hands behind my neck, and it's been so long since someone clung to me like this, like she needs me and only me in this moment. Her teeth scrape over my lower lip and I chuckle, my palms flattening against her back. So she wants to play rough?

Sudden light plays against my closed lids. I lift my head from Freddie's, blinking against the brightness.

A clipped voice echoes from the panel. "We're very sorry about this inconvenience. We should have the elevator moving again shortly."

"Thank you," I call out.

The line clicks off and I turn my attention to Freddie, still straddling my legs. Her eyes are red and wet, her lips puffy, and I know the latter is my doing. "How are you doing?"

"Good," she says, but the harrowed look in her eyes doesn't leave. I smooth my hands over hers and loosen the death grip on my coat.

"Let's stand."

She gives me a look that makes it clear she thinks I'm crazy for suggesting it, but I help her up, my arm around her waist. We sway as the elevator begins to move with a faint jerk.

She buries her face in my jacket, and I smooth a hand over her back. Over and over again until the elevator slides to a smooth halt at the top floor. It's a tangle of arms and haste in making it out into the narrow corridor, and then Freddie's hand finds mine and she's pulling me to a door at the end. Her hands tremble as she pulls out her keys, so I take them from her and unlock the door.

All of her is trembling. She pauses in the middle of her tiny studio and covers her face with her hands. There's not a sound, but her shoulders shake.

I shut the door behind me and wrap my arms around her. "You're okay now," I tell her. "You're home."

"This is so silly," she says in between racketing sobs. "I'm sorry, Tristan, I don't know…"

"It's not silly. That was a stressful situation, and now it's over. Of course you're reacting to it." I look around the room for a couch, but there is none, only a bed tucked into a corner of the room. It's neatly decorated with a gray spread and colorful pillows.

I pull us toward it, and we sink down together, her still in my arms.

"You're not," she accuses.

"I'm not reacting?" I smooth my hand over her hair, looking up at the ceiling in the tiny studio. The bed smells like her, of floral perfume and shampoo and the woman clinging to me. I'm most definitely reacting. "I wouldn't say that. That wasn't a pleasant experience."

She shudders in my arms. "I'm only taking the stairs from now on."

"You live on the fourteenth floor."

"Then I suppose I'll get in great shape."

I chuckle, curving my fingers around her waist and holding her as she calms down. Her crying abates as quickly as it had come on, a consequence now of released tension and not fear. It's gone entirely when she props her head in her hand and looks at me.

I smooth my thumb over her cheek, over the lightly smudged mascara. "You're okay," I murmur.

Her smile is small but true. Traces of amusement play in her eyes. "This is really not how I wanted you to think of me."

"I can think of you anyway I want," I say. "Not for you to decide."

Her faint laughter is breathless. "Right."

"And your fear of heights hasn't made me think less of you, if that's what you're worried about." My fingers shift to her ear, tracing the smooth edge of her jaw. Her skin is like silk beneath my fingers. No, this has only made her more human to me, real and fallible and sweet and nuanced, with frailty to counter the ambitious fire.

And it just makes me want her more.

Freddie leans into my hand and closes her eyes. "How did you know what to do?"

"What to do?"

"To calm me down," she says. "Have you talked people away from a panic attack before?"

My hand slips from her cheek. "My sister used to have them."

"Oh, I see." Giving me an apologetic smile, Freddie gets up from the bed and gets a tissue to wipe her eyes and nose. She kicks off her shoes and shrugs out of her beige coat. A turtleneck and dark jeans cling to her body, to the shapely thighs and hips, the dip of her waist.

I close my eyes, but it's no use, because she settles against me on the bed. Her hand on my chest, her leg over mine, as if we lie like this all the time.

"Used to?" she asks. "How did she get them to stop?"

I look up at the ceiling. "She died a few years ago."

"Oh. Tristan, I'm sorry, I didn't mean to bring it up."

"You couldn't have known."

"Still. I'm sorry."

"Thank you," I say. My coat is unbuttoned and there's

nothing but the fabric of my shirt between her fingers and my skin. I close my eyes. "I've never kissed anyone to stop them from having a panic attack, though."

"I can't believe that worked," she says. The warmth of her exhale against my neck makes my body tighten. Awareness of her is everywhere, from the pads of my fingers to the tingling in my lips. My fingers brush over a strip of bare skin where her sweater has ridden up. "It worked pretty well, I'd say."

"If you're looking for flattery, you won't get it from me," she says. But she tucks her face against my neck in a gesture that feels more flattering than words ever could.

My hand slides clean under her sweater, palm against her lower back. Once, twice, I run my fingers over her skin. Freddie presses a soft kiss to my neck.

I graze the clasp of her bra and trace the length of her spine. "Freddie…"

Her lips continue to move, tracing the edge of my jaw, finding my lips with her own. She tastes like sweetness and comfort, like sincere thank-yous and I-want-yous. I kiss her back, our mouths meeting. What starts soft takes no time at all to ignite. My hand tangles in the length of her dark hair.

Freddie moans into my mouth, surrendering to the kiss in a way that is so trusting it threatens to shatter me. It's too precious. I shift, stretching her out beneath me. Her dark hair is a beautiful wilderness on the comforter beneath us, but it's her eyes I can't look away from.

They hold desire and trust, tentative and wonderful.

Her hands pull me back down and I kiss her like I need her more than air, more than life itself, because that's how it feels. After yesterday's close call, the jealousy, the elevator, holding her trembling in my arms—the desire to make her mine is damn near all-consuming. I want her skin against mine and her moans in my ear.

And that's exactly why I can't. Not while there are dried tears on her cheeks, not when adrenaline and fear are still pulsing through her system. I shift my kisses from her lips to her neck, smoothing her sweater back down over the taut expanse of her stomach.

She turns into me with a frustrated sigh and I hold her, kissing her forehead. We lie like that for a long time.

"What are we going to do, Tristan?" she finally asks.

I'm wondering the same thing myself. "I don't know."

"We can't have anyone finding out about this."

"I know." I shut my eyes tight, fighting with the arousal still alive in my veins.

Freddie takes a deep breath. "I've worked so hard to be where I am. And I have so much work still to do. I can't be the trainee who sleeps with the CEO to get ahead."

The perfectly reasonable words cut. It's what I've known for weeks. She has so much left to experience that doesn't include someone like me.

"And I need to have control, Freddie, but with you I have none."

There's a resigned smile in her voice when she speaks again. "So what are we going to do with ourselves, then?"

"We're going to be friends," I say, smoothing my hand over her hair and hating the word. "Outside of work. Perhaps just from afar... but we'll be friends."

"Friends," she repeats, like she's tasting the word.

I wonder if she finds it as bitter as I do.

15

FREDDIE

I know my weaknesses well, know where I fracture and break. Sharing them with Tristan had never been my plan. But in the span of one evening, I'd given him all of it. My panic attacks, my fear of heights, even my fear of dating, the way I clung to him more than I needed to for the simple pleasure of holding him close. He'd seen it all.

What we are now doesn't exist, a word that can't be found in the dictionary. Two people who met as strangers. Who enjoyed one another as strangers, but who have gotten to know one another as friends.

Two people who live very different lives and have to abide by workplace rules.

And yet, yesterday had happened. I'd given him all of my fragility, and he'd held it in the palm of his hand until I was strong enough to take it back.

There's no way I can forget that. No way I want to forget that.

I rest my head in my hands, turning away from the painful thoughts and the numbers on my screen. We'd been wise in stopping yesterday, in establishing rules and boundaries. I'm only two months into a one-year internship. He's a single dad with a company to run.

The world would only see one thing.

But why, then, does it feel like we made a mistake?

"Frederica."

I look up. "Yes?"

"I need you for a client meeting. We're meeting with Nicour in—" Eleanor glances at her watch—"less than thirty minutes, and Clive couldn't make it. I just love it when he cancels last minute."

I reach for my binder, my handbag, following her out of the office. Toby gives me a thumbs-up and a mouthed *good luck*. Not a single part of me thinks he might be the mole. My gaze drifts over the back of Quentin, but for all his mutterings and bad moods, I don't think it's him either.

"Frederica?"

"Coming." I hurry after Eleanor to Strategy's conference room. In the spirit of saving time as well as miles to travel, this is a digital meeting. Exciteur has an entire camera setup just for this sort of thing.

When they work, that is.

Eleanor grows increasingly stressed as the technician struggles with the electronics.

"They're waiting for us," she hisses.

"Any second now…" he murmurs.

I open my laptop and prepare for taking notes, drawing up all the info I have on Nicour. The door to the conference room opens. I don't look up, focused as I am on the numbers on the screen.

"Mr. Conway?" Eleanor asks. "I wasn't aware you were joining this meeting."

"Filling in for Clive," he says. A chair is pulled out next to me, a familiar cologne scenting the air. Something knots in my stomach.

I look over, but Tristan's gaze is focused on Eleanor and the techie. Cool, casual power on his face. Here he's a man made for boardrooms and thousand-dollar watches, no trace of the handsome stranger from the Gilded Room or the caring man in my elevator yesterday.

I turn my focus back on Eleanor.

"There we go," the technician says, stepping back. The projector screen flickers once, and then the good people at Nicour come into view, sitting at a conference table much like ours. Discussions begin, so I turn to my note-taking, focusing on the words being said and *not* on the man sitting a few feet from me.

It's difficult, when he's all I can concentrate on.

Eleanor defers to him when he deigns to speak, but he mostly lets her handle the show. Has he come to watch her performance? Or had he come to watch mine?

Perhaps he'd decided I haven't been effective at finding the mole and chose to take matters into his own capable hands.

Tristan is the one who ends the meeting. My hands still on the keyboard of my laptop as he speaks, the depth of his voice filling the room.

"It's been good to touch base with you," he says. "Our team will have a new business strategy to present to you in a month's time."

"Looking forward to it, Mr. Conway. Thank you for taking the time."

"Of course, Howard," Tristan says. "Talk to you soon."

The conversation clicks off and sudden silence reigns supreme. He taps his fingers along the table. "Nicour is one of our biggest clients."

"And they'll get nothing but our best," Eleanor promises.

I close my laptop and look between them. Tristan still hasn't given me a single glance since he entered the room. Is it only professionalism?

"Excellent," he says and moves to stand, but Eleanor stops him with a cleared throat.

"While I have you here, might I ask a favor for the conference in Boston this week?"

He sinks back down, raising an eyebrow. "Yes?"

"I'm sure you remember our junior trainee, Frederica Bilson," she says, nodding to me. "I'm aware that Strategy is only approved for four attendees for the conference, but she has a lot to recommend her. I've nothing but high praise for her and I'd like to include her from my department as well."

Wow.

The praise makes my cheeks heat, but I meet Tristan's gaze with a level one of my own. His eyes are bottomless, unfathomable. No hint that he recognizes me beyond the courteous.

"That would make your department the biggest we're sending to the event," he says.

"I'm aware," Eleanor responds, "but she's worth it."

A pang of warmth spreads through my chest. Praise from her is rare indeed, but here she is, going to the mat for me.

Tristan pushes his chair back. "Very well. You're going to the conference in Boston, Miss Bilson."

"Thank you, Mr. Conway."

"Thank your trainee supervisor," he says dryly and nods to Eleanor. Another hit of his cologne strikes me as he walks past, and without as much as a goodbye, he disappears out the door. It shuts behind him with finality.

I open my mouth, but Eleanor stops me with a wry smile. "Don't thank me yet, Freddie. It'll be a lot of work."

"I'm a fan of hard work."

"Yes, I've noticed. That's part of why I want you there. We'll need all hands on deck."

I nod, reaching for my laptop.

Eleanor smiles. "I've never met a more diligent note-taker."

"It came in handy in college and it comes in handy now."

"It sure does." She gathers her own papers, standing. A frown mars her lips. "Mr. Conway's not usually so… short."

I focus very hard on looking pleasantly interested. "Who knows what bothers management?"

"Who knows, indeed." She shakes her head, the clean-cut bob swaying. "Oh well. He'll be excellent at the conference regardless, I'm sure."

"Is he ever anything else?"

Eleanor shoots me a surprised glance. "Indeed, Freddie. I've sometimes wondered that myself."

As I return to my desk, my hands tremble. Not with fear or nerves, not even with anticipation. The mess of emotions inside me includes far too many to be classified.

Yesterday, he'd held me like I was all he wanted. Yesterday, all I'd wanted had been him. And yet we'd stopped it. For me, it had been on account of this job, my career, my sense of self-worth. He's not someone who dates, but I can't forget the words seared into my mind—the sad way he spoke about why women want him. I can't forget the way he is with his son.

Had I been wrong?

"I just heard the good news!" Toby says, sliding into view on his desk chair. "You're going to Boston with us this week!"

"Another pair of hands on deck," Quentin says from his desk, not turning around.

"Not to mention another soul ready to party on Thursday evening." Toby does a little dance in his chair. "Are you ready, Freddie?"

"Yes," I say weakly. "I was born ready."

16

FREDDIE

Toby grips the conference badge hanging on a lanyard around my neck, turning it one way and then the other. "It still looks pretty good."

"It does not," I protest. "It looks like it's taken a dip in a cup of coffee, because it has."

"Well, it sort of works with your dress. It's blush-colored."

"It's supposed to be peach." I reach out and put a hand on Toby's shoulder. "I really appreciate the pep talk, but let's face it. I'm just going to have to give up on the idea of one day framing this."

He laughs. "Can you imagine the sociopath who would do that?"

"You mean me?"

"If the shoe fits," he says, leaning on the high drinks table we're standing by. Not fifteen minutes after the last workshop ended, and the conference hall had been transformed into a professional meet-and-greet.

"Where's Quentin?"

"Off networking," Toby says, waving a dismissive hand.

I raise an eyebrow at him. "Quentin? *Networking?*"

"He's good at schmoozing when he wants to be. Others, like me, aren't."

"Toby, you're the most sociable person I know."

"Yes, but see, that's the problem." He raises his glass of wine to me in triumph. "I'm unable to be anyone but who I am, and in places like this, no one's really interested in getting to know *you*. They just want to get to know the you that will help them get ahead."

"Wow. That was astoundingly cynical."

He grins at me. "I'm only two years older than you, Freddie, and yet so much wiser."

"And so humble," I laugh, raising my wineglass to his. It's the one free drink included in our conference package, but I already see attendees heading to the bar to pay for their second.

"So?" he asks. "What did you think of your first day?"

I mimic wiping sweat off my brow, and he grins. "Yeah, Strategy is always sent to every single meeting, just in case there are new tactics to pick up on."

"Eleanor asked me to go to two workshops. At the same time. When I pointed out that I couldn't, she actually growled down at her phone."

He snorts. "Yeah, the bosses get a bit intense here. This is where they recruit new clients and do a bit of schmoozing themselves."

My eyes catch on a familiar figure over Toby's shoulder, far in the distance. Quentin. His gaze is fixed on us... or at least on Toby. There are none of the usual traces of wryness on his face. As soon as he catches me watching, he turns, disappearing into the mingling crowd.

"Uh-oh," Toby says by my side, obvious relish in his voice. "Your date is coming our way."

"What?"

"Luke, at eleven o'clock."

"I didn't think Sales would be here."

"Love will find a way," Toby teases, too loud for my liking, and then Luke reaches us. He gives us both a wide grin and runs a hand over his short hair.

"Of course Strategy is here," he says.

"You know it." I raise my glass to his. We've texted a bit after our day spent in New York, but I've made it clear that I'm only looking for friendship.

"Sales made it too?" Toby asks.

"Yeah, it was a last-minute thing. Not planned or anything, but when my boss asked me, I jumped at the chance." He moves next to me, our elbows touching.

"Of course you did," I joke. "Who can resist twelve-hour workdays and lanyards?"

"Don't forget a complimentary drink," Toby points out. "That's key."

"But only one," I say. "We don't want attendees getting rowdy."

Toby rolls his eyes. "God, I can't wait to get rowdy. There's a bar next to the hotel... so you know where people will migrate when this is done."

"And they'll be paying for it tomorrow," Luke says with a chuckle, looking over at me. "Think you'll join?"

I shrug. "Probably, but I won't be out late."

"You're so young," Toby says. "So idealistic, so motivated. I remember those days."

I grin at him. "Sorry, I forgot how cynical you've become."

"I'm the worst."

"Well, maybe not the *worst*," Luke says. "Did you hear Conway up there on the panel?"

"I thought he was good," I say.

"Oh, of course he was. He could convince anyone of anything when he deigns to try," Toby says. "But you're right. His view of the industry wasn't necessarily... optimistic, not for us little guys."

"I'm sure he'd call it realistic," I say.

"That only makes it worse."

"Well, he's a venture capitalist," Toby says. "He took over Exciteur to ensure it makes money, and when it does, he'll leave. That's their role."

I take a sip of my glass and make my tone casual. "Think it'll happen soon?"

Toby shakes his head. "I doubt it, but I can't claim to know what goes on in management."

"He's not here, is he?" Luke asks. "I haven't seen Upper Management since the last panel."

"I don't think so," I reply, and I've been keeping an eye out. Tristan has been in meetings not open to the likes of us most of the day, but I've seen him striding down hallways and of course, working the microphone during the panel discussion. The difference couldn't be clearer—me, in the back, taking notes. Him, being interviewed on the future of consultancy.

Luke drains the last of his wine, putting it down decisively on the table in front of us. He leans in close enough that I can smell his aftershave. "We should head to that bar soon."

I make a noncommittal sound. Damn Toby for grinning beside me, for knowing about our date and for finding it hilarious.

My eyes search for a possible out. But they lock on a pair across the crowded room, a pair that blaze with intensity. The burn scalds.

Tristan's here.

His gaze travels from me to Luke, standing closer than he should. There's none of the professional civility of the last couple of days. Despite the distance, I can read his face perfectly. He's burning, he's angry, and he's not as indifferent as he pretends.

My hand trembles as I put my wineglass down.

Tristan turns, parting the mingling crowd like the Red Sea as he strides toward the elevators.

I force my gaze away. "I'll be right back," I tell Luke and Toby. If they reply, I don't catch it, hurrying through the packed crowd.

Like a moth drawn to a flame, I know I shouldn't, but I can't resist.

He's gone when I reach the elevators. Only one is still in motion, and as I watch, it stops at floor twenty-six.

The top floor.

Putting steel in my spine, I step into a free elevator and press the same button. The doors close behind me and I focus on breathing, in and out, in and out, my gaze on every floor that passes. Elevators have been harder than ever since the one in my building stalled. I've avoided them whenever I can, but here and now, there's no way around it.

I can do this.

Nothing is going to happen.

Don't think of the possible drop.

The elevator gives a cheery sound when it reaches the top floor and I breathe a shaky sigh of relief, emerging in a narrow corridor. A sign points to the right with the words *Rooftop Terrace* emblazoned in gold letters.

Balconies and rooftops are my kryptonite. I hedge toward the glass door. It's dark outside, it's December, it's cold.

Why had he gone up here?

Wrapping an arm around my midsection, I pull open the glass door and immediately regret it. Goose bumps race over my bare arms at the chill in the air.

One step out onto the terrace.

Another step.

I'm far away from the ledge, but I can still see it, fenced and menacing in the distance. A dark figure is standing with his hands on the railing and head bowed against the chilly wind.

I brave another step forward. "Tristan?"

He turns his head. "Freddie?"

"Yeah."

Releasing the railing, he runs a hand through his hair. Wind whips at his suit jacket. "Christ, you followed me up here?"

"Yes. Ta-da."

His mouth quirks, but it's brief. Then he's shrugging out

of his jacket and wrapping it around me. It's warm from his body heat and I drown in it. "Thank you," I murmur, my fingers curling around the fabric. "Why are you up here?"

He shakes his head, looking away from me to the soft Bostonian skyline. It's less crowded than New York's. "You'll catch a cold," he says.

"You looked like something was on your mind."

His mouth twists in a not-smile. "Someone was."

My stomach feels like it might give out. "Oh."

"You, in fact." His jaw clenches, working tight. "I saw you and the other trainee, and the jealousy hit me like a fucking freight train."

"It's not... Tristan—"

"I know," he says. "I have no right, Freddie. You told me you can't go there with me. Not to mention the two of you were just talking. I know the jealousy is irrational, but it lives inside of me nonetheless."

"I don't want him."

He closes his eyes. "All those people down there, all of them wanting to talk to me. Not for *me*, but for what I represent. And the only person I wanted to talk to was you, but approaching you was unthinkable. I was jealous of that, too. They could talk and laugh with you and I couldn't."

"I'm here now."

"Why are you?" he asks. "Why follow me up here?"

"We're friends."

"Friends, yes. Friends. And yet I think about you all the time. How you felt in my arms, the taste of you, the sounds you made. I want you so fucking much, Freddie, and I can't have you, and it's driving me up the walls."

My breath hitches, every word of his a blow against my resolve. "I didn't tell you I wanted to be friends because I don't want that either, Tristan. I go to bed hoping you'll call me and ask me to meet you at the deli. I walk the corridors at work hoping to bump into you. I think about you *all the time*."

His eyes are focused and sharp on mine. "I used to be in control before you," he accuses.

"So was I. You've ruined all of that for me."

"I can't say I'm sorry."

"Neither can I," I breathe.

He closes the distance between us and fits a large hand to my cheek. Tilts my head up, until he blocks out the city lights around us. "Be with me tonight," he says. "Just the two of us in my hotel room. We can just be us. Frederica and Tristan, and not who we are at work."

The raw note of need in his voice sparks the same chord in me, beckoning me to join in the symphony. And oh, how I want to. "Yes," I murmur.

His hand slides down to grip mine. He leads the way, opening the glass door and bringing us both back into the warmth. Tristan pauses by the elevator. "You didn't take the stairs?"

"No," I say, shaking my head. "I didn't want to risk missing you."

He kisses me with startling intensity then, bruising my lips with the force. I savor the taste of him, the strength of his body against mine. Every nerve ending feels electrocuted by his touch. "God, I want you," he murmurs.

My hands dig into his shirt. "I want you too."

"We're taking the stairs this time." His hand slips down to mine and then we're walking, taking stairs devoid of people. We shouldn't walk like this in public, but the idea of pulling my hand out of his feels akin to losing a limb.

We're not going far. He pushes open the door to the twenty-fourth floor and we walk down rows of identical hotel doors.

Tristan unlocks the door at the end. "My suite," he says.

A quick glance back at the corridor tells me what I already know. Nobody's watching. There's no one to see us, to see me, no one to spread rumors. I step inside, and he closes the door behind me.

17

FREDDIE

His hands smooth up my arms, strong and sure. "You walked out onto a rooftop terrace."

I lean against him. "I did."

"Thank you."

"You're worth a bit of fear."

Tristan's chuckle sends shivers over my skin. "What a compliment, Frederica." His hands slip down, over the sleeves of his jacket, tracing my bare skin beneath.

I tip my head back against his shoulder. "I've missed you."

"It hasn't been that long," he murmurs, his hand sliding inside his suit jacket to rest on my stomach. His thumb brushes over the underside of my breast.

"Yes," I say. "It has."

Another hoarse chuckle, and then his lips brush over my exposed neck. "You're right. And every night since I was at your apartment, I've thought of how you felt against me."

My eyes slide closed. "Tristan…"

"Yes?"

"What are the rules?"

"The rules, sweetheart?" He smooths his suit jacket off my shoulders and it drops to the floor between us.

Unable to bear it any longer, I turn to him. "You told me about the rules at the Gilded Room. What about tonight?"

Tristan tips my head back, running a thumb over my lower lip. "No rules," he murmurs. His kiss is powerful in its slowness. Deliberate and methodical. The need from the stairwell is still there, but it's leashed now. Held in careful check but brimming beneath the surface.

Tristan walks us backwards until my knees hit the edge of the hotel bed. He lifts his head, hands gripping my waist. "Freddie..."

"I know," I tell him, pulling his head back down. Because I do. The need is crawling beneath my skin, an itch that's bone deep. "Come here..."

He groans against my lips. I'm lifted up and then I'm horizontal, all in one smooth motion, and Tristan never stops kissing me. His hand slides beneath the hem of my dress and finds the back of my knee. Notches it around his hip.

Stretched out like this, even fully clothed, our bodies align like they're meant for one another. Like it's all they've ever been meant for.

His hips roll once. Twice. Even through the fabric, the feel of him against me is enough to send an ache through my body.

"Off," I tell him, my hands moving across the expanse of his chest. I need to touch his skin. Tristan sits back on his knees and tears the shirt off in one smooth motion, not bothering with the buttons. His chest rises and falls with the force of his breathing. A smattering of hair dances across his chest.

"Freddie," he says hoarsely, hands digging into my thighs. "I need you too much to go slow."

I reach for the zipper on the side of my dress. "You think I'd let you go slow?"

A savage grin crosses his face and then he's there, tugging the sheath off me. The fabric snags at my breasts. I wiggle to help it slide down and he growls, eyes tracking the movement.

His hands linger at my ankles, over the straps that keep my heels in place. "These stay on."

I nod, stretched out on the bed in front of him. "Anything."

The way he watches me is my undoing. There's nothing he could ask of me now that I'd say no to, nothing I wouldn't seek to satisfy. His want fuels mine, and mine enflames his, a cycle I can't wait to lose myself in.

Tristan trails kisses down my neck, my collarbone, the sharpness of his stubble grazing the swells of my breasts. He buries his face between them with a growl, hands reaching for the bra clasp. I arch my back and sigh with relief when it comes undone.

Tristan lifts himself up on one arm, eyes on my chest as he peels the bra off me. Freed, my breasts rise and fall with my breath, my nipples hard.

"I've missed these, Freddie."

My breathless laughter is cut off as he dips his head, sucking one of my nipples into his mouth. Every aching pull spreads liquid fire through me. He shifts between my legs, the hard length of him pressing against me once more.

"Tristan…" I beg, burying my hand in his thick hair.

He switches, taking my other nipple in his mouth. But he hears me, because his hand dives beneath the waistband of my panties.

My breath turns shaky as he cups me, fingers parting, stroking. I roll my hips against his hand in the search for more friction. He doesn't give it to me. No, he pulls my panties clean off instead, tossing them to the side.

Once again, I'm spread out naked in front of him in a hotel room while he's half-dressed.

But this time, he's not wasting any time playing. Tristan undoes his zipper and the swollen length of him springs free.

"I'm so hard for you, you have no idea." He opens his wallet, fishing out a foil wrapper. "Do you know how many nights I've gotten off just thinking about our night together at the Gilded Room?"

I shake my head, the image his words elicit making my throat dry. "Tell me."

He rolls the condom on with a low groan. A line of hair runs up to his navel, muscles tensed beneath still-tan skin. "So many. I've been hard and cursing myself for leaving as early as I did that night," he says. "For not taking the time to fuck you more than once. Thinking that if I had, I wouldn't crave you like I do."

I sit up, reaching for his arms, the rock-hard muscles shifting underneath my hands. "It wouldn't have been enough," I say. "Once, twice. I would have wanted you again."

He takes my mouth in agreement. It's a kiss to devour. A kiss to seal.

A kiss to claim.

He grips my thighs and pushes them apart, settling between my legs. Thank God for high hotel beds and tall men, because the angle is perfect. He grips my hips and uses them as leverage, burying himself inside me with one strong thrust.

I gasp at the sudden sensation, but it's drowned by Tristan's hoarse groan. His eyes drift closed in pained bliss as he pauses, buried to the hilt.

"Tristan," I murmur.

He grins and looks at me, because he knows exactly what he's doing by denying us both movement. But two can play this game.

I arch my back, reveling in the way his eyes track the movement. The way they widen when I cup my breasts. He groans at the sight and flexes his hips, thrusting hard inside me.

"Gorgeous," he mutters, his fingers digging into my hips as he strokes in and out.

I arch my back further. "Do you know how good you feel inside me?"

He thrusts so deeply the air is knocked out of my chest. I reach out blindly and grip the comforter, holding on as he responds by pushing us both closer to the brink.

I've never been driven out of my mind by a man like this. There's no room in my head for doubts or thoughts, just this connection and the growing pleasure. He hooks my knees under his arms and bends forward, until I'm folded in half and his face is inches from mine.

"Oh my God," I breathe. "That's deep."

"Too deep?"

I shake my head and he resumes his thrusts, hips moving like a piston against me. The muscles in his arms strain, bulging on either side of my neck. I latch on to his neck and kiss the heated skin. Tell him exactly what I'm thinking in the moment.

"I can feel you so deep inside me."

He growls into my ear. "You can't fucking talk dirty to me, Freddie, or I won't last."

I wrap my arms around his back. My body is near the breaking point with pleasure and intensity, so close to my own release, but I can't help myself.

I still want to be the best sex he's ever had.

So I tighten my muscles around him and press my lips to his ear. "I want to feel you come inside of me."

He gives a hoarse groan, his muscles tensing up. I hold him through the force of his release, as he pushes harder against me, bruising my inner thighs. It's the most glorious thing I've ever experienced.

Tristan, undone like this, undone in the same way I've been unravelling for weeks. A complete loss of control.

I dig my fingers into the wide expanse of his back as if I can keep him by force, fuse the two of us together.

He's crushing me, but I think I'll die if he moves.

"Holy shit," he whispers. Our heartbeats thunder against

one another, chest to chest, his hair-roughened skin against my nipples.

I take a deep, nourishing breath. Tristan must feel it against him, because he lifts himself up.

"You okay?"

I nod.

He raises a questioning eyebrow, thick hair falling over his brow. The gesture tugs at my heart.

"You didn't hurt me," I insist, flexing my legs around his hips. There'll be soreness tomorrow, sure, but none of it uncomfortable.

Tristan grips the base of the condom as he pulls out. I wince at the lack of him. It's just as jarring as his intrusion had been.

He returns to me within moments and stretches out beside me on the bed. I turn on my side, but he stops me with a hand on my hip.

"Not yet, you don't," he murmurs, bending his head to my nipple. It's still taut.

"But—"

"I'd never leave you hanging." His hand skates down my stomach, and oh God, he's circling that spot again. I close my eyes against the sensations building inside me. I'd been right at the edge before, and now...

Tristan tugs me effortlessly to the side and curls his hands around my thighs, spreading them. Bending his head. I break apart at the touch of his lips and tongue, fracturing and reassembling as pleasure ripples through me.

He doesn't stop touching me, either. It just shifts from rapid to soothing.

I struggle to catch my breath, staring up at the eggshell-white ceiling. My hand knots in his thick hair. "I hope nobody was in the hotel room next to ours."

He chuckles against my thigh, his eyes telling me exactly how he feels about himself right now, and it's pretty damn good. "I don't care if they were."

I give him a crooked smile. "How come you're always the one who goes down on me? I want a shot too, you know."

"There'll be time for that." He pushes off the bed and walks to the minibar. I flip onto my stomach and watch him pour us both a glass of sparkling water. Admire the long, strong lines of his legs. The muscled expanse of his back, widening into broad shoulders. Every inch of him speaks of confidence and masculinity, a body inhabited by someone who revels in life. Tristan hands me a glass of water and watches as I drink, his eyes never leaving mine.

Nerves flutter in my stomach as we both come back down after our orgasmic high. What does this mean?

Tristan reaches down and runs his thumb over my bottom lip. "I have to say, I didn't expect this, Strait-laced."

I catch his thumb between my lips and bite down softly.

He grins. "I won't stop calling you that, you know, no matter how much you bite."

My teeth dig into his thumb and he pulls it out with a chuckle. "Heathen."

"I didn't expect it either," I say. "To be honest, I didn't think much further ahead than making it to the roof."

"About that," he says, setting down his glass on the small table in-between two leather chairs. This suite has to be three times the size of mine. "Where did that phobia come from?"

I rest my head in my hands. "You'll laugh."

"I very much doubt that."

"Promise me you won't?"

"I promise," Tristan says, stretching out beside me on the bed.

I take a deep breath. "I liked to climb trees when I was little. Large ones, small ones, didn't matter. I climbed them all."

"Non-discriminatory," Tristan notes with a nod. "Admirable."

I knock him with my shoulder and he laughs, draping his

arm over my bare back. Fingers trace down my spine. "What happened?"

"Well, I fell out of one."

"Did you break anything?"

"No."

"That's good," he murmurs. "But Freddie, why would I laugh at that?"

"Because I fell five feet."

His eyebrows rise and I shake my head at him. "I know, it's *nothing*. I climbed higher trees than that all the time. But after that, I stopped, and somehow the fear just grew and grew in my head."

Tristan presses a kiss to my forehead. "We all have scars. I won't judge where yours came from."

"And what would—" The shrill sound of my cell phone cuts off my response. It's jarring and sharp in this little bubble we've created.

I fly off the bed and fumble through my handbag for the offensive thing, all while Tristan is watching me.

It's Toby. "Hey?"

"Freddie!" he calls. "Where are you? You said you'd join us at the bar!"

Someone cuts in, and then I recognize Quentin's voice. "Please come save me from having to talk to any more strangers. I'm all strangered out."

"Did you hear that?" Toby asks. "Quentin said *please!* Where are you?"

"In my hotel room."

"What? Are you feeling okay?"

"Yes, yes, I'm not—"

"Good! Either you're joining us or we're coming to get you!"

"I'll be right there," I hear myself saying, reaching for my discarded dress on the floor. "Buy me a drink."

Toby hoots. "The bar next to the hotel. We'll save you a seat!"

"See you soon." I click off and scramble in search of my underwear. Toby and Quentin's voices in my ear were like a slap of reality, a cold bucket of water. The entire conference center, not to mention the hotel, is crawling with people we know. People who are all too eager to put two and two together and arrive at twenty-eight.

"Heading out?" Tristan asks. He's lying on the bed, an arm behind his head and a knee bent, like nothing bothers him. But his face is unreadable again.

Have I jeopardized everything? Not just my job, but the two of us, too. The budding friendship, the way he looked at me in my apartment just a few days ago. That look is gone at the moment.

"Yes," I say. "We can't have people knowing about this."

"They're not in this hotel room with us."

"No, but they are in the hotel." I shimmy into my dress, and he watches me struggle with the zipper in silence. Why on earth had I decided to do this at a *work conference?*

Had people seen me following him up to the roof?

He watches me search for my panties. He'd tossed them to the side, but the carpet is infuriatingly panty-free.

"Over there," he mutters, pointing to the chairs in the corner. My bright-red lace panties hang off the edge of one. A blush creeps up my cheeks as I shimmy them up my legs and beneath my dress.

"I'm sorry I have to run so fast," I tell him. "I just, I don't…"

"You don't want them to suspect anything," he finishes. "I get it. We'll talk later."

I give him my widest smile, but even I can hear the faint panic that flavors my voice. "Thank you."

He nods. "Go."

So I do, the door shutting behind me with a solid thud. The corridor is still empty, and nobody sees me race for the elevators in an attempt to get off a floor I have no business being on.

18

TRISTAN

"We could get Grandma another set of knitting needles. She likes that," Joshua comments. He kicks at a stray lump of snow on the sidewalk, one of the final remnants from last weekend's weather.

"That's not a bad idea," I say. "Perhaps a pattern book. String, too, maybe. Or is it yarn?"

"You're just making stuff up, Dad. You have no idea how to knit."

I grip his shoulder, giving him a playful shake. "Who made you an expert, huh?"

He laughs and pushes away from me, grinning under the thick head of curls. "I know a ton of things. Like I know I'll get another sweater from her!"

"Oh, you sure will. Makes sense, too, since we're going somewhere cold for Christmas."

It takes a moment, but then his face lights up as he gets the joke. We've been working on sarcasm and irony.

"Do you have any clever ideas for what Linda might want?" I ask him. "You were there just last night."

His godmother had been my sister's best friend, and after Jenny died, she's stepped in as often as she can. Despite having two kids of her own, she'd helped me navigate the first few years of parenthood in a way that made her more god than godmother in my eyes.

Joshua takes a moment to think. "She complained about the dishwasher."

"You want us to give Linda a new dishwasher? She'd love that." As often as I can, I've tried to let Linda and her husband know I'm here to help just as much as they are with me.

I reach out and tug Joshua's jacket back in place. It's cold out. He lets me, despite hating how snugly it fits around his neck. "You'll be in charge of what we buy her kids," I tell him. "I'm delegating that to you."

His smile is back. "Really?"

"Absolutely." Well, within reason. But he knows better than me what they'd like, not to mention this Christmas shopping expedition should be fun. Another notch in my grand scheme of creating more holiday memories.

Jenny and I used to bake gingerbread cookies with Mom the night before Christmas. We'd race down the steps the next morning to the Christmas tree, one side of it decorated with our ornaments and the other side with Mom's collectibles.

A pang of familiar guilt hits me. Joshua looks just as he always does, walking next to me with a bounce in his step. But he's never known what it's like to have a sibling or two parents. All he'll remember of his childhood is me, and I'm not Jenny and Michael.

"Look!" Joshua says. "It's the elephant lady!"

I'm so focused on him that I don't notice who's walking towards us until he points her out. Freddie's coat is bundled tight around her body, a hat pulled low over her dark hair. Her feet are in giant boots, unlike anything I've seen her wear in the office. Gone are the sleek skirts and heels.

It's a Saturday, and we live in the same neighborhood.

Her gaze drifts from mine to Joshua's, and then a smile spreads on her face. "Hi there!"

"Hi," he says back. "We're out doing our Christmas shopping."

Freddie makes a show of looking between the two of us. "But where are the bags?"

"We just left home," I reply. Freddie's eyes dance, not quite meeting mine. Redness starts to tinge her olive-toned cheeks. "How're you doing?"

"Good. Great, I mean. I've spent the morning doing laundry." Her gaze flicks from me to Joshua. "I was at the same conference as your dad this week."

"In Boston?"

"Yes," she says. "He spoke in front of several hundred people."

Joshua turns to look up at me. "Really, Dad?"

"Yeah, I suppose."

"That's pretty cool," he says, with the air of someone who can make such judgements. "Did you do it too?"

Freddie shakes her head. "No, I don't think I'd dare."

"You would," I interject. "I have no doubt you would."

Her eyes return to mine, and there's a question in them I can't decipher. Not when she'd been the one to rush out of my hotel room in Boston as if we'd committed a sin. We haven't spoken in the days since.

"We're going to Tahiti for Christmas break," Joshua tells her. "Dad's taking me to swim with whales."

"Really? That's so exciting!"

"Yes, we've done a lot of research," I say.

Joshua nods. "There should be humpback whales there this time of year, migrating from Antarctica. They stop in French…"

"Polynesia," I fill in.

"Right, they stop there to have their calves. And there are whale sharks. And dolphins."

Freddie's eyes widens. "And you'll swim with them? That sounds a bit scary."

"No, it just seems really, really cool," Joshua says.

I can't help but smile at the bluster. We've had long discussions about this very topic, because even if he won't admit it, he thinks it sounds a bit scary too. I've told him it's fine to stay on the boat, but he's committed to getting into the water.

"It sounds out-of-this-world cool," Freddie confirms. "How awesome of your dad to take you there."

"Yeah, and my grandma is coming too," Joshua adds.

I clear my throat. "Where are you going for the holidays, Freddie?"

"Probably back home to Philadelphia. My extended family celebrates together every year, with all of my aunts and uncles and cousins." She shrugs, a wry smile on her face, as if she's described something dull and ordinary. "It's not swimming with whales in French Polynesia, but it'll do."

"It sounds lovely," I say. I mean it, too. Her gaze warms, her hands falling still where they'd fiddled with the sleeve of her coat. Looking at her, I realize just how much of a fool I've been for being hurt she rushed out of my hotel room in Boston like that.

Perhaps she's regretting what she did. Thinking about her job, the possible consequences if someone finds out… If she's having doubts, I'm not helping.

Joshua's voice cuts through the silence. "Do you have a lot of aunts and uncles?"

Freddie refocuses on my son. The winter sunlight glints off her raven hair. "I have a few, yes. Let's see… three uncles and two aunts. Do you have any?"

Oh, no.

"Yes," Joshua replies. "Dad is actually my uncle *and* my dad. I think that's pretty cool."

I close my eyes. He doesn't understand how that sounds to people, and I've never wanted to enlighten him about it. But that leaves us with encounters like this. God help me if he goes around saying that without context at school.

Freddie's silence is shocked.

I clear my throat. "Joshua is biologically the son of my sister and her husband. After they passed, I adopted him."

"I was tiny back then," Joshua adds, helpfully holding up his index finger and thumb to indicate *just* how small he was.

"I'm really sorry about that," Freddie says, and then doesn't seem to think of anything else to say. I don't blame her. Most people have the same response whenever Joshua wants to let them know. I always let him decide if and when, both with friends and adults.

I put a hand on his shoulder. "Thank you. We do all right, don't we, kid?"

"We do," he confirms.

"We also didn't mean to keep you here. Are you heading somewhere…?"

Freddie's smile turns rueful. "Just the grocery store. Good luck with your Christmas shopping."

"We'll probably need it," I say. "Here's hoping the stores won't be full yet."

Freddie smiles and takes a step to the side. "I'll let you go, then. Enjoy your day."

"You too."

"I'll see you at work," she tells me.

It's the last place we'll see each other, with the floors and red tape separating us. As much as I've wanted to over the last couple of weeks, walking into the Strategy Department and talking to one of their trainees is verboten for me. All the power of the CEO, and yet I can't choose which of my employees I want to talk to.

"We'll talk later," I say.

"Bye!" Joshua calls.

She heads past us down the street. Joshua peers over his shoulder before tugging on the sleeve of my jacket. "She's really nice."

"I think so, too."

"She's your friend, right?"

I nod. "Yeah."

He gives me a solemn two-eyed wink, not yet having mastered the art of using only one. "I get it, Dad. You want to become her best friend *first*, before you tell her you like her."

My mouth opens, my brain drawing a blank. He's using my own words against me. Clever kid.

"But you have to talk a bit more," he advises me, dropping my sleeve. "You were too quiet!"

With the startling revelation that my kid just gave me advice about women, I follow him down the street, wondering if the world has completely turned on its head.

———

Joshua and I return to the apartment late that afternoon, carrying bags of stuff. Scented candles, gift cards, toys for Linda's kids, a book on knitting for my mother. Joshua heads to his room as soon as we get home and leaves me with my thoughts. And like all roads lead to Rome, my thoughts take me to Freddie.

The idea of her regretting the night in Boston is a sharp pain sliding between my ribs, lodging somewhere between soft tissue and my pride. It hurt that she'd rushed out like she did. But it hurt more to think she wished it had never happened at all.

Joshua is sound asleep when I call her that evening. She answers after the third eternity-long signal. "Tristan?"

"Hey."

"Hi."

"Are you busy?"

She clears her throat. "No, I'm not."

"Laundry's all done? Grocery shopping?"

"Yes," she says, sighing. "Of all the people in New York, I run into you two. What are the odds?"

"We're pretty great people to run into."

"You are," she confirms.

I close my eyes as I ask the question, as if it makes it easier to imagine her face before me. Easier to picture what her eyes will look like as she replies. "Do you want to meet up tonight? I'd like to talk to you."

The pause is excruciating.

"Okay," Freddie says.

Blessed relief sweeps through me. "The deli?"

Another pause, this one more delicate. "Yeah. Or you could come to my place, if you'd like?"

"Absolutely. I can be there in fifteen minutes."

"I'll buzz you in."

My nerves are on fire as I pull on my coat, as I let Marianne know I'll be out. The brisk winter air doesn't cool me down either.

Freddie's pull is undeniable. My feet take me to her apartment door without conscious thought, my mind spinning possibilities in kaleidoscopic patterns.

She opens the door in a pair of black sweatpants and a sweater, her dark hair unbound around her face. "Hi," she murmurs.

"Hey," I say, a hand on the door. "Can I come in?"

She lets me in. The simple sound of the lock sliding in place behind me sends hot, erotic anticipation through me. Can't be helped.

I reach for her, powerless in the face of her nearness. Her hands are warm in mine. "I know the other night wasn't what you'd planned. What either of us had planned," I say.

Her mouth opens on a soft exhale, but I barrel on. "Did your co-workers suspect anything when you met them?"

"No. Not at all, actually."

"Good," I say, and I mean it. "I understand why you'd want to keep it from them."

She frowns. "I didn't mean to rush out like that. The idea of them being in the same hotel, of potentially having to answer questions… of HR finding out…"

"I understand."

"It was panic. I don't like to panic." Her eyes turn to our

intertwined hands. A soft thumb smooths over the back of my hand, the smallest, tiniest of caresses.

"As long as you don't regret it," I say. My body feels like it might break if she says she does.

But Freddie shakes her head. "I don't regret it."

My eyes close at the relief of those four words.

"How could I?" she continues. "When it was everything I've wanted for weeks? You're not the only one who's been burning since the Gilded Room."

She reaches up and runs the cool touch of her fingertips along my jaw. Soft. Sure. I bend my head and kiss her, and her arms twine around my neck, leaning into me with the same trust she's shown from the start. The same trust that undoes me.

As much as I loved her body in the tight dress and heels, the feel of her in loungewear is almost better. It's easy to slide a hand under the hem of her sweater, smoothing across the skin on her lower back.

She tugs off my coat, and I toss it over the single chair in her studio.

"I'm happy you're here," she says, running her hands over my chest.

"I wasn't too forward in inviting myself over?"

Her grin widens. "No."

Kissing her is like losing myself. All the titles, the roles, the worries, they melt away. She pulls me forward until we're back on her bed, devoting ourselves to kissing. Freddie bends a knee to fit me more snugly against her, but my hand never rises further beneath her sweater than the curve of her hip.

When I finally lift my head, her lips are rosy and swollen. "I didn't come here just for this, you know," I murmur.

"I know," she says, her hands sliding under the collar of my shirt. "But you're not complaining, are you?"

"Never."

Her smile beneath me is intoxicating, beckoning me back down. We lose another few minutes to kisses, but any time lost in that way is never wasted. She's the one who tugs the sweater over her head.

I watch as it inches over olive-toned skin, and Christ, she's not wearing a bra. The magnificence on display derails all my thoughts of being a gentleman.

They derail all thoughts, period.

She laughs as I bend my head and suck one of her nipples into my mouth, worrying it hard between my teeth. We slip effortlessly into an intimacy deeper than any we shared the first night at the Gilded Room, a repeat of Boston without the urgency or the hesitancy.

Freddie explodes before I do, clinging to my shoulders and moaning against my ear. I give in, burying myself deep and shaking from the pleasure-pain of my release.

I rest against her until the thundering of my heart has quieted, until I can see straight again. It's somewhat reluctantly I lift myself off and shift beside her, wrapping my arm around her waist. "I know we shouldn't," I say, "but I can't imagine ever tiring of this."

Freddie's smile is heavy with pleasure. "Me neither."

I glance around the tiny apartment. Last time I'd been in here, I hadn't given it much thought, focused as I'd been on her. She'd been trembling from the stalled elevator.

Now she's relaxed and languid beside me, and the trembling this time hadn't been from fear. "So this is your kingdom," I note.

She chuckles. "Yes, if a kingdom can be considered less than two hundred square feet. Sorry about the chill in here, by the way. The heating system isn't great."

"Hadn't noticed." I lean over and press a kiss to her shoulder. "You kept me warm."

Her smile widens. "What a line, Mr. Conway."

"Does it give me bonus points?"

"Half of one, perhaps."

"You'll have to show me the heater later. We forgot that

last time." I nod to her dresser, the framed photographs standing there. "Who are they?"

She settles into the crook of my arm. "My parents and my grandfather."

"From Philadelphia."

"Yes. Well, my grandfather was technically from Palermo."

"Italy?"

"Yes. He came here after the war. Had nothing, really, but his studies as a technician and a few English phrases. Learned to speak the language within months."

"That's impressive," I say, and I mean it.

Her voice warms. "He started working in a small clothing store, and within a few years, he became the manager. Opened his own store a few years later."

I curve my hand over her hip. "And his granddaughter got an MBA?"

"Yes. He passed a few years ago, but we used to talk a lot about business. He liked to give me the name of a company, and a week later, he'd ask me why I thought they were successful. I'd have to give him my analysis. He'd listen, nodding every now and then, eyes thoughtful behind his glasses. And then he'd tell me what I'd missed and correct any Italian grammar I'd messed up."

The warmth in the picture she paints is enough to make me smile. "He sounds brilliant," I say. "You speak Italian?"

"Yes, but anyone can tell I'm American from my accent."

"That's still more Italian than I speak." My fingers trail across her bare ribs, her skin like silk. "How do you become more interesting every time I talk to you?"

She raises an eyebrow, the smile on her face glorious. "I'm multi-faceted like that."

"You most definitely are, Strait-laced. So, tell me. What's your own great business idea?"

"I'm not telling you, you venture capitalist. You'll just steal it."

I press a hand to my chest. "You wound me."

Laughing, Freddie turns over on her stomach and rests her chin in her hand. Dark, silken hair slips over her shoulder and tickles my bare chest.

"That was my snarky way of saying I don't have one, at least not yet. Perhaps my thing is helping already existing companies rather than starting my own."

"Now that sounds like a venture capitalist in the making," I point out.

She grins. "I want to work at a Fortune 500 company someday. I'd love to live in Italy for a few years and work at a company there. Perhaps somewhere in Asia, too. Singapore?"

"It's lovely there," I comment.

"Of course you've been."

I make my voice lofty. "Many, many times."

Her grin widens. I reach up and trace the smattering of faint freckles across her nose. Long, bare eyelashes flutter over her cheeks. "I won't be able to stay away," I tell her. "Not when I know you want me too."

Freddie's eyes soften. "I don't want you to stay away."

My thumb slides down to her lips, tracing the outline. "Outside the office, then."

"Yes."

"When it's just you and me," I murmur.

"Just us," she agrees, her lips brushing mine with promise.

19

TRISTAN

My cards are terrible. Two sevens and a five, not to mention a two, and there's not a unified suit amongst them. The only possible strategy is to bluff, but looking around the table, I doubt any of my business partners at Acture Capital will buy it. We've played too many times.

Carter reaches for his glass of whiskey, smiling a bit too widely to himself.

I narrow my eyes at him. "You're the worst at bluffing."

"Or the best," he counters.

"He's certainly the least consistent," Victor says dryly. "You change your tactics every few months."

"I have to keep you sharp," Carter says, raising his glass to us. "You're welcome."

Anthony says nothing, just shakes his head at our youngest partner. Carter burns with the same kind of energy I had at twenty-eight.

Victor looks at me over his cards. "How are things in the consulting world? Tired of being for sale?"

"Not yet. The beast is just starting to turn around."

"Just? Exciteur has been profitable for months."

"It was profitable when we bought it," I point out. "The aim is to make it more so."

The decision to acquire the majority share in Exciteur had been joint, but Acture always offers human capital as well as financial. I'd insisted on being the one to take on the CEO position.

Carter tosses his cards onto the table. "I fold."

I grin. "So you were bluffing after all?"

"I'll never tell."

Victor looks down at his cards and there's not a smile in sight. The bastard might be ice cold, but he knows his business. "Have you found a media company you think is right for us yet?"

Carter leans back in one of my leather chairs. "No, but I'm monitoring a few. I'll email the short list to all of you when I have it."

"Good," I say. "Because you know that if you're not running point on something, we're going to foist a company on you."

"Like that matchmaking business," Anthony says, the threat hanging in the air.

Carter groans. "Please don't. I'll find a media company for us to buy tomorrow."

"We joke about it," Victor points out, "but Opate Match could go off the market any day now. If we're going to make an offer, we need to do it soon."

I reach for my own glass of whiskey. "It has global potential. Very small overhead. Minimal effort. Victor's right, Carter, we should buy it soon."

"I can draw up the papers for you tomorrow," Anthony adds.

Carter's eyes narrow with betrayal. "Don't think I don't get what you're doing. I'm not opposed to running point on this one, but I'll be damned if I let you all win on walkover."

"You folded," I point out.

"That was before I knew this was on the cards." He gestures to the wads of cash in the center of the fold-up table. I stash it in the closet when Joshua is home, but he'd begged to spend the night at Linda's, talking about her son's new video game.

"If we're playing poker for who has to run point on Opate Match," Carter continues, "I demand a rematch. One where the stakes are clear."

I run a hand over my jaw, the stubble rough against my hand. "You're not wrong."

Victor shoots me a withering look. "Your sense of fairness is appalling sometimes."

"Just because you lack one," I retort. Victor St. Clair is all caustic humor and underhand business deals, and has been since the moment I met him on the other side of a negotiating table years ago. Half the time, I'm not sure why we tolerate him at all. The other half, he reminds me by bringing in an obscene amount of money through hostile takeovers.

"One final game," Anthony decides. "The weakest hand has to run point on Opate. Fuck, that's a stupid name."

I drum my fingers against the velvet-clad table. "We make them an offer of purchase on Monday. No procrastination this time, either."

"No procrastination," Carter echoes, shuffling the cards. "I won't fold this time, boys."

Anthony snorts, crossing his arms beside me. If Victor is ice cold bordering on rude, Anthony is skepticism personified. Joshua once referred to him as "my sad friend" in a bout of childlike insight. He'd also been my friend through all of it. Jenny and Michael's airplane crash and Joshua's adoption.

I lean against him. "I'll bet you ten thousand that Carter will fold in the first five minutes."

"I heard that," Carter grinds out, handing out the cards.

I tilt mine close to my chest, watching as the others do the same. The table falls into tense silence. As opposed to when we play for money, this has real stakes. I don't have time to take on the running of a secondary company, even if it is a small, easy flip.

Judging by the cards I've been given, I probably won't have to, either. Two queens and a four.

"Dealing the river," Carter says, flipping up card after card in the center of the table.

It seems like we're all holding our breaths.

"You know," I say, "I think there's an inherent value in having the one of us who's best at romance running point on this. It is a matchmaking company, after all."

Victor and Anthony catch on instantly.

"Imperative," the former agrees. "For business's sake."

Anthony nods. "I'd be just as likely to wreck the business as I'd be to make it profitable. Matchmaking for the rich? You know I think it's bullshit."

Carter keeps his eyes on his cards. "I hate all of you."

Laughing, I reach for a card in the river and exchange my four. Two queens and a king, now. I could lose, but the others would have to have a hell of a hand for that.

"Thanks for having us here tonight," Anthony tells me as he reaches for his own card.

"Yes," Victor drawls. "The kid's out tonight?"

"Out of the apartment, yes, but hopefully not out on the town. He's nine."

"Right, right."

"He's at his godmother's. Begged me to go, really. Something about her kids having a game that he really wants to play."

"He's getting big," Anthony says.

"Yes. Only a few more years and I'll have a teenager to deal with."

"My condolences," Carter says. "I remember how I was, and I don't envy you."

"Let's hope he's a better kid than you were."

Carter grins at me. "Let's hope."

It's over an hour later when the game comes to an end. Carter has folded, as was expected, and he's already enjoyed a solid fifteen minutes of jokes on the topic.

Anthony is the last to show his cards. He spreads them out on the velvet table and leans back in his chair. "Sorry, Carter."

But the cards he's displaying aren't good.

"Wait a minute, though." Victor leans over and inspects the mismatch of cards. It's *almost* a flush, but it consists of both spades and clubs. "That's not a flush. The suits are mixed up."

Anthony lifts up his cards, eyes narrowing. "Well, fuck. I could have sworn those two were the same."

"Shit," Carter says. "Seems like you're our love expert after all."

"Anthony 'the Matchmaker' Winter," Victor adds. "It has a nice ring to it."

Anthony runs a hand over his face, pushing back from the chair. "I need another drink. And Tristan, I'm blaming this entire thing on you."

"On me?"

"A ten-million-dollar apartment, and you have lighting dim enough to make a man lose at poker." He stops by the bar-cart I keep in the corner, pouring himself another brandy. "A matchmaking company. Christ."

"See it as an opportunity!" Carter calls. "You can use it to find love!"

"One more word out of you, and you're out of this company," Anthony responds.

I reach for the cards on the table and start to shuffle. "Do we go back to money?"

"There's nothing better," Victor agrees.

The sound of my phone cuts through the room, drowning out the low music from my speaker system. I push back from the table. "One moment."

The familiar number sends a thrill through me. "Hello?"

"Hi," Freddie says. "I'm sorry to call you this late. I know you said you had plans for the night."

"Not a problem at all. What's happened?"

Her voice turns apologetic. "Well, you know how you made that joke about the heater?"

My mind sorts through our previous conversations, the jokes and jabs and flirtation. The joke about fixing her heater. It had been an excuse tossed out between us, testing the waters.

"I remember," I say.

"Well, it's actually broken."

The snow swirls outside the windows, draping the street in a heavy white blanket. "It's freezing tonight."

"Yes, the heater chose the worst possible moment. The super's not working tonight, and I can't find an electronics store that might sell a space heater open this late."

"Your apartment must be an icebox, Freddie."

"It's not warm, no," she says with a small chuckle. "That's why I'm calling. Do you happen to have a space heater I could borrow? Just for a few days."

I glance over my shoulder at the three men I work with. They're at the poker table, drinking and talking and pretending like they're not listening to every word I say.

"I don't, but I have something better. A warm apartment."

"Tristan, I couldn't ask—"

"You're not asking, I'm offering. Come to mine. We'll fix your heater tomorrow."

"Are you sure?"

"Absolutely. Pack a bag and get here as soon as you can."

She breathes a sigh of relief that makes me feel ten feet tall. "Okay," she says. "I'll see you soon."

"You will."

Anthony and Carter give theatrical groans as soon as I hang up.

"Well, boys," Victor says. "I guess this means we're being kicked out."

Carter shakes his head. "He has to make the most of his kidless night. I suppose we should just be happy we got worked into the rotation."

"Fuck you guys."

Anthony shakes his head, but there's no real resentment in his eyes. If anything, he looks pleased. "Who is she?"

The answer to that is more complicated than I care to share. Someone I work with. A trainee, technically. She's eight years younger than me.

And she's the best thing that's happened to me in years.

"A friend," I respond. "She lives close, and her heater just broke."

"A friend," Carter drawls, draining the last of his glass. "Right, well, have fun with your friend."

"Don't be jealous," I tell him.

He gives me a wolfish grin right back. "I'm not. Anthony might be, though."

"Why on earth would *I* be jealous?" he asks, leading the trio to my hallway.

"Because you're about to enter the world of elite dating as a single man. The ladies will be on you like vultures."

"Just when I'd managed to forget about it," Anthony says, "you bring it right back up again."

"I'd apologize, but, you know…"

"You're not actually sorry?"

"No."

The doors close behind them and then they're gone, without any genuine complaints about being kicked out. I wait a few minutes before I head into the lobby to wait for her. When she arrives, her giant coat is wrapped tight to protect her from the chill, snowflakes dusting her dark hair like the freckles on her cheeks.

They're rosy from the cold wind.

I reach out and take the bag she's carrying. "Hey."

"Hi," she says. "I'm really sorry about this, you know."

"I'm not," I say, typing in the keycode for the elevator. "We'll have your heater fixed tomorrow."

"I don't even know what happened. One moment, it was making a lot of noise and heat, and the next… complete silence. It won't start," she says. She gets into the elevator with me, but there's hesitation in her features that she can't quite hide.

"This is my private elevator," I tell her. "It only goes to my apartment. I have it serviced twice a year."

A shaky smile. "You're telling me no elevator of yours would ever malfunction?"

"That's exactly what I'm saying, yes. It wouldn't dare to."

And just like that, the ride is over. The doors open into my hallway. Freddie steps out, looking around, before turning to me with alarm in her eyes. "Your son. What did you tell him?"

"He's not home tonight."

Her eyes soften. "Right. Sorry, I just realized I had no idea what I was walking into."

"No need to worry."

"What were you doing tonight?"

"Come. I'll show you."

She follows me into the living room, lined with floor-to-ceiling windows that look over the park. The poker table is still in the middle, the coffee table shoved unceremoniously to the side. Four chairs are empty and abandoned around it.

Through Freddie's eyes, this might look ostentatious. Showy. It screams of everything her apartment didn't. Every descriptor an antonym.

"Wow," she breathes. "The view must be amazing during the day."

"It is. Especially after it's snowed, actually. The entire park is white."

She trails a hand along the green velvet that lines the poker table. Her eyes rest on the pile of hundred-dollar bills in the center. The guys must have forgotten to collect their winnings on the way out.

It looks obscene to me too, suddenly. But Freddie doesn't comment, continuing on toward the gallery wall by the TV. Black and white pictures, all in dark frames.

I watch in silence as she takes them all in, seeing everything I've done in the past few years. Everything Joshua and I are, all that we've seen and all that we've lost.

Surprisingly, I don't get the urge to cover them up.

"This one is gorgeous," Freddie murmurs, stepping closer to a large, black and white photograph of a volcanic coastline.

I clear my throat. "Hawaii."

"Oh?"

"Joshua and I took a helicopter. The photo's taken from the air."

Freddie studies the surrounding photographs. Joshua, standing at the foot of a waterfall in Yosemite. He's grinning from ear to ear as the water cascades behind him at a ninety-feet drop. Something tiny compared to something huge. Another is Joshua, smaller than he is now, and myself on a boat in the Caribbean. Half of his small face is covered by a snorkel. He's giving the camera a thumbs up and a smile lacking both front teeth.

"You really do take him everywhere," Freddie murmurs.

"I try to, at least."

"How come?" She works her way down the gallery wall, studying each photograph in turn.

"Well, I want him to see the world," I say. It's the truth, but it's not all of it, and my response hangs in the air between us. Inadequate.

Freddie comes to a halt by the final black and white photograph. Jenny is smiling wide, her eyes laughing at the camera. The braid down her back has come half-undone in the whipping wind and tendrils of hair curve around her head like a halo.

She's standing on a bridge with a harness strapped around her.

"My sister," I tell Freddie.

"Joshua's mother?"

"Yes. I took that picture right before she bungee-jumped for the first time." It feels like Jenny is seeing us, looking out from beyond the years, the miles, the chasm that separates us today and her then. On the Rio Grande Bridge in New Mexico.

Freddie shivers. "Wow. I can't imagine doing anything like that."

"I jumped after her."

Her eyes swirl back to me. "You did what?"

"Jenny wouldn't have let me come that far with her and then *not* jump."

"You said for the first time. She bungee-jumped more than once?"

"Oh, yes. She loved adventure." I nod toward the wall of photographs, the testaments to our travels, Joshua and I. After Tahiti, I'll send off another picture to be framed. "She'd have wanted her son to experience the world. To see it like she did, as a beautiful, complex, ever-changing playground."

Freddie's hand brushes against mine. Her fingers curl around it in the lightest of grips. "Did you travel with her often?"

I shake my head. "I was focused on Acture Capital. On growing the companies I took over. She was the one who couldn't sit still. Who had a list as long as she was tall with all the places she wanted to visit and things to do."

Freddie's fingers tighten, and I look from Jenny's familiar portrait to eyes that are soft, and strong, and kind.

"Joshua looks like her," she says.

"He does."

"He looks a bit like you, too."

"Well, I am his uncle."

A smile plays on her lips. "And his dad, as he informed me."

I close my eyes. "I have to tell him one day how that sounds when he says it. Sometimes I imagine him telling teachers and other kids just that piece of information, no context. One day I'll have police showing up here."

"It's sweet," she says. "He didn't seem upset when he told me."

My fingers thread through hers into a latticework. "It's not real to him."

Freddie's eyebrow rises in a silent question, so I serve up another painful slice of me, aided by the whiskey I've had and the kindness in her eyes. "He was just shy of turning three when Jenny and Michael died. He doesn't remember them. All he knows about them comes from stories, things he's been told. He knows he had a mother and a father before me."

Her fingers tighten around mine. *Go on*, the gesture says. And I find the words pouring out. "Trying to keep their memory alive is impossible. I've tried. But talking about them is like talking about legends to him. He enjoys stories of their adventures, but they're not... *real*. And if I force us to dwell on it, will I just make him sad? Do I keep reminding him of what he lost or let him embrace the life he has now?" I look back at Jenny on the bridge. She gazes boldly back at me through the void, but has no answers to give. No guidance or opinions on how I'm raising her son. The boy she'd called her greatest adventure.

"When he started calling me Dad... it was rough."

"Was it?"

My gaze shifts to the black and white picture of Michael. His hangs higher than Jenny's, his mouth serious but eyes smiling into the camera. Jenny took that picture, but she never told me where.

"He knows he doesn't have a mother. I can't take Jenny's place. But I have taken Michael's, in all the ways Joshua will remember."

"You haven't taken anyone's place," Freddie tells me. "You stepped in, at a time when it was necessary. Don't you think Jenny and Michael would understand that?"

"They would." I run my free hand over my face, all the ways I'm not good enough racing through my head. The nights I'm not home in time for dinner with Joshua and Marianne. The curious questions I haven't answered as well as Jenny would have. A soft tug of Freddie's hand takes us past the discarded poker table, toward the cloud couch in the corner.

We sink down onto the softness together, like we've done it a thousand times before. Like her body was meant to curl up next to mine.

And the words keep coming.

"I know every day that they'd do a better job, too. I know I'm a replacement. Being the best father to Joshua is something I'll fail at." I rest my head on top of hers, scenting floral shampoo and Frederica. "You came over for heat, and you got this heaviness instead."

There's a smile in her voice when she responds. "I don't mind heaviness, Tristan. And I enjoy getting to know you better."

My eyes drift closed at the words. Innocent, simple words, but they haven't been spoken to me with sincerity for years. I wonder if they ever have.

Her hand drifts to the nape of my neck and fingers slide into my hair. Touch for touch's sake.

"My last relationship ended when I adopted Joshua," I admit.

Freddie's fingers still for a moment, but then they plunge deeper, nails raking softly over my scalp. "Hmmm," she says. "I imagine it was a difficult time."

"I wasn't a good partner in the months after Jenny and Michael died. And she... well. She apologized for it, but she wasn't ready to become a stepmother." I close my eyes, wondering at how a simple touch can feel so good. "I can see now that she wasn't in it for the right reasons."

Freddie makes another humming sound, shifting closer. Seconds later and her lips brush softly against the edge of my jaw. "The right reasons," she repeats. "What are the wrong ones?"

"Money, prestige. Status." I give a shrug. "Jenny never liked her."

"You told me that's why you go to the Gilded Room parties."

"Mhm, so I did. At a time when I wanted to distract you."

She smiles. "It was appreciated. And remembered."

"Clearly."

"You said at least women want you for your body there."

I close my eyes at my own words reflected back at me. "Lovely sentiment."

Freddie chuckles, and I shift us so she's in my lap, knees on either side of me. The soft fabric of her sweater has ridden up and my fingers brush against the skin of her lower back.

"Tell me," she insists, her dark hair falling forward like a curtain. "Do you think you could live without them?"

"Without the Gilded Room parties?"

"Yes. They're fun, and I understand that they provide... thrilling entertainment, but... is it really want you want?"

My fingers dig deeper into her hips, hearing a question she hasn't asked. A question I haven't asked.

One that hovers close to defining what we are.

"No," I murmur. "It's not what I really want. But I don't think I'm capable of taking care of what I do want, even if I were to get it."

Her breath hitches, full lips falling open. But her eyes don't stray from mine. "I think," she murmurs, "that you've made it pretty clear you never give anything less than your best."

The air warms between us, her compliment stirring inside me. It forces me to bend my head to her neck and press my lips against the sensitive spot beneath her ear. Her fingers tighten in my hair, a soft sigh escaping her.

And I know I always want to be the man she sighs like this for. The man she confides her fears in. The man she trusts and holds on to.

So I grip her tighter and pull us both into standing.

Her hands slide down my chest. "We're going somewhere?"

"Yes." I pull her through the living room, down the hall, passing Joshua's closed door. Further down to mine.

"Hungry?" I ask her.

She shakes her head. "I ate earlier."

"How long was your heater off for?"

"A few hours."

"A few hours before you called me?"

Freddie gives a sheepish shrug. "Yes."

That's it. I grip her around the waist and grin as she squeals, tossing her onto my bed. She bounces once on the wide surface and spreads her arms, like she's about to make a snow angel. Her hair is a dark halo. "You told me you were busy tonight. I didn't want to bother you if it wasn't important."

"You not freezing to death is pretty important."

She reaches for me, pulling me down on the bed. "Do you know," she asks, her smile a beautifully wicked thing, "that I agree with that?"

"One more thing we have in common." I brace myself on my elbows above her, and while her breasts press tantalizingly against my chest, it's her smile I can't look away from.

"Do you want to know something?" she asks.

"I do," I say, bending to press my lips to the soft skin of her neck. She lets out a soft sound, somewhere between a sigh and a moan.

"From where I stand, you've done a pretty good job with everything, Tristan," she murmurs. "Things don't need to be perfect to be worth doing."

20

FREDDIE

I wake up in a bed that's large enough for five, snuggled deep under soft linen comforters. A heavy arm is draped around my waist. My legs threaded through someone else's.

I smile sleepily. I'm with Tristan in his bed, having spent the night. The intimacy we'd shared has settled into my bones, thorough relaxation throughout my body. Lingering pleasure from the night before. A light, pleasurable soreness.

The giant room is cast in soft shadows and flickers of faint December light. The strong lines of Tristan's face are smoothed into softness, the thick hair mussed. A man used to being watched, here where no one can watch him.

Tenderness clenches in my chest at the sight. He might be my boss. There might be a thousand things standing in our way. But I want this man, with all of his doubts and flaws and strengths and skills.

His arm tightens around my waist. "You're awake," he murmurs, not opening his eyes.

"So are you."

His arm inches higher, a hand settling around one of my breasts. I've quickly learned it's one of his favorite handholds.

I run a hand over his chest. "Thanks for being my heater."

"Hmm," he says, hand squeezing. "I do my best."

"You must run a degree or two hotter than me."

"We all have our skills." He rises on an elbow, his shoulders a contrast of sharp, masculine angles against the softness of the comforter. "You really have amazing breasts, you know."

It's such an offhand comment that I laugh.

He raises an eyebrow. "It's true. Perhaps not a skill, but very true."

I peer underneath the comforter, where his hand covers one of them from view. "They're all right," I agree. "But the size can get pretty annoying. I can't really buy sports bras from normal stores, for example. Shirts often gape at the buttons."

Tristan frowns. "Must be difficult."

"It's a nuisance sometimes."

"One wonders if they're worth it." He pulls the comforter back, folding it at my waist, and inspects my breasts. His hand switches from one to the other and my laughter makes them bounce.

"Yes," he finally announces. "From my perspective, they're worth it."

"I'm so happy to hear that," I tease.

He grins as he bends his head, taking one of my nipples in his mouth. A sharp sting of arousal rushes through my body at the heat. "Can't resist," he tells me, as he switches breasts.

"You did warn me," I murmur, sliding my hand into his hair. Closing my eyes as his hand moves down my stomach and over my bare thighs.

"It's a Saturday morning."

"That's right," I echo. "We don't have to be anywhere."

"Your heater's not running away."

My breathing hitches as he pushes my legs apart beneath the comforter, his fingers finding me as naked as I'd been last night.

"No," I breathe. "It'll be just as broken in a couple of hours."

"No need to rush."

"None at all." My back arches at the smooth circling of his fingers. My pleasure comes easily, a path well-trodden in the past few weeks with him.

"That's it." He bites down softly around a nipple and I shudder against him, my fingers knotted in his hair. Lazy, unhurried, unrushed. Intimate.

Tristan in the morning, I'm learning, is a glorious thing.

I try to reach for the hardness resting against my hip, but his fingers stop me. One of them sinks deliciously deep inside me.

His mouth slides up to my neck. "Do you know how good you feel?"

"Mmm."

"Sore?"

I shake my head, my hands curving around his wide shoulder. "Just a little."

"Good," he murmurs, adding another finger. His movements are still light and teasing. I twist my hips and he shakes his head. "I'll never tire of this, Freddie. Never stop needing you."

"That doesn't sound like a problem."

A hoarse chuckle. Then his hand disappears, leaving me bereft and wanting. He pulls the comforter back and reaches for a pillow. "On your stomach," he orders, voice rough from sleep and want. I look down at him, hard and aching, and obey. He slides the pillow beneath my hips and I look over my shoulder to see him there, straddling my legs, tightly pressed together.

"Tristan," I tell him. A plea and a question.

He gives me the wide, unfiltered grin I love the most. The one of a man who loves being in control. And then he pushes into me from behind.

The fit is snug like this, the pressure inside me rising with each disappearing inch. Only when he's buried to the hilt does he lie down on top of me, elbows on either side of my face to bear his weight.

He's everywhere. His body on top of mine, touching from foot to crown, his hair-roughened chest against my back.

It's the most delicious thing I've ever experienced.

"Yes," I breathe as he starts to move. With my legs still pressed close together, I can feel every ridge of him.

He bends his head and gently bites into my shoulder. Laughter escapes me, one he echoes, before it turns into a groan. I turn my head against the mattress and wrap my arms around his, the muscles taut and bulging as he carries his own weight. Press my lips against his arm.

"Never stop wanting you," he murmurs, voice pained.

"Me neither." He's bearing me into the bed, and with the pillow beneath my hips... The pressure is right where I need it. "Don't stop."

"Never."

The pleasure spreads through me in shockwaves, my hands turning into claws around his braced arms. I can't move, can't think around the pleasure of my orgasm and Tristan moving inside me. My whole world narrows to sensations. Like the sound of his hoarse groan in my ear. The feel of his hot skin against mine.

He rests his cheek against mine and grinds out the words. "It's too good."

"Let go," I urge him, borne into the mattress with the force of his full-body thrusts. "Come for me."

His hips lose rhythm as he explodes, growling in my ear with the force of it. Both of us left panting and loose-limbed on the giant bed, his body covering mine like a blanket.

It's a long moment before either of us speaks. Tristan goes first, laughing softly into my hair. "Felt like you were squeezing the life out of me, Freddie."

"Not all of it, I hope?"

"No, but it was damn close." He presses another kiss to the nape of my neck before lifting himself off. I give a sound of protest and he laughs again, a large hand playfully slapping my hip. "I'd be very upset with myself if I crushed you."

There's such buoyancy in his voice, so different from the heaviness it had contained last night. I roll onto my back and reach for a pillow to prop up my head. "You're welcome to wake me up like that anytime."

His eyes warm as they slide over my body. "I wouldn't mind that myself," he says. "You are unbelievably gorgeous, you know. Have I told you that? Just how attractive I find you?"

Despite what we've just done, a blush creeps over my cheeks at the frankness in his tone. At this man, kneeling naked on the bed beside me, who isn't the least bit afraid of saying what he's thinking.

No games, no hesitations.

"You've made it pretty clear," I say, "but I'll never tire of hearing it."

He grins. "Good. I won't tire of saying it, either."

"I don't think I've told you how handsome I find you."

"Oh?"

"That's what I called you in my head, when we met. Handsome." I reach for his hand, playing with his fingers. "So much better than Strait-laced, by the way."

"Oh, but I love undoing your laces, Frederica. It's my favorite pastime."

"Not complaining about that." My thumb smooths over his. "I didn't know it was possible to want someone this much."

His gaze warms. "You didn't?"

"No. It's never been this way before. This easy, or this natural."

"Effortless," he echoes. "I understand."

"You do?"

A single, clear nod of his head, as our gazes lock and hold. This is more than either of us had anticipated when we gave in to the attraction again. But judging from the way he's looking at me, he's not the least bit unhappy about that. Neither am I.

A trickling sensation snaps me out of my thoughts. "Oh! I have to go clean up."

He glances down between my legs. "Mmm. We were irresponsible."

"Yes. I'm on the pill, at least."

"And I'm sure you take it regularly."

"I do. I had a checkup a little more than a year ago, and I haven't slept with anyone since then."

"Three months ago for me," Tristan says. "But even before, I hadn't been with anyone without a condom for years."

His gaze drifts back between my legs, lingering over the evidence visible there. "Glad we can skip them from here on out," he says, satisfaction in his voice.

"So am I," I say, snapping my legs together. "If you're done inspecting your handiwork, I think we should shower."

He pulls me off the bed with a laugh. "You want to wash away my pretty signature?"

"I'm sure you'll sign me again soon enough," I retort, threading our fingers together. "Now show me the water pressure you must have here. I'm expecting perfection."

"That was the pretext all along, wasn't it? I bet your heater isn't even broken."

I push open the door to his en suite. *Bingo.* The giant marble shower is more than large enough for the two of us. "It was all a hustle," I tease.

Tristan reaches past me to turn on the waterfall showerhead. "Then consider me a very happy mark."

———

I pull on one of Tristan's shirts, and it falls halfway to my thigh. "Should I get started on coffee?" I call.

He's in the bathroom, brushing his teeth.

"Sure!"

I fold up his sleeves, one at a time, as I pad through the enormous apartment. Long hallways, rooms off to the side. One looks like a home office, another a laundry room. A guest bedroom.

The kitchen is a gleaming landscape of stainless-steel appliances and marble kitchen counters. Someone has meticulously organized the cereals into glass jars on the counter. The one labelled *Cocoa Pops* has a tiny sign next to it. **Only on weekends.**

It makes me smile. As does the schedule attached to the fridge, clearly outlining a child's school year. I stop in front of Tristan's coffeemaker. The appliance looks more monster than machine.

"Do you have to be a licensed barista to use this thing?" I call in the general direction of his bedroom, but there's no response. Right. You probably need walkie-talkies in this apartment.

I've just figured out where you add water when a sharp elevator ding sounds from the living room. Someone's here. I tug at the hem of Tristan's shirt and head into the living room. He's told me he has a housekeeper and a driver. It's mildly embarrassing to be seen like this, though.

The woman I encounter in Tristan's living room is very clearly neither. Snow clings to her black puffer jacket, flakes in the blonde curls of her hair. She's a few years older than me, perhaps, a pair of mittens in hand.

She stares at me like I stare at her. From the shock in her gaze, she might as well have been confronted with a unicorn or a yeti.

"Hello," I attempt. "I realize I'm not who you were expecting. Tristan's in the bathroom."

"Right," she says. "Okay."

"I'm Frederica." Manners kick in and I step forward, offering her my hand. She shakes it woodenly, her gaze drifting to my shirt. It's very clearly not mine.

"Linda. I'm his son's godmother."

I smile. "Oh, that's right. He's told me about you. Joshua stayed with you last night?"

Her eyes widen further, but then she gives me a tentative smile back. "That's right. He's downstairs."

"Well, that's good. I should probably change." I glance down at my shirt. Mortification nips at my heels, but I don't let it in. Tristan and I have done nothing wrong.

Well, not unless this woman is also an Exciteur HR rep.

"Probably," she says.

"Tristan should be done any minute now."

"Right," she says. "I have to say, I wasn't expecting to meet anyone. He doesn't often have guests over."

"I see."

"With his work and his son, he's a busy man."

I nod. "Yeah, he is that. Did you perhaps want a cup of coffee? I was going to make one, but I can't seem to figure out the machine."

"No, thank you. I just came up because—"

"Freddie?" Tristan's strong voice echoes from the hallway, and then he emerges, dressed in slacks and a barely buttoned shirt. His eyebrows rise at the sight of Linda. "Is everything okay?"

"Yes," she assures him. "Absolutely. Joshua's downstairs."

"Right." The question is clear in his voice, now colder. "Didn't know you were coming up."

"I tried to call ahead. A few times, actually. But there was no answer."

He nods. "Sorry about that."

Linda gives us both a genuine smile. "It's snowed. Look outside."

We turn toward the window-clad wall, and yes, Central Park is covered in a blanket of thick, white snow. My breath catches in my throat.

"It's gorgeous."

"Joshua is downstairs with Mark and Andrew. They've got a head start into the park. The boys want to have a snowball fight. Or build a snowman. Or a fort. They kept changing their minds."

Tristan snorts at my side. "Of course."

"I just came upstairs to tell you about it, and to grab Joshua's mittens and snow pants. He told me where they are."

Tristan nods. "I'll join you. I'll bring his stuff, too."

"That works." She steps back toward the elevator. "We'll be by the ice-cream shop, but just call if you can't find us."

"Will do."

She gives me a little wave. "It was nice to meet you, Frederica."

"Likewise."

The elevator doors close behind her, and then we're once again alone. Tristan runs a hand through his hair and steps past me to the coffee machine. A few wan clicks of his fingers and it whirls to life. Responding to its master in a way it had refused to do for me.

"I know I can't be angry at her for coming up, but I still am." He shakes his head, back turned. "All for snow pants."

"Was it bad that she saw me?"

He hands me a cup of freshly brewed coffee. "No."

"Thanks," I say, the heat warming my hands. "I'll leave in a few minutes, Tristan."

"I don't want you to," he says, but the conflict is there on his face.

"I know. But you need to go meet your son and play in the snow."

"Your apartment has no heat," he retorts. "I still haven't called my electrician to have a look at it."

"That's okay, I'll figure something out."

His jaw works with the force of his thinking. "I've never introduced him to a woman I'm seeing before. I'm not sure it's a good idea to tell him about us unless it's… well."

"Unless it's serious," I finish, putting the cup down. "God, I understand, Tristan. Completely. Let me just pack my stuff."

He follows me down the hallway, clearly displeased with the situation. But I mean what I said. I understand. He's a father. He has someone else to think about. While it's not at all the same, I have my career and reputation, too. Neither one of us is entirely free to do as we please.

He leans against the doorway and watches me get dressed. "Joshua's already met you," he says.

"Yeah, I suppose so. Twice."

"Right. Look, this is what we'll do. I'll call the electrician right away. Have him come over as soon as he can to look at your heater. It should be no more than a few hours."

"That's perfect, thank you."

"Meanwhile, you join us in Central Park."

My hands pause on the zipper of my jeans. "You're sure?"

"He knows you and I are friends, and he's met friends of mine before. I'll introduce you as that."

"Okay."

"Okay?"

I smile at him. "Absolutely. But only if you're okay with it."

"I am. But just because I want to make sure, and I'm always honest with him..." Tristan pulls out his phone and shoots me a chagrined smile as he raises it to his ear. "Joshua has a phone for emergencies. Not that it's always charged, but it's worth a—oh. Hi, kiddo."

A pause.

"Yeah, I'm coming down with your ski pants and boots in a few minutes. Do you have your hat?"

I pull on my shirt and hunt through his bedroom for my socks.

"Good. I have a question for you. Do you remember my friend? The elephant lady?"

My smile comes unbidden at that, and I look over at where he's standing. Tristan is smiling right back at me. "Yes, that's her. What do you think about her meeting us in Central Park?"

I sit down on his bed and pull on my socks, still looking at him.

He chuckles. "Only if she's okay with having a snowball fight. Okay, I think that's fair."

I pretend to lob a ball at Tristan's head, and he ducks to the side, grinning wide. "Okay, kid. I'll see you in a few minutes."

He clicks off the phone and leans back against the wall. "He thought it was a great idea."

"That's terrific," I say. "But elephant lady?"

"Is it better than strait-laced?"

"No. You really need to work on your nicknames."

Tristan catches me around the waist as I pass, pressing a soft kiss to my lips. "Sweetheart," he says. "I like that one."

Something flutters in my stomach. "So do I, handsome."

Grinning, he pulls me along down the corridor. "Let's go. We have snowballs to throw."

21

FREDDIE

I close the door behind me. My studio is toasty compared to the cold New York air, courtesy of Tristan's electrician and the newly installed heater. I kick off my boots and hang up my coat before I call him.

"You're back home?" he asks.

"Yes," I tell him. "And you're overprotective."

He sighs on the other line. "Walking home at night is still a risk."

"A small one. I was just at the bar next to work. It takes me fifteen minutes to walk."

"With your co-workers?"

"Yes." I sit down on my bed and pull up my legs. "You know, after having worked with them for a few months, I really don't think the mole is in my department."

There's a smile in his voice. "I'm not surprised you'd think that."

"It's not because I'm biased."

"Of course it's not."

"I've really been paying attention, you know. To their schedules and what calls they take. How they talk about projects. More so, how they talk about you or Exciteur when we're alone together. But all of them seem loyal to the bone."

"That's good to know," he says.

I fluff up a pillow behind me. "I can be a great corporate spy. I don't know why you doubt me."

He laughs then, warm and rich, and the sound washes away the days since we'd last seen each other. Since our snowball fight on Saturday, we'd only managed one late-night meeting since, here in my apartment. It's been nearly four days since then.

"I don't doubt you, Freddie. I know better than that. But I think you bring out the best in people, including someone who might be leaking information."

"Hmm." I take a sip of my tea, contemplating his words. "Perhaps I'm the one who has to make the first move. If I start talking crap about the company and your takeover, they'll feel more comfortable to let their traitor flag fly."

He laughs again. "You're that good of an actress?"

"I'm good at everything. Haven't you heard?"

"I have," he says. "The pitch you helped Eleanor deliver today has received raving reviews."

"Really?"

"Really," he echoes. "I heard the head of sales talk about it, not to mention the email we received from the clients afterwards."

I breathe out a sigh of relief. "Oh, that's amazing. We really worked so hard on this one, and the strategy we came up with was *excellent*."

"You'll have to give the pitch to me one day."

"Yes, well, I spent several evenings working on it this week. It better be good after all that time," I say. On the other end, I hear the sound of his feet, and then the closing of a door. "You're in your bedroom?"

"My home office," he says. "You remind me of me when I was your age."

"When you were *my age*? You're not that much older than me, mister."

"I suppose not," he admits. "But the ambition, I mean. Working evenings and being eager to rise in the ranks."

My gaze snags on the pictures on my dresser, the shrine to success. My parents. My grandfather. "I know you work evenings too, Tristan. And what you've accomplished is really inspiring. Exciteur is doing better now than it ever did before you took over the leadership."

He brushes past the compliment. "I used to have your hunger."

"Don't you still?"

There's a smile in his voice. "I'm not twenty-six anymore. There are responsibilities I can't forsake for a few extra hours at the office."

He's talking about his son. Joshua, whose smile comes wide and easy and has the confidence of a kid raised with love. I make my voice teasing. "Then why do you have a home office? Something tells me you spend evenings there every now and then."

"And what would make you think that?"

"Oh, I don't know, just knowing you? Tell me I'm wrong."

"You're not," he admits. "I'm often answering the emails at night. Why do I get so many?"

I laugh, turning over onto my back. Stare up at the ceiling and feel perfectly happy. "Have you received any from a disobedient trainee lately?"

"As a matter of fact, I haven't. I keep expecting it, but no dice."

"Expecting it?"

"It would spice things up. Rise right to the top of my priority list."

I smile. "I can't believe you thought I was a man."

"Frederica, you're called *Freddie.*"

"I know. But it was amusing, all the same."

He sighs, but it's laced with pleasure. "It's been too long since I've seen you. And it's only been a few days."

"I'm glad you said it first."

"You don't want to admit it?" he asks.

I run a hand through my hair, wishing he was in front of me. "Yeah, I like to play hard-to-get like that. I'd hate for you to think I like you."

"What a horrible thought," he says. "So, you like me?"

"I might, yes."

"Hmm. Well, I might like you too," he says. My heart swells in my chest at the words, smooth despite the rough baritone of his voice. "And I want to take you out. Properly, on a date, just the two of us. Somewhere in New York."

I close my eyes. "We can't do that. We never know when someone might see us. See you, especially."

"And that would be bad."

"Yes, unfortunately. My co-workers, the ones I had drinks with tonight? They were gossiping about two people at Exciteur who slept together once, after last year's holiday party. And they're in different departments. You and me? As far as gossip goes, we're meat and potatoes compared to that little appetizer."

Tristan's rich chuckle fills my ear. "We're tastier?"

"Infinitely."

"I understand, you know."

"About the not-being-seen-in-public-together part?"

He hmms in agreement, and I close my eyes to picture him, sitting in the leather desk chair in his apartment. Arms crossed over his chest and a smile on his face. "We both have things to lose, but the reputational toll would be harder for you."

"Probably true," I admit. "Unfortunately."

"But I won't be the boss of Exciteur forever," he continues. "And you won't be the trainee forever."

"Do you think we can... keep going until then? Hiding it?"

"I can," he says. "I'm not saying it'll be easy, but for you, of course I can. The question is, can you?"

My heart speeds up. "Yes. If you can, why couldn't I?"

"Because you're the one with a career to build, a social life to establish. I wouldn't be giving anything up, Freddie, but you... you might be. Only seeing me in the evenings every now and then. Not dating anyone else. Because that would have to be part of it."

"Of course," I murmur, voice dry. His words sink in, but there's no hesitation in me. No fears. "But I'd be gaining you, Tristan. Even if it's only behind closed doors."

He's quiet for a beat, the silence heavy on the line between us. "You're sure, Freddie?"

"Yes."

"All right," he says, and now there's a smile in his voice. "I can't offer you champagne and candlelit dinners in restaurants around New York yet, but I can offer you home-cooked meals and companionship. Not cooked by me, really, and companionship includes my son. You're welcome to dinner tomorrow evening if you want to."

I have to swallow before I can answer. "Are you sure?"

"Yes," he says. "He had more fun with you at the snowball fight than with me. Besides, I think he's more observant than I give him credit for. The other day he offered to be my wingman, and I have no idea where he learned that term. He's nine, for Christ's sake."

I laugh, turning on my side in the bed. "That's sweet."

"Or creepy. Haven't decided yet."

"I'll be there, Tristan. Tomorrow."

"I can't wait," he says. "You've turned me into a teenager, Freddie, and a few days without you are suddenly far too many."

"Tell me about it. I work every day in a building with you in it and I can't see you."

"I've thought about bending the rules."

I bite my lip. "More than we already have?"

"Oh yes. The past week, I conjured up ten different reasons I had to go down to Strategy."

"I didn't see you."

"I didn't go through with any of them," he admits. "I understand how important it is for you that no one finds out. Truly, I do. So I keep myself to the thirty-fourth floor."

"Your ivory tower," I murmur. "Thank you for that." We might be crossing all kinds of lines, but he has never been anything but respectful every step of the way.

He clears his throat. "Tell me more about your grandfather."

"Really?"

"Yes, or your parents, or where you grew up in Philadelphia. Anything to keep me from having to answer these damn emails."

Laughing, I turn onto my back. "I think I can save you from that fate, handsome."

22

FREDDIE

"We could go to the salad place," I tell Quentin. "Or the sushi one next door."

He frowns. "No, they're always packed for lunch. Toby, do you remember when we had to stand in line for thirty minutes?"

Toby gives a noncommittal grunt from his desk.

Quentin doesn't comment. No snide *aren't you done soon?* Or *what's keeping you?* Nothing at all. I glance at him, but his face gives nothing away. Still, I'm convinced something has happened. The tension between them has changed flavor.

I lean against Quentin's desk. "How late did you guys stay at the bar the other night?"

His gaze slides to mine. "Not that late."

"Uh-huh." My face is neutral, but he narrows his eyes regardless. I give him an innocent look. *I don't know anything, won't say anything.* A flush creeps up his ruddy cheeks.

He turns from me to Toby. "Are you done soon?"

"Yep, I just need to send this email off to Clive. He's up my ass about the Stanton project, wants all the details… I don't even know why," he grumbles. "I'm reporting to Sharon on this case. But I'll be a few minutes late for lunch."

Quentin groans beside me, but it's not as dramatic as it

would've been a week ago. Call me Sherlock, but I'm on to something here. "We don't mind waiting," I tell Toby. "Isn't that right, Quentin?"

He shoots me another withering stare. I grin gladly back at him.

But then his gaze drifts over my shoulder, eyes widening. It's the classic *oh shit* look.

Eleanor's voice falls like a scythe. "Frederica. Do you have a moment?"

"Of course," I say, pushing from the desk. "In your office?"

"Yes." Not waiting for me, she turns on her high heel.

I grab my notebook and pen. "Go ahead and have lunch without me, boys."

Quentin groans. "Unlikely. At this pace, my stomach will devour itself, and you two will be responsible for my death."

"In that case," Toby responds, fingers typing furiously, "I suggest you start working on your eulogy."

I leave them to their bickering and head into Eleanor's office, closing the glass door behind me. She gestures to the chair in her office and looks over at me from the edge of steel-rimmed glasses. She rarely wears them, but when she does, she goes from ice-cold raptor to intimidating librarian.

"Excellent job on the pitch the other day."

The unexpected praise makes me smile. "Thank you."

"The clients were impressed, and I've sent word along to my superiors about how important your contribution was."

"Thank you for that," I say. "That was very thoughtful."

She holds up a finger. "Not thoughtful. I was being fair. And if I hadn't been, you would have been in the right to ask me to do so."

I nod. "Okay, noted."

"To tell you the truth, Freddie, you've surpassed my expectations during your time here already."

"I appreciate that."

She gives me a thoughtful look. "This is a bit unusual, but

I recognize an ambitious woman when I see one. A position has become available, one we need filled soon."

Her words set off a storm of excitement. "This sounds interesting."

She gives me a rare smile. "Yes, one could say so. One of the international consultants at our Milan office will go on eight-month-long maternity leave. We need to replace her for that time… and when I saw the email, I of course thought of you."

My stomach squeezes into a tight fist. "You did?"

"You speak Italian. Now, it is uncommon to hire a junior trainee like this, but I think there's some real potential here. This would be a full-time, fixed position, and after your eight months there, I can promise you the company will want to retain you. Either in Italy or back here at headquarters."

"This is incredibly kind of you."

She raises a finger, but there's a smile in her eyes. "Not kind," she says. "Remember, just like I wasn't being thoughtful before."

"Right, I'll remember," I say, smiling. "I'm glad you see the potential in me."

"That's better," she says. "I wouldn't do this if I didn't want to ensure the company keeps you. So, if I have your permission, I'm going to recommend you to HR and the Milan office immediately."

My throat dries.

Milan. Italy. Eight months. A full-time job and a salary that's higher than what a trainee makes. A more permanent foot into this company and a chance to live in Italy.

The giant, man-shaped *but* is like a dagger inside of me. Tristan.

I have to talk to him about it.

I have to think about it.

"Can I have until Monday?" I ask.

Eleanor's eyebrows rise, but not in dismay. "Absolutely. Very wise, to take some time to think about your options."

"Yes, I want to do a bit more reading about Milan. But I won't keep you waiting longer than that."

"I appreciate it." She stands, and so do I, surprised when she extends me a hand. Like we've concluded an informal interview, which I suppose in a way, we have. "Good to see another strong woman joining Exciteur."

Her words reach right inside and twist the innermost core of me. Everything I want, everything I've dreamed about, is within reach. And I'm not sure which of the two options I should choose.

"Thank you," I say. It feels like a lie. "I appreciate it."

———

The offer churns inside me for the rest of the day. Everything inside me is leaning toward no, that I can't give up what I've just started with Tristan. But saying no to an opportunity because of a man feels like a betrayal of everything I've worked so hard for. My MBA. My grandfather. My family who believes in me. Myself, for working long hours.

My head and my heart, torn. It's so cliché it would have been funny if it wasn't my life. If it wasn't real.

Tristan smiles at me when I arrive at his apartment for dinner with him and Joshua. He's leaning against the wall in his hallway, hands in his pockets, the top buttons of his shirt undone. No suit jacket. Casual, masculine elegance, power in the frames of his shoulders.

A soft welcome in his eyes.

"Hi," he says. "How was the elevator ride?"

He always remembers. "It went surprisingly well. I haven't forgotten that it's your elevator, so it never malfunctions."

"That's right," he says, eyes warming.

"Something smells delicious." Oregano and garlic float like divine essence through the air. "What's for dinner?"

"Marianne is making lasagna."

"Do you like lasagna?" Joshua's voice echoes into the hallway a second before he appears, rounding the corner in a pair of jeans and a T-shirt with a safari-themed print on it. Another place they've visited?

The giant smile on his face makes me smile in return. "I love lasagna," I tell him. "With lots and lots of cheese on it."

"Cheese is my favorite meal."

"It's not really a meal," Tristan tells him.

"Yes, it is," Joshua replies with the tone of someone who's had to explain this multiple times. "We should give you a tour."

"A tour?"

Joshua nods, and Tristan steps in, a wide smile on his face. "You're right, buddy. Of course we should."

Ah, because I haven't been here before. Not in Joshua's eyes, anyway. I nod in the direction of the living room. "Lead the way, guys."

Joshua is just as relaxed and funny, the same happy-go-lucky kid he'd been the past weekend in the park. He doesn't seem to mind my presence, talking to his dad about things he'd likely talk about even if I wasn't there.

Seeing the two of them interact twists something inside me. For all his fears, Tristan is a really great dad. One look at how confident and kind his son is makes that crystal clear.

His housekeeper doesn't comment on my presence, but treats me with the same natural, effortless level of comfort as she does the other two.

"Dad," Joshua says when he's done, pushing his plate away. "Let's make s'mores for dessert."

Tristan looks like he's fighting a smile. "S'mores... but we're not camping."

"You don't have to be camping to have them," Joshua explains, turning to me. "Do you like s'mores?"

"They're pretty great," I admit. "I made them in the microwave the other night."

"*You did?*"

"Oh yes. It's one of my favorite things."

Joshua's eyes widen and he turns to Tristan. "See? Our guest loves s'mores! So it's kind of our responsibility, too. As hosts."

Tristan laughs, reaching over to run his hand through Joshua's hair. "We'll make s'mores, kid. Over the fireplace?"

"Yes!"

Joshua goes to his room to play after dinner, with the happy words that s'mores are only half an hour away. We've been instructed to tell him as soon as it's time.

I don't want to leave this. Not when I'm just learning their lives, their secrets. Captivated by their charm.

Tristan nods toward his office and I step past him into the man-cave. "Thanks for dinner," I say.

He crosses the distance to me. "Was it too much?"

"Too much?"

"Dinner, here. Me and Joshua."

I shake my head. "Not at all."

He reaches up to run a tendril of my hair between his fingers. "You're sure? You've been distracted all through dinner." His jaw works, the only sign of discomfort. "I know it must be difficult to date a man who's a father. Not having time just to... date."

"No, Tristan, that's not it." I reach out and curl my fingers around the soft fabric of his shirt. "Not at all."

His thumb curves down to my chin. "Then what is it?"

"Eleanor wanted to speak to me today," I say. Needing to say the words aloud, wanting to hear his calm, collected input on it. Tristan can make sense of this.

"Did she?"

"Yes. There's an opening in your Milan office."

His thumb stills along my jawline. "That's right. I saw it in an email today, from HR. Did they approach you?"

I nod. "Eleanor wants to recommend me for it. It's a full-time position. And I don't know what to do."

His hand moves again, his gaze watching it travel down my neck. "It's a good opportunity for you."

"Yes, it is."

"And you'd get to experience living in Italy. Honor your grandfather. Speak the language."

"Yes, but—"

Tristan shakes his head. "This is fantastic, Freddie. I understand why they approached you."

I nod, mute.

His smile slants. "I know you want to go."

I do, but as I look into the deep blue of his eyes, the decision isn't an easy one. It's not really a decision at all, not when I feel bonded to the man in front of me. To my co-workers and the life I've started to build here.

My throat closes. "I asked for the weekend to think about it."

"Good," he says." Very professional."

"Yes."

"You're ambitious, Freddie. And brave. Two of the things I like most about you. You'll do brilliantly in Italy."

"I'll miss you, though." Somehow, I manage to keep my voice light. My smile crooked. "Amongst all the gelato shops and the Vespas."

He smiles right back at me. "So will I. But I'd hate myself for holding you back."

I find myself nodding. Like we've agreed on this, as if the decision is made, even as my heart feels like fracturing. He's not reacting the way I'd hoped. The way I'd needed.

Tristan tips my head back and presses a kiss to my lips. It's full of the same quiet confidence as usual, but something about it makes me want to cry. "Come on," he murmurs. "Let's have s'mores. They don't have that in Italy, do they?"

23

TRISTAN

I rest my head in my hands, turning away from the bright glare of unread emails in my inbox. The same fucking inbox that's full every time I look, no matter how many emails I keep reading.

Jenny's voice comes back to me, as it does from time to time. Little things she used to say. *Don't work to live,* she'd say. Right before leaving on one of her adventures around the globe, taking her to Southeast Asia or Bermuda or the coral reefs that shelter Australia's Gold Coast. I didn't start listening to her advice until after she'd gone. What would she tell me in this situation?

Freddie's beautiful, elfin face drifts into my view. Olive-toned skin and brown eyes, dark hair, a beauty with fire in her eyes. And now she's been offered her dream job. Oh, I'd recognized the tentative hope in her eyes as she told me. The warring of emotions. She's conflicted, and it's because of me.

I can see so much of myself in Freddie. The hunger in her eyes. I'd had the same desire, undiluted and powerful, when I was her age. Before I'd received Joshua. I will never regret taking care of him, never regret signing those papers. He's Jenny's greatest lesson and greatest gift, as if she'd handed me the note *slow down, brother* in human form. He's a wonder.

And yet I remember the initial feeling of being held back. Of making concessions, of sacrificing pieces of your old dream as you try to make sense of the new one. I can't ask Freddie to do that, and we can't build a relationship that's heavy with that decision, weighed down by her sacrifice. I don't know if it would survive it.

She might resent me one day, not to mention how I might resent myself, because it would kill me to be the reason she doesn't get what she dreams of.

I reach for the phone on my desk. Dial the number to the chief HR rep.

To do what, though? Instruct them to give her the job?

Or tell them to choose someone else?

Slowly, I put the phone down. For a long moment I just stare at it in horrified silence.

I can't interfere with this. Whatever happens, it's Freddie's decision, and it has to be on her merits alone. My fingerprints can't be anywhere near this. Not if we're to have a hope of surviving past it, as friends.

Friends. Could I stand just being her friend? Receiving polite little postcards from Italy?

Never has the knowledge that she's in the same building as me burned the way it does today. Sitting just a few floors below me, but she might as well be on the other side of the globe already for all the good it does. I can't take her to lunch. I can't show her the city.

I'm powerless.

And I hate feeling powerless. So I open my emails and type a quick one to Gwen in HR, still keeping my internal promise not to interfere. **Let me know when you have a viable candidate for Milan,** I write. **I want the position filled as soon as possible.**

The emotions inside me still as soon as I've sent it. At least I'll be notified when she's made a decision. Should give me an opportunity to put on my game face for when she comes to tell me. To break up with me gently. Tell me she's following her dreams, the way I want for her. Even if it'll hurt.

I don't know if it makes it easier or harder that we won't have much time to spend together before she goes. The company's holiday party is tomorrow night. Then I fly to Tahiti with Joshua, and she heads to Philadelphia to celebrate Christmas with her family.

A quick, rapid-fire succession of knocks on my office door, the pattern familiar. "Come in."

Clive's navy-blue suit is a bit too large for his form. He's wearing the same bland smile as always, but it widens when he notices my scowl.

"You look like you want to punch someone," he comments. "Should I leave? Because I'm not a volunteer."

"No, I'm good."

"You sure?"

"Yes. What do you need?"

He doesn't waste any time. That's one of the things I've always appreciated with Clive as a COO, that he isn't here for idle chitchat or trying to get to know me. We run a business, so let's get down to running it.

"Actually," he says, sinking down in the chair in front of my desk, "what I want is an update on the mole situation."

My mood sours further. The fucking leak had struck again, at least if the article Anthony sent me this morning was correct. A rival company in the biotech sphere just unveiled their new five-year plan, and it's nearly point for point the same as the business strategy we'd developed for a client.

I run a hand through my hair. "I think it's time we start broadening our horizons away from just Strategy."

He frowns. "Logically, Strategy makes the most sense. They're the only ones with access, if one excludes the executive branch. And it's not amongst us."

"I have it on good authority that it's most likely not an employee in Strategy."

"You do?"

"Yes. I want you to draw up a list of everyone who knew about the biotech strategy for Finley. Leave no one out, including the two of us."

His eyebrows rise. "Okay, sure thing. But just out of curiosity… who is your source in the Strategy Department?"

The name hovers on my tongue, but something about Clive's interest halts me. Freddie doesn't deserve to be dragged into this. "I'll keep that to myself."

"Yes, sir."

Clive shuts the door behind him as he leaves, the silence of my office complete. The way I usually like it, but today, the absence of sound grates. It leaves too much space for my thoughts.

A click on my keyboard wakes my computer to life, and there's already a peppy email waiting there for me from Gwen in HR.

Great news! We've found a trainee from the New York office who would be excellent for the position. We just need to dot some i's and cross a few t's, but we'll have the position filled shortly!

I close my eyes and push back from the desk, telling myself I'm happy for Freddie, but all I feel is happiness slipping out of my grasp.

24

FREDDIE

I spin the frosted glass of white wine around, the red imprint from my lipstick sharp against the rim. He isn't here, and yet I can't stop glancing around the packed holiday party, searching for a glimpse of the man I'd first locked eyes with across the Gilded Room. The man who grilled s'mores with his adopted son in the fireplace of a multi-million-dollar apartment. The man who'd refused to be categorized from the very start.

"Earth to Freddie," Toby says. "Are you okay?"

"Oh, yes. Absolutely."

"You looked lost in thought," he says. "I hope you were somewhere far better."

"Better than this?" I sweep an arm out at the lavishness. One of Exciteur's office spaces has been transformed, and food-laden tables surround a tastefully decorated Christmas tree. "What more do we need?"

"Oh, I don't know. A beach. A raise. A longer vacation to look forward to," Toby suggests with a grin.

"God, I'd love a longer vacation. What are you doing for yours?" I ask. "Both of you?"

Quentin frowns into his glass, but he shoots a sideways glance at Toby. Toby, who is almost forcefully cheery. Who hasn't made a single snide, cheeky remark about Quentin. "I'm staying in New York. Well, I'm going to my family in Jersey for the holidays, but that's only thirty minutes away."

I glance at Quentin, but he doesn't rise to the bait, doesn't make a comment about how Jersey isn't New York. "I'm staying here," he tells us both.

"That's nice. You two have someone to hang out with, then," I say. "Just in case, I mean. I know I spent some lonely weekends here when I first arrived."

They don't look at each other, but nervousness flavors the air. Perhaps they're navigating the same turmoil that Tristan and I have, working at the same firm. But for them it might amount to no more than a slap on the wrist. For me and Tristan? A junior trainee and the company's CEO looks awful, from both perspectives.

"But not anymore, not when you have us," Toby says. "Because we're going to the opera in January."

Quentin groans at this, but I don't. "Really?"

"Yes," Toby says, clinking his glass with mine. "I'm going to make a real New Yorker out of you."

"And this comes from someone raised in Jersey," Quentin mutters, but his voice is fond. My attention slides from their ensuing banter to our mingling co-workers. To the company I've just started to get to know.

And there he is, across the room. The man I'm falling in love with.

He's talking to Sharon and Clive in the far distance of the employee-packed room. There's an uncomfortable tilt to his shoulders, like he doesn't want to be here. He shakes both of their hands and disappears toward the hallway.

I watch him retreat just like I did at the conference in Boston. We don't have a rooftop terrace here, though. And he's not going home, not when he hasn't grabbed the mic yet and wished everyone here a Merry Christmas.

My heart speeds up as I tell Quentin and Toby I forgot something at my desk. I ride the elevator to the thirty-fourth floor instead. There's so much churning emotion inside of me that I barely register the familiar fear.

Milan is my decision, and yet Tristan hadn't wanted me to make the one my heart is telling me to. *You're ambitious and brave, and that's what I like about you.* Would he think less of me if I turned Italy down?

And worse, would I think less of myself?

I walk down the empty hall on the top floor, passing offices I've never entered. Heading to the large one at the end of the hall with the emblazoned letters on the door.

Tristan Conway.

I knock and he responds a few seconds later. His voice is familiar, and yet not. Because this professional tone isn't one I've heard him use toward me since… well. Ever.

Even in the Gilded Room, he had his walls lowered more than he does here, in the company he owns and operates.

He closes his laptop when he sees me. "Freddie?"

"Hi." I push the door shut. "Are you hiding from the party?"

"I couldn't be down there. Besides, they don't want me there."

"They don't?"

He pushes back the chair and rises. "No. They want to gossip and blow off steam. They want to talk *about* me, not with me."

I frown. "That sounds sad."

He waves a dismissive hand, coming around to lean against his desk. Not crossing the distance to me. Not wrapping his arms around me or pressing a kiss to my temple. Just calm, collected, restrained. A man who's made up his mind.

"We haven't spoken this weekend," I say.

"I've been busy. So, I take it, have you?" The voice isn't unkind, but it is determined. "I heard you accepted the job."

"No, I haven't. Eleanor gave me an extension. I have until the end of the week," I say, taking a step closer, and hating the unusual formality between us.

Tristan meets me halfway. I lean against his chest and he wraps his arms around me, pressing a kiss to my forehead. The bristles of his rough-shaven jaw tickle my skin. "You're hesitating?" he asks.

"I am, yes."

"I hope you're not hesitating because of me," he says. The hand on my back is soft, but the steel in his voice is not.

Something in my chest cracks. "And why not?"

He sighs, both arms coming around me. "Because we're in different times of our lives," he murmurs. "Because I can't be the one who holds you back. Because this is a dream of yours, Freddie, and it would kill me if you regretted saying no."

My next words aren't well-thought out. They're a fear given words, and like a genie, they can't be put back into a bottle. "What happens if I go? Does that mean we'd be over?"

The single nod against my head is heart-breaking. "How can it be differently?" he asks.

There are a million things in my mind. *I can stay here instead.* Or *you can quit being the CEO. We can do long-distance.* Or, worst of all, *Why don't you come with me to Italy?*

But it wouldn't be fair to ask him that, not when I know what he'd have to sacrifice in return. The value he places on being a good father and a good boss are his very best qualities, and I wouldn't want him to break them even if he was inclined to.

My eyes burn and I clench them tight, but it only speeds the tears on their journey down my cheeks.

"Frederica?" Tristan murmurs, a hand smoothing over the back of my head. "Are you okay?"

I shake my head against his chest, and he sighs, pressing me closer. He might not say a word, but I can feel it in the strength of his arms. *I know,* he's saying. *I know exactly.*

"When do they want you there?" he murmurs.

My words come out muffled. "First of February. I understand if you don't want us to continue seeing each other, you know. If I'm moving."

He leans back, eyes widening as he takes in my face. They grow soft as he cups my cheek, a thumb smoothing over my tear-tracked cheek. "We can," he says. "But it will make things harder for us both when you go."

"Yes, it might."

"So you'll go to Philadelphia to celebrate with your family."

"And you'll go to Tahiti to see the whales," I whisper, my hands locked in his shirt.

He nods. "And when we get back in January... we can see. We'll meet to say goodbye, if nothing else. I'm here, Freddie. Always. Just not to hold you back."

But what if you're not? I want to ask. *What if Italy's the thing that's holding me back?*

The trust in me I see in his eyes stops my words. Combined with the look in Eleanor's eyes when she said how much she believed in me. My grandfather, with more business savvy in his pinkie than most people had in their entire body.

"Don't go back to the Gilded Room," I blurt.

Tristan's eyes widen. "Where did that come from?"

I take a step back from him. "Tristan, you're worth so much more than someone who only wants you for your body, *or* for your money. Than something that's just for a night."

His jaw works, and he leans back from me, hands braced against the edge of his desk. "You... you want me to start dating properly?"

The words make my eyes burn with tears. "No. Yes. I don't know, but I want you to be happy. You deserve to be happy."

"So do you," he tells me, voice hoarse. "More than anyone. But forgive me, Freddie, if I'm not quite at the stage yet where I can wish you happy dating."

My attention narrows to small, discernible things. The miserable lines on his face. The way he's holding himself back. My own feelings spinning out of control.

And I have to get out of here before I lose my own determination, asking him to be okay with me instead. With *letting* him hold me back, as he put it. But how can I do that?

"Bye, Tristan," I say. My voice breaks on his name.

His voice reaches me as I open the door out of his office. Against the New York lights streaming in through his window, he looks like a sentinel. A quiet guardian, a warrior of old. "Bye, Freddie," he murmurs.

The door shuts behind me with a finality that bruises and I race down the hallway toward the elevators, the hated, blasted things, and for the first time I think I'd be happy if they drop me all the thirty-four floors to the bottom.

A hard chest stops me and I stagger back, looking up at the man who's stepped out of his office. "Oh, I'm sorry."

Clive holds my elbow a second too long to steady me. "That's all right," he says, eyes widening as he sees the tears on my face. "Are you okay?"

"Yes, yes, absolutely. Just… allergies." It sounds just as stupid spoken out loud as it did in my head.

"Allergies?" Clive looks from me to the office down the corridor, at those incriminating letters emblazoned on the oak door. His eyes widen. "Ah. I see. Did he hurt you?"

What? "No, of course not. We were discussing work."

"Work?" He releases me and steps back, eyes narrowing. "You work in Strategy, right? One of the junior trainees. You organized that Thanksgiving thing he suddenly decided to throw."

There's no way to surreptitiously wipe tears from your cheek, so I just go for it, forcing spine into my steel. "That's right."

Clive nods. "Interesting. And you're sure, absolutely sure, that he didn't hurt you?"

It's an odd question. So is the gleam in his eyes, a gleam that turns my stomach from sad to uncomfortable. Suspicions form in my mind. "He didn't."

"Good. Had to ask."

"I'm heading out," I say, stepping past him. "Goodnight, Mr. Wheeler."

Clive gives me a nod, gaze lingering. "Goodnight, Miss…"

"Frederica Bilson."

"Frederica Bilson," he echoes. "That's right. Good night, then."

———

I make it home without sobbing, but the tears burn at the back of my eyes like a party-crasher or an unwelcome guest. They're in good company with the suspicions Clive had brought up, twisting into fear in my stomach. He'd realized right away that there's something between Tristan and me.

My hand trembles around my phone. I can't talk to him. Not so soon.

Not yet.

And yet I've worked for this career, and so has he. If my suspicions are correct… I have no other choice but to be professional and suck it up.

I dial Tristan's number.

It takes him five long signals to pick up. Had he been back at the holiday party? Still in the sheltered silence of his office?

There's no knowing, but the voice on the other end is weary. "Freddie…" he murmurs.

"Clive saw me on the way out of your office. He saw me, and he saw my… he saw that I was crying. I think he put two and two together."

Tristan's voice snaps into competence. "Okay. What makes you think that?"

I pace the tiny space of my apartment. "He knew. He asked me if you hurt me."

"He asked *what*?"

"He asked it twice."

Tristan's shock on the other end of the line is profound.

Mine, however, isn't. I can't keep silent as the suspicions bubble out of me. "Are you sure he's not the mole?"

"Of course I'm sure," is the response, but something about it sounds reflexive. Rehearsed.

"He's been asking Toby, one of my co-workers, for information. Information about projects that Toby doesn't usually report to him about. That last time I heard, it was regarding the Stanton case."

"Ah."

"And remember that meeting, over a month ago, where he couldn't make it? You went in his stead."

"I remember." A hard note creeps into Tristan's voice. "Yes, the pattern matches up. He was away that day for personal reasons, and a week later we found out that... Well. He could have been selling the strategy you pitched to our competitors."

"So you believe me?"

"It's plausible." A rough sigh, and it's everything I feel too. It's a sigh of *I can't take any more of this shit.* "Clive was with me from the very beginning. He was my right-hand man when I took over, the one person who seemed to welcome it when Acture Capital bought the company from the old management."

"Maybe he wasn't so welcoming after all."

"No, maybe he wasn't."

"But, Tristan, he *knows*. About us." My voice grows feverish. "He might use it somehow. It could cause some really bad publicity for you."

"He won't use it."

"How do we know that? Can we stop him?"

"We will," Tristan repeats, and this time there's no mistaking the steel in his voice. It's unbending. "If he's the mole, the things this company can do... I'll take care of him. No one will find out about us, Freddie. Your reputation is safe."

"Okay." I sink down on the edge of my bed. "But *how*?"

As far as days go, this one has been too intense for my liking. If I slept for a week, I doubt it would be enough.

"I'll tell him you were my eyes and ears in Strategy. Give him one truth to keep his eyes off the other."

I nod slowly. "Okay."

"I'll handle it, Freddie. Go to your family," Tristan says. "I'll keep you informed if anything happens, but it shouldn't. Not after I'm done with him." Perhaps the calm ruthlessness beneath his voice should scare me, the mixture of threat and reassurance. But I know him, and I know his values, and it leaves me with a sense of peace.

"Thank you," I breathe.

"Are you in your apartment?"

"Yes."

"Good. Thanks for calling me," Tristan murmurs. "I understand that it was… difficult. I appreciate it."

"Of course. You did ask me to find your mole, you know."

His voice softens. "So I did."

"And I always deliver."

"You always do," he agrees. "Sleep tight, Freddie."

"I will, thanks."

"And Freddie?"

"Yes?"

"Merry Christmas."

I open my mouth to wish him and Joshua the same, but by the time the words emerge, he's already hung up. So I close my eyes and lean back on my bed, the fixed heater humming loudly beside me, and let the tears flow.

25

TRISTAN

Fish in vivid colors swirl beneath me on the dock, dancing in the crystalline waters like they're performing a ballet recital to music only they can hear. Like so much on Tahiti, they're beautiful. We couldn't have asked for a better seaside bungalow, built right on the shoreline.

The place is a marvel in the Pacific, an untouched paradise, and I've already promised Joshua we'd start donating to marine conservation as soon as we get home to preserve pristine places like this.

And yet.

Because isn't there always a but?

The phone in my hand lies cold, empty and near signalless. I'd had to walk to the hilltop in the small settlement to get enough signal to call Freddie on New Year's Eve.

But she hadn't responded. Hadn't called or texted back, either.

So I hadn't tried to reach her again, instead keeping my promise to avoid making this harder for her. Even if the idea of her moving away feels like a splinter, burrowing deeper every day. In the short months I'd known Frederica, she'd wormed her way under my skin in a way no one else had. No woman, none since my ex, and that was before Joshua. Years ago.

I open the emails on my phone. I haven't looked at them in days, and only then in the evenings, when Joshua has already gone to bed. But now he's resting inside the bungalow and I'm allowed to sneak a few minutes of work in.

My lawyer has responded, assuring me we've got Clive in hand. Selling company secrets is a violation with some serious legal ramifications, and we're going to pursue them all.

I close my eyes at the memory of the conversation. Of Clive's usually bland, obsequious face turning red with rage.

I was second in line to take over this company. Management had groomed me for CEO. And then you and your friends took over, and I was pushed back down the chain.

It had been there, under the surface, for over a year. The hate and the envy. And I hadn't seen it.

So you tried to destroy the company as revenge? I'd asked him. *Is that any way to honor this firm or the employees?*

He'd shook my words off as if they meant nothing. Lost in his resentment, they probably didn't.

I have dirt, he'd said with obvious pleasure. *Sleeping with a trainee, Conway? How do you think that'll look in the press? You'll be barred from every event and function in the city, with the current climate. All they'll see is a dirty, powerful man, abusing his—*

I'd cut him off.

If he wanted to hurt me with Freddie, he would have to try harder than insinuating anything had ever been coerced or sinister about us. If there's one thing it wasn't, it had been that.

It had been one the purest experiences of my life.

She was my informant in Strategy, I'd told him. *You're reaching, trying to discredit the employee who helped unmask you. If you think anyone will believe your attempts to save face, you're delusional.*

And that had been that. He'd been escorted off the

premises, all of his company accounts shut down, his email communication on company servers seized.

The very next call I'd made had been to Eleanor. I had briefed her on the situation, letting her know Freddie had been reporting to me. Phrased correctly, it wasn't a big deal. I'd simply been impressed with Freddie's abilities after Thanksgiving and asked her to keep her ears and eyes open.

Eleanor had been quietly impressed, rather than offended that I'd bypassed her. "I never liked Clive," she told me. "Something about his manners always felt too sugary." I'd sent her the email asking her to replace Clive as my COO the very next day.

I put my phone down and close my eyes against the Polynesian sun. The anger at Clive still burns, even if it's more at his threats than his betrayal. His complete disregard for Freddie, who had never done him a single wrong.

Freddie.

All thoughts start and end there, it seems.

A child's skipping footsteps on the dock makes me turn. Joshua's in a T-shirt and shorts, his hair mussed from where he's been lying on the giant hotel bed. He'd watched a bit of a nature documentary on his iPad after we'd gotten back from whale-watching.

"What are you doing?" he asks me.

"Just thinking. Looking at the ocean."

He sits down cross-legged beside me on the dock. Beneath us, soft waves break against the pillars. "Can we go swimming later?"

"You bet we will. Is Grandma inside?"

He nods. "She's resting. She said she's been on enough boats this week to last her for life."

I laugh, mussing his salt-roughened hair. "She's not a boat person."

"She said she took pictures today, when you and I snorkeled."

"But not as good as ours."

He gives me a cheeky smile. The underwater camera we'd brought had come in handy today, when we'd finally swum next to a whale shark.

"We're hanging that one up at home, right, Dad?"

"We sure are, kid."

We grin at each other for a few seconds, and damn, my kid really is the best. My phone pings and his grin turns into a frown. "Dad, were you *working?*"

He says the word like I've been busy committing violent crimes out here on the dock. "Just answered a few emails," I tell him, grabbing my phone. "I'll put it on silent... oh. It's from Anthony."

Joshua's frown disappears. My son knows and likes Anthony, having seen him often over the years. He might be quiet, and he's often scowling, but Anthony is a good man through and through.

"What did he say?" Joshua asks. "Did you tell him about the whale shark?"

"Not yet, but I'll tell him now." Smiling, I click open the text. And laugh. "He's being cranky."

"Why?"

"Because of the company we told him he had to take over next."

"He doesn't want to?"

"No." Seeing Joshua's expression, I hurry to explain. "No, he does. It's a good opportunity. But it's in an industry he thinks is a bit... silly."

"What is it?"

"A matchmaking company."

Joshua frowns, a tiny furrow between his brows. "A what?"

"It's for grown-ups who want to meet a wife or a husband, but are having trouble finding one on their own."

"Oh." Joshua lets out a chuckle, swinging his legs above the water. "That *is* silly."

"Anthony thinks so too."

"There are a ton of grown-ups. Shouldn't it be easy to find someone to marry?"

I run a hand over my rough jaw. I hadn't bothered to shave this week, and the feeling is foreign against my hand. "Well, grown-ups don't want to just marry anyone. It's difficult to find the right person."

Joshua gives a wise nod. "Is that why you haven't gotten married, Dad?"

"Part of it, I suppose. And I work a lot too."

His glance down at my phone makes it clear my kid thinks the very same thing. No doubt emphasized by Linda's well-meaning comments. "Do you wanna get married?"

"Well, kid, I don't know. I suppose I do, if I meet the right woman."

He shades his eyes and looks out across the endless water ahead of us. He's a little red at the nape of the neck despite the copious amounts of sunscreen my mother is careful to slather him in. "I like your friend who came to dinner. Freddie."

I try to keep my tone level when I answer. "She's really nice, isn't she?"

He looks down at the fish beneath us. "Yes. When she comes over again, I think I might give her my giant stuffed elephant, the one I won at the Thanksgiving Fair."

"Oh? How come?"

"She liked elephants more than me, and besides, I'm almost too old for stuffed toys." He turns to me with a smile that looks so much like Jenny's that I suddenly feel seven years old again, looking up at my older sister at his age. "Besides, you want to marry her, don't you, Dad? I can help you convince her."

My heart squeezes tight in my chest and perhaps my answering smile is a bit sad, because his falters. "Don't you want to?"

"I do," I admit. "But she's moving away."

"What?"

"Yeah. To Italy."

He sighs, looking down at his bare feet. "Danielle might move back to France."

"Really?"

"She told me before we went on break. She'd heard her parents say they weren't going to stay in America forever."

I smile. "That might still be a while. They could stay here for years."

He shrugs. "I told her I didn't want her to go."

"You did?"

"Yes." A private smile forms on his lips, and I know he's far away. Lost in the memories of his first crush. I wonder when he'll stop confiding this sort of thing to me.

I hope it's never.

"So you still like her," I comment.

He nods. "And I think she likes me too. She's stopped spending time with Dexter. She always sits next to me."

"That's great, kid."

His smile widens. "Yes. Did you ask Freddie not to move away?"

I shake my head slowly. "No."

"Why not? Perhaps she won't. You know, if she likes you too."

It's so simple, coming from Joshua. Obvious. The clarity in his voice isn't hindered by adult concerns or nuance.

I run a hand through my hair, and it's just as salt-roughened as my kid's. "If I say it, she might stay. And as much as I want that, I also know that moving to Italy is her dream."

Joshua frowns in concentration. He's really considering this, gears turning in his mind. "But Dad," he says, "if you don't tell her, perhaps she doesn't *know* you want her to stay."

"I think she knows."

"Thinking and knowing isn't the same thing," he informs me, legs swinging. "Mrs. Kim always says that in science class."

My lips tug. "Well, she's right about that."

"I think you should tell her. Then she knows, and she can make up her mind."

So simple.

So clear.

And yet his words lead me into a different direction, one I hadn't considered before. By not asking her, by not telling her explicitly how I feel, I'm not trusting her to make her own decisions. I haven't given her the full picture. All the words I haven't spoken suddenly fill my chest, clog my throat, until they feel like they're going to choke me.

Joshua gives me a wide smile. "I'm right?"

"You are," I tell him. "You really are."

"See, Dad, I know things too."

"Oh, you sure do, kiddo."

He's his own person, someone unique and separate from me, Michael and Jenny. And yet I get the strangest feeling that Jenny has told me off again, this time from the grave and through her son.

And this time, I'm going to heed her advice to throw caution to the wind. Joshua stretches out on the dock beside me, putting his skinny arms beneath his head. It's such a teenage pose, showcasing the length of his legs and torso. The shorts we'd bought him for this trip already look a bit short.

But he's only nine.

Is this the precursor of a growth spurt?

"You gotta stop growing, kid," I tell him. "It's going too fast."

He grins up at the sky, a boy without a care in the world. A boy who was brave enough to swim with a whale shark today. His smile had been ecstatic when we'd been back on the boat, my arms wrapped tightly around his shoulders to keep him from shivering.

"I'll be ten in a few months," he informs me.

"Don't remind me."

"You want me to be a kid forever?"

I lie back on the dock beside him, my feet hanging off the edge. The sky is as turquoise above us as the Pacific beyond.

"I want you to be my kid forever."

He laughs. "I'll still be your kid when I'm a grown-up."

"Yes, I suppose you're right."

"You're being stupid, Dad." He shakes his head, nudging me with his elbow. "And we'll go on adventures then, too."

My heart aches with love for him, and for the first time in years, something pricks behind my eyes. I look up at the heavens above. *Thank you, Jenny.*

"Yes," I assure him. "We always will."

26

FREDDIE

"Who knows?" Toby asks. "It could have been anything. Breach of contract. Insider trading. Perhaps he just pissed Mr. Conway off one time too many."

Quentin shakes his head. "No, the man wouldn't fire someone who's productive just because of his attitude. Ten bucks it's because he harassed someone."

"Are we really taking bets on this?" I ask, my hand tight around my glass of whiskey. The first day back after the Christmas holidays, and the entire office had been abuzz with speculation about the personnel changes. It's a weight off my shoulders that nothing relates to me.

"You don't have any theories?" Toby asks me. He's sitting across from me, his arm brushing Quentin's on the bar table. Both seem entirely relaxed with this casual touch.

"I don't," I say. "And to tell you the truth, I doubt we'll ever find out. Management is being really tight-lipped about it."

"These things leak. They always do."

"Mmm, not all things," I murmur, nodding to them. I can't help letting them know what I suspect, not when we work so closely.

Quentin goes still. Toby, however, doesn't. He laughs. "Freddie, you know?"

I shrug. "I always thought you two would be cute together."

Quentin looks away from our booth to the crowded bar, a flush rising on his cheeks. "Cute," he mutters.

Toby elbows him, still looking at me. "Although now we have a new problem."

"You do?"

Quentin looks back at me, face fondly resigned. "I was offered a job today."

My eyebrows rise. "What? Really?"

"Yes. Apparently Eleanor's been offered a position higher up, so to speak."

Clive's job. It has to be. "Oh God, are you saying what I think you're saying?"

"I'm not saying anything," is his cool response, "as I'm not yet allowed to."

"But you see what this means, right?" Toby asks. "We're not just co-workers who are dating. I will now be dating my boss. That's a whole different ballgame with HR."

I can't help but laugh, and there's no stopping it, despite my happiness for them. The irony is too much. Toby joins in, even if he's laughing for a different reason. "It's like a bad movie, isn't it? What do I do?"

"You're an MBA grad," Quentin comments, and it's the first time I've heard him say it without a trace of scorn. "You're in high demand in all the other departments too."

"But then I'd leave Freddie behind," Toby says, touching his glass to mine. "How would she survive without my guidance?"

"I'd flounder," I say, my smile growing wider. As happy as I am for them, I'm just as nervous about talking to Tristan again. When I see him next, I'll have to tell him what I decided.

What I'd told Eleanor the day before I left for Philadelphia.

That while I truly appreciated the offer, I was committed to staying at the Exciteur headquarters and fulfilling the position for which I was hired.

The second I'd said it, and the moment I'd seen the begrudging acceptance and respect in Eleanor's eyes, I'd felt completely at ease with my decisions. Happy, even. Italy will still be there in a few years. In decades, too. But what I have going on now feels more important.

Tristan feels more important.

But I don't know if he'll think less of my ambition because of it.

My phone rings, vibrating on the table between us. I give Quentin and Toby an apologetic smile and slide off the stool.

My heart stops in my chest when the familiar caller ID appears.

I weave my way through the people in the bar as I answer, still in the outfit I'd worn at work.

"Hello?"

"Hi, Freddie." His deep voice is familiar in my ear, like the past two weeks of separation hadn't happened. "I'd very much like to see you."

I swallow. "I'd like that too. Did you just get back from Tahiti?"

"Yes, a few hours ago. I can come to the bodega on your street, if you'd like."

Someone screams beside me in post-work bliss and drink, and I hold my hand to my ear. "Sorry, sorry, I'm heading for the exit."

"You're at a bar? Oh. The one close to work."

"Yes, but I'll be leaving soon."

"No need, I'm already out. I'll meet you there."

"Tristan, I—"

But he's already hung up.

I stare at the phone in my hand, blindly, wondering if that

just happened. But there's no denying the effect his voice and words have had on me. Adrenaline floods my system and launches me into action.

He's coming here.

When I return to our table, I reach for the coat hung over the back of my chair. "I'm sorry, guys, truly, but I have to head out."

"What? Why?"

"We just got here."

"I know," I say, "and I'm sorry. But we'll have other nights. Congrats again, Quentin."

He gives me a rare smile. "Thank you."

"And don't worry, I'll keep it to myself until it's official."

"Thank you. Both of the things I know."

Toby winks. "And don't... oh my God. What is *he* doing here?"

Their eyes are both locked on a point somewhere over my shoulder, and I still, too scared to turn around.

"Frederica," he says, drowning out the sounds around us. My hands shake as I tie the waistband of my coat. When I turn... there he is, standing in a suit and a navy overcoat, his thick hair dusted with snowflakes. A tan across his skin.

Seeing him feels like coming home, like something clicks inside of me, and I know I've made the right decision to stay in New York.

"You came here," I say.

"I did," he confirms, looking past me to Toby and Quentin. He gives a single, professional nod in their direction.

"Gentlemen."

A glance over my shoulder tells me they're in a complete and utter state of shock.

"I need to speak to Ms. Bilson for a moment," he says. "Enjoy the rest of your evening." He steps aside and motions to the exit, the length and breadth of him easily giving us space in the crowded bar. I wonder who else in here is from the office. Who might be watching.

But I can't find it in myself to care.

"See you tomorrow," I tell Toby and Quentin.

"Um, sure. Have fun?"

Tristan holds the front door open for me and we emerge on the busy sidewalk, the cold New York air a comfort to my fevered senses.

"Thank you for meeting me," he says.

"Of course. Wasn't expecting you to be here so quickly, though."

"I was in the area already."

"Oh." I take a deep breath. "It's actually perfect, this, because I have to tell—"

Tristan shakes his head. "Let me go first, please. I need to tell you what I should have told you weeks ago, before you accepted the job in Italy. What I wanted to say."

My mouth closes on my words. "You do?"

"I've been an idiot."

"You have?"

A smile spreads across his features, and combined with the tan and the look in his eyes, he's breathtaking. Every inch the handsome stranger I'd met at the Gilded Room all those months ago. "Freddie... Frederica. I want you, and I've vowed to never stop telling you just how much. Fuck, Freddie, do you know how deep inside of me you've crawled?"

A shake of my head and his words pour out, passion blazing in his gaze.

"I was in the crystal blue waters of Tahiti with my son. I was determined that I wasn't going to hold you back in any way. I tried to be happy for you, genuinely. But you were there on that trip along with me, next to me the whole time, a phantom you. One I couldn't reach out and grasp, couldn't share my thoughts with, couldn't sleep at night for thinking of."

My throat is dry, a desert of emotion. "Tristan, I want you too. You know I do."

"I do, Freddie, and I'll never take it for granted again. So

I'll tell you what I felt like I couldn't before, and perhaps it's selfish of me, and if so, you're free to hate me for it. But I don't want you to go to Milan. I want you to stay here in New York with me."

I open my mouth to respond, but he shakes his head. "But," he interjects, "I know you have your dreams and goals, and I will never stand in the way of that. So if you'd like, go to Milan. I'll be there as often as I can. As often as you'll let me."

I shake my head at him, but I'm smiling. "Tristan, I turned down the job."

"You did what?"

"I turned it down," I say. Above us, snow whirls in indecipherable patterns under the streetlight. "I just got to New York, and I want to stay here. I want to work at the headquarters and I want to live in my tiny apartment a bit longer."

Tristan grips me around the waist. "You're serious."

"I am, oh I definitely am."

He laughs, a deep, unbelieving sound, and then he bends his face to mine. Perhaps I should mind. There might be people from work passing by. But I can't, and I don't, because the feeling of his lips against mine is a promise and a balm after two weeks of uncertainty. He kisses me like it's the first of many, many, many.

"I've already called my co-owners," he murmurs as he lifts his head, thumb grazing my chin.

"Okay. Uhm, why?"

"Because I'm renouncing my title as CEO of Exciteur."

"You're doing *what?*"

"I'm not going to spend the coming ten months of your internship hiding, Freddie." His hand slides down my arm to grip my hand. Long fingers twine through mine. "I want to show you around the city. Take you to my favorite spots, have dinner with you at restaurants, Sundays in the park. All of it."

I grip the lapels of his coat. "But what about Exciteur?"

"One of my business partners will take over as CEO." A

trace of sly confidence appears in his smile. "I'll still be able to influence decisions behind the scenes."

"Of course you will," I tease, but there's no emotion behind it. Nothing can drown out the happiness bursting through me like a broken dam. "What will you do instead?"

"Perhaps," he murmurs, lowering his head again, "I'll take some time off."

"Oh, will you?"

"Mhm. And if that doesn't work, there's a publishing company I've been looking to buy."

Laughing, I rise up on my tiptoes and kiss him. He can deny his hunger all he wants, but he's just as ambitious as me, and that hasn't changed with fatherhood. "Let's get out of this cold," I tell him when he finally raises his head again, both of us breathing hard. "I have a brand-new heater in my apartment."

He lets me pull him down the street, smiling. "Oh, do you?"

"Yes, and I don't think you've seen it."

"I better come up, then," he says. "To inspect it."

27

TRISTAN

Four months later

The damned mask chafes at my skin, reminding me why I've rarely worn the thing. I tuck it into the inner pocket of my suit jacket instead. The incense hangs thick in the air, the scent of citrus and chamomile familiar but not unpleasant. I gaze out over the writhing bodies in the warehouse the Gilded Room chose for this occasion.

Women in lingerie serve drinks out of highball glasses while a man trails them in nothing but a police hat and shorts. I watch as one of the city's top bankers invites a model to sit on his lap. She agrees, smiling with false modesty.

My gaze continues, past the performance, until I find the one woman I'm here for.

She's leaning against the opposite wall. The silky fabric of her red dress clings to every exquisite curve, draped around her chest in a way that beckons a man to drown himself between those breasts. Dark, thick hair hangs in loose waves down her bare arms and shoulders. I know how it feels over my skin as she rides me, and how it must be tickling hers even now.

The mask she wears hides most of her face from view, but I'd recognize Frederica anywhere.

I motion for a waiter and replace my empty whiskey glass with another. Coming here tonight had been her suggestion. It's been six months since we first met, and when I'd proposed dinner to celebrate the occasion, she'd suggested this.

I'd been shocked. Intrigued. And what the lady wants, she gets.

A sultry voice to my right forces me to break eye contact with Freddie. A woman has her hand on my arm, nails digging into the fabric of my suit.

"Hello, stranger. I haven't seen you around in a long while."

She's vaguely familiar, with ice-cold blue eyes and a pointed chin. "It has been a while," I agree.

The old days when I'd attend a few of these parties a year seem like they belong to a different life. One where interactions with women were short, to the point, always fun, but never serious.

A way to keep relationships at arm's-length, until Freddie refused to stay away. Until I couldn't let her go.

"I'm going to head into one of the bedrooms soon," the woman drawls, her hand inching down to wrap itself around my hand. "If you'd care to join…"

I release her with a placid smile. "Sorry, but I'm taken for the night."

Her eyes scan the area. "And she's left you here alone?"

"For the time being, yes."

"A pity," ice-blue eyes says with a shrug. "She'd better come to her senses soon."

As she meanders off, my gaze returns to where Freddie had been. But she's gone. I take a sip of my whiskey and relish the familiar burn down my throat, amplifying the punch of lust in my stomach. She's here, somewhere, being admired by all the men.

But she'll pick me.

Her strength, ambition and fierce intellect hasn't stopped impressing me yet. With Victor in charge of Exciteur, the talented son-of-a-bitch, I'm still kept informed by both him and Freddie. So I know she's been offered Quentin's old job in Strategy, a position that would guarantee a full-time job after her internship ends.

I lean against the wall and scan the crowd for a spark of red silk and dark hair. Some of the women here are in lingerie, but even fully naked they'd have nothing on Freddie's allure.

Her voice reaches me first. "Hi there, handsome."

I turn to find her leaning against the wall beside me, her arms tucked underneath her breasts. The move gives me an even deeper view of her cleavage. "Hello," I say.

She re-adjusts her mask, a flash of territorialism in her eyes. "You've already been spoken to."

The urge to grin in triumph grows stronger, but I play along, crossing my arms over my own chest. "So I have."

"She looked... interesting."

"I told her I was already with someone."

Freddie's composure cracks and her lips break into the smile I love the most. Wide and unrestrained and just a bit fierce. A mouth that is kind, but never weak. "I'm happy to hear that," she says.

I take her hand in mine, fingers brushing over the diamond tennis bracelet on her wrist. It had been a gift for her twenty-seventh birthday.

She hasn't taken it off since. "Have you seen how the men have watched you here tonight?"

"No," she says.

My thumb smooths over the rapid pulse in her wrist. "I have. I've seen them all look at you, at how that dress clings to your body, at your hair. They've all been hoping they'd be the one you came and spoke to."

"Yet here I am," she murmurs, shifting her hand in mine. "Talking to you."

I incline my head. "Here you are. And do you want to know something?"

"What?"

I lean forward, brushing her ear with my lips. "I'll never tire of being chosen by you."

A shiver ghosts across her skin, and it'll never stop turning me on, seeing how I can affect her, even after these months of ever-growing intimacy. Freddie slips her fingers in between the buttons of my shirt. "Thank you for agreeing to come here with me tonight."

"Anything you want," I say, moving my lips down to her neck. "But would you mind telling me why?"

"Why not?" she asks. "It's fun."

"It is indeed."

Her fingers tighten in my shirt. "You once told me you don't need this anymore, not while we're together. Is that still true?"

"Unequivocally," I tell her. Through the thin fabric of her silk dress, my hand traces the outline of her hip. I love these handholds.

"Good. Then this is our last time here."

I smile against her skin. "I won't miss it."

"We're saying goodbye to it tonight," she murmurs. "And I'm claiming you."

I tip her head back to give me better access to her collar-bones. I won't go further than this, not with all these people looking... but there's no denying a part of me longs to with the fall of her chest so close to my face. My teeth graze over the thin spaghetti strap.

"Claiming me?" I ask.

Freddie gives a single nod. "Yes. The last thing these men and women are going to see tonight is me, leading Tristan Conway out of the Gilded Room."

I smile against her skin, this fierce, brave woman who

went to a sex party she wasn't invited to, who seduced a man who thought himself un-seducible, and who stood up to her boss when she accidentally emailed him with an insult. "You've come a far way, Strait-laced."

Her hand slides up to grip my hair. A slight, unmistakable tug.

But my grin doesn't falter. "You don't hate that nickname anymore," I challenge.

"No," she admits, the hand softening. "I don't."

"Tell me when you want to lead me out of here, and I'll follow you."

Her smile turns crooked as she pulls my head down for a kiss. It quickly turns heated with her body beneath my hands. A tug and she's pressed against me, those gorgeous breasts a delicious weight on my chest.

"Now," she murmurs. Her hand slips down to grip mine as she turns, leading me with confident determination through the populated warehouse.

And people do watch us.

How could they not? Her, drop-dead gorgeous and on sky-high heels, a woman on a mission. And me, following her with my hand linked to hers. My conqueror is showing off, and yet I feel nothing but pride.

Let them see her take me off the market for good.

We get our phones back from the attendant by the door and leave the party behind. Freddie steps into the elevator ahead of me without hesitation. I squeeze her hand in mine and she looks up, smiling. She rarely looks at the monitor counting the floors anymore.

She's challenging her limits all the time, now. We've even been out on my balcony a few times.

"What?" she asks me, but she's smiling.

I take her in my arms and tip her head back. "You did great in there."

She licks her bottom lip. A clear invitation, and my body

rises to it. The things I'll do to her when we get back to her studio… I've learned to work with the size constraints.

Her mouth softens into a delighted smile. "You're looking at me like that again."

"Like what?" I brush her lips with mine once, twice. "Like I love you, sweetheart?"

Her breath hitches. "Yes. Like that."

"Well," I murmur, kissing the corner of her lips. "Perhaps that's because I do."

The sultry seductress before me transforms into my smiling girlfriend. "I love you too," she murmurs, arms around my neck. "So much. I didn't know when to tell you."

"Well, is there ever a bad time?" I kiss her again. This must be the longest elevator ride in history, but I'm not complaining. She laughs in my arms, a sun exploding, and I'm the only one here to soak up the rays. "The first time you kissed me after the first night was in my elevator, when it stalled. Do you remember? Now the first time you tell me you love me is in an elevator. Are you trying to get rid of my fear by positive reinforcement?"

"Maybe. Is it working?"

"It might be." She presses her lips to mine again, still half-smiling. "There's just one thing we have left to do in one."

My eyebrows rise. "Are you saying what I think you are?"

The elevator doors open to reveal the candlelit lobby of the old Brooklyn warehouse. Freddie laughs, pulls me toward the exit. "You do have a private elevator," she says.

"You're right, I do. It's almost the same size as your studio."

"Be nice," she chides me, eyes glittering. "There's something else I think we should do too."

I push open the front door for her. "Tell me."

"Well, remember the previous tenant in my apartment? Rebecca Hartford?"

"The one whose invitation to the Gilded Room you stole? I remember."

"I didn't steal it," Freddie protests.

I bite my tongue to keep from smiling. "Of course not, Strait-laced."

"Well, I was thinking we should send her flowers," she says, her hand tightening on mine. "We owe her a lot, don't we?"

I smile back at her. "We owe her everything."

EPILOGUE

Six years later

The strong wind whips at my hair and pulls tendrils out of my tight braid. The New Mexican air is dry and hot, the glittering Rio Grande a thin snake of water more than five hundred feet beneath me. It's the exact spot Tristan and his sister bungee-jumped from more than twenty years ago.

Tristan and Joshua had planned our trip here since he was ten, but it had taken time, because you had to be fourteen to be allowed to jump. Tristan had insisted on waiting one more year.

Sweat drips down my spine and I give the harness I'm in a tentative tug.

"It'll hold," Tristan says by my side. His calm, familiar voice steadies me. Of course it'll hold.

Breathe in.

Breathe out.

Two bungee-jump operators unstrap Tristan's own harness with quick hands and I grip the railing tight. "And you're sure you enjoyed it?"

His grin is wide beneath his wind-tousled hair, handsome

streaks of gray at his temples. "A rush like no other," he assures me.

Joshua gives me a nearly identical smile. "It was *amazing*, Freddie. You won't regret it."

I peer over the edge of the bridge to the five hundred feet drop. It had been hard enough to watch my husband and stepson jump, both of them screaming at the top of their lungs. "You were so brave," I say. "Both of you."

Joshua runs a hand through his curls and smiles down at me. Down, because he's now taller than me, and I still haven't gotten used to it. "It wasn't as scary as I expected. Not when I'd actually jumped."

At fifteen, he's not yet at the age where we are terribly embarrassing to be around... but it's getting closer. Every trip we still go on where he's enthusiastic and invested is one to treasure. Tristan slings an arm around his son's shoulders. A few years more and they'll be the same height.

"Your mom would have been so proud of you," he tells Joshua. "Or angry at me, for letting you jump."

"Perhaps both?"

"Very likely," he agrees, tugging Joshua closer. "At any rate, I'm proud of you, kid."

Joshua laughs. "I'm proud of you too, Dad. Thought you'd chicken out at the last minute."

"Who, me?"

"Yes."

"I'd never," Tristan says grandly, but we're all grinning. The adrenaline of the day has pushed us all to the edge in more ways than one, here on the bridge to honor Jenny and to overcome fears.

Tristan gives Joshua's shoulders a final squeeze. "Do you want to go wait by Grandma and Julie?"

He nods, shooting me one last smile. "You can do it."

"Thanks, honey."

Tristan and I watch him walk the twenty feet or so back to where Maud is standing, our two-year-old safe and snug in her arms. Julie watches us with the rapt attention only an awed toddler possesses. We both give her a little wave, and she waves back, dark hair whipping in the wind, just like mine.

Mommy jumping too? she'd asked earlier. It had been easy then to give her a confident affirmative.

Tristan turns me away from our family, his hands steadying weights on my shoulders. "Frederica," he murmurs.

"Tristan," I murmur back.

"You don't have to do this, you know."

"I know, but I want to."

He doesn't raise a questioning eyebrow, doesn't comment. Just steadies me with the familiar gaze that promises truth, and kindness, and loyalty. "You don't struggle with elevators anymore. You can sit on a balcony without feeling anxious, and we even zip-lined in Costa Rica. I'd say you've already conquered this fear."

I shake my head. "This is the final step."

"All right. But if you're wondering... you're already the bravest person I know. By far, Freddie. You took that spot squarely when I watched you give birth to Jules. There's nothing left to prove, sweetheart. And no one will think less of you if you unsnap this harness."

"You're supposed to talk me *into* this, not out of it."

His grin flashes. "All right. I'm sorry."

I close my eyes and take a deep breath. "It'll be over so fast."

"Real fast," he says. "In the blink of an eye, really."

"And after that I'll always be the person who bungee-jumped. I can say that for the rest of my life."

"You sure can."

Behind my closed eyes, I conjure the picture that hung in Tristan's apartment. It hangs in our new home now on the ever-expanding gallery wall. Jenny strapped into a harness, smiling into the camera, standing on this very bridge. I'm doing this jump for me. For me, for my husband, for my children, and for my son's parents, who I never had a chance to get to know.

"It's one hundred percent safe," Tristan says. "You know I wouldn't have let Joshua or you jump here if it wasn't."

Yes, I do know that. He'd done extensive research before we came here, and we've rented the bridge and the bungee-jumping company for the full day. Everything has been quadruple-checked.

"You won't be strait-laced anymore if you do this."

"Give me another reason?"

His smile turns crooked. "Well, this might be your last shot at doing something like this for a while, sweetheart."

"That's right." I nod. "I want to start trying again right after this."

"We will," he vows. Both of us want to give Julie and Joshua another sibling, and once we start, this will be off-limits. If there's one thing pregnant women shouldn't do, it's bungee jump.

"Okay," I tell him.

"Okay?"

"I'm ready. I'm doing this."

He tips my head back and presses a confident, determined kiss to my lips. "You can do absolutely anything, Freddie."

He steps back and motions for the professionals. Ben and Allan hustle into action immediately. Strap me in, tightening carabiners and pulling ropes taut. Tristan is the last to tug at my checks and balances.

"It'll be over so fast," he says.

"Conquering my fear," I murmur.

We give each other a single nod of determination, because we're in this together, even if it's my turn to jump now. Since we got married, it's been the two of us, a team tackling life. Work. Joshua. Pregnancy. Birth. Julie. At every step of the way it's been us, and despite the lack of sleep and the stress of becoming a stepmother, we love each other more now than we ever did that first year. With the right person, love only gets deeper with time.

So it's with confidence that I walk toward the edge of the bridge, knowing he's got my back. The tips of my toes extend past the edge of the bridge. The Rio Grande beckons like a ribbon of light blue at the bottom, further than I'll reach.

"Whenever you're ready!" Allan calls.

I think of Joshua and Tristan, brave enough to let me into their life. Of Maud, who lost a daughter but fought her way back to a new, sunny outlook on the world.

I think of my grandfather, the hardest-working man I know, who took risks I couldn't imagine. What's jumping off a bridge compared to leaving your homeland behind?

And I think of me, daring to take that first step with Tristan all those years ago, the two of us strangers in a crowded room. What's a fear of heights compared to the fear of the unknown? And I've already conquered that with my family by my side. As scary as jumping might be, they'll be right up here when I return.

My hand slides from the railing as I let go, stepping out into the unknown, a smile on my lips.

———

Want more Tristan and Freddie?

Join my newsletter to read a 4000-word short story told from Tristan's perspective. He and Freddie are newly married, settled... and trying. For a baby, that is. Follow along.

THE STORY CONTINUES

Saved by the Boss follows Anthony Winter as he reluctantly takes control of a matchmaking company catering to the city's elite.

Love isn't for him.

But Summer Davis has yet to meet an impossible case, and she knows love can conquer all.

Including her surly new boss…

Grab **Saved by the Boss** now or read on for the first chapter!

CHAPTER 1

SUMMER

"A boss a day keeps bankruptcy away," my aunt says. She's perched on the edge of my desk with a wide smile on her face. "Isn't that what we've always said? And Anthony Winter is the biggest boss of them all!"

"Yes, but he's not signing on as a high-paying client. He's our new owner."

"No," Vivienne corrects me. *"Co-owner."*

"With a fifty-one percent stake."

"Still an important distinction." She walks to the gilded mirror in the corner of my office, one of two at Opate Match. We're small, but we deliver love to New York's elite. Started by Vivienne Davis twenty-five years ago.

Now sold by Vivienne Davis, two days ago.

And she doesn't seem the least bit concerned the venture capitalists she's sold it to will dismantle us.

I try a different route. "It's your life's work."

"Yes," she agrees, fixing her lipstick in the mirror. Rearranging her honey-wheat hair, styled into shoulder-length curls. "But we've been close to bankruptcy for years. I hate that word. After today, let's never use it again."

"We have plenty of clients."

"Not enough, Summer. You're worrying, darling, and it'll give you wrinkles if you're not careful."

I sigh. Ace lifts his golden head from the floor at the sound and flicks his ears, attuned to my moods. "I wish I could be as happy about this as you are. I know it's a good thing, it's just... well, there will be changes."

"Dear, I'm the one who should worry, not you!"

"I know, I know."

"They're not allowed to fire any employees in the first three years, I made them put that into the contract. You'll meet Mr. Winter when he drops by the office tomorrow. He's the serious, grumpy type. Definitely committed to turning our numbers around." She gives a small laugh. "In truth, I think our ability to turn a profit is the only reason he's willing to stand me."

I meet her smile with one of my own. My aunt is an excellent judge of character. "He's too good for a matchmaking company?"

"He thinks he is," she says. "We'll see about that. But I don't doubt his commitment to turning this ship right side up. We need some business savvy, Summer, and we need their capital."

I sigh. "Yeah, you're right. I look forward to meeting him tomorrow."

"Good." She puts her vintage handbag over her shoulder and gives me a winning smile. "I have to head out for lunch, or risk keeping the Walters waiting even longer. Did you hear they're celebrating their twentieth wedding anniversary this summer?"

"I did, yes. That's fantastic."

"One of my triumphs. Suzy is out of the office too, had to run some errands. You'll take a break, won't you, darling?"

"Yes, I will. Ace and I will hit the park for lunch."

"That's a good dog," she says, patting Ace's head on the way out. "How about we have lunch at Olive next week? It's been a while."

"I'd love that," I say.

"Then it's a date," she says, smiling. There's the sound of heels on hardwood and then the decisive snap of our front door closing.

I lean back in my office chair and look down at Ace. My golden retriever looks back at me.

"Opate Match," I tell him. "Sold, like a piece of furniture. To a venture capitalist."

He cocks his head like only a dog can, as if he's trying to solve a puzzle. But this is one I don't have the answer to. Opate is Vivienne's pride and joy. She's poured her sweat, blood and tears into making it work for decades.

I know the decision to take in outside investors hadn't been easy, even if we needed it. But her optimism seems unfailing.

Ace trails me as I head to the coffeemaker in the reception. Suzy's desk is abandoned and the door to my aunt's office left ajar. The three of us have tried to save this sinking ship for over a year, but competing with free dating apps, well... it hasn't been easy.

I look out the window at the sun-drenched New York street and take a sip of my freshly brewed espresso. Selling out feels like the end of an era.

The buzzer rings on our front door. I frown, heading to Suzy's desk. None of us have clients scheduled for the rest of the day.

I press down the answer button. "Opate Match, how can I help you?"

The voice is masculine and clipped. "I'm here for a meeting."

A meeting? We don't have anyone scheduled, but Suzy's made mistakes before.

"Of course," I say. "Come on in."

I hide the coffee cup behind a steel statue of Cupid and brush away some biscuit crumbs from my skirt before opening the door.

I don't recognize the man who enters. He's also tall enough that I have to tilt my head back to meet his gaze. Dark-haired and suit-clad, but so are most of the men who come seeking our matchmaking services. No hints at his profession there.

Early thirties, I'm guessing.

I extend a hand and give him my warm, professional smile. "I'm Summer Davis. It's a pleasure to meet you."

He looks at my hand a second too long before clasping it in his for a brief shake. "I'm here for a meeting with Vivienne Davis."

There's a frown on his lips, as if the prospect tastes sour on his tongue. He's one of the more reluctant clients, then.

"Yes, that's right," I say. "She delegated the meeting to me, but I'm sure we'll get off to a great start. I take it this is your first time here?"

His scowl deepens. "It is."

"Excellent. Let's get you sorted. You're welcome to step into my office, just through here... would you like a cup of coffee?"

"No."

"All righty. Just let me know if you change your mind." I close the door behind me and motion for him to have a seat. Despite the scowl, he has a good look. Not classically handsome, I'll admit. There's something too rough-hewn about his facial features for that. But he's tall and broad-shouldered, with an old-world masculine look. Not to mention he has the dark, scowling thing down pat, and there are tons of women who like that.

Yes, I think. I can work with this.

I take a seat opposite him and fold my hands together on the oak desk. "First and foremost, I'd like to thank you for coming in today. It's the first step, after all."

The stare he levels at me is unnerving. "Right."

"I'm aware of how difficult it can be to try something like this, especially if you haven't used any form of matchmaking services before. But we're complete professionals, and I promise you that our service is always first-class. We'll never pair you with someone we don't believe will be a good fit."

He leans back in his chair, hands curving around the armrests. Something flashes in his eyes. Is it amusement? This man is impossible to read, but I'll figure out his language.

"Good to know," he says.

"Not to mention we have complete client confidentiality."

"Right." His gaze travels from me to the framed images on the wall beside me. They're wedding photographs.

A real chatty Cathy, this guy.

"All successes," I tell him. Couples who meet through Opate often send their wedding photos to us, together with handwritten thank-you notes. I'd saved every one. "What made you approach Opate Match?"

He looks down at the sleeves of his suit jacket, re-adjusting them. Is he smiling? Offended? He's giving me nothing to work with, and it's not like I have access to his initial emails with Vivienne. No, I'm flying blind, but I'll have to pretend I'm not. Is he a stockbroker or an oil tycoon? Interested in men or women?

I'm walking a tightrope over here.

"What made me approach Opate Match..." he repeats, his deep voice filling my office. "Truthfully, I've never had much respect for agencies such as yours. I've long been somewhat of a... skeptic, you might say."

I nod. This is not unusual. "That's understandable when you've never been a client of one before."

"Most dating services and websites seem to be quick ways for people to find sexual partners," he says, looking straight at me, a glint in his eyes. It's clear he thinks he's offending me.

I lean back in my chair. If he thinks he'll unnerve me, he has no idea of the matches I've brokered. Three times divorced? I'll find someone perfect for them. Can't date in public for fear of the press? Bring it on.

"There are certainly some who use dating services for that end," I agree. "But Opate is not one of those services."

"Oh?"

"No. We pride ourselves on making lasting matches, ones our clients are pleased with long-term. Naturally, what people do with their free time is outside of our hands, but once we know what a client wants, we'll never set them up with someone looking for a different level of commitment."

He gives a slow nod. "And the couples on the wall there? They all wanted the same level of commitment from the beginning?"

"For the most part, yes."

"Hmm."

"You don't seem convinced," I say, adding my widest smile. "I understand that blind dating can be unusual, intimidating even, when you're not used to it."

He drums his fingers along the armrest. "You believe in this company. In what you offer."

"Of course I do," I say. "I wouldn't work here if I didn't."

"Many people work with things they dislike."

"Not me."

He gives another quiet hum and glances from me to the room around us. The hardwood floors and white walls, polished tables and expensive armchairs, filled with the elegant minimalism so common in high-end decor. "Opate Match profiles itself as a company for elite matchmaking. Matches for the rich and famous, I believe, is one of the tag lines."

"Our clientele is well-heeled, yes." I tip my head in his direction. "Like you."

When in doubt, flatter a client.

The look on his face makes me think he's fighting against rolling his eyes. "Right. Well, I understand the merits of that... but it doesn't convince me the company deals in true love."

I've had clients in my office who have cried, screamed,

cursed the person they were just on a date with for not wanting to continue. This man might be obstinate, but he's far from the most difficult case I've had. Has he been burned in the past?

"How so?"

"It's prestige dating," he says. "Trophy wives and rich men, or Upper-East-Siders who didn't have the good fortune of meeting their future spouse at an Ivy League college. They're not here for love, Ms. Davis. They're here for an arranged marriage."

My hands fall flat on the desk in front of me.

It's one thing to be accused of being a service setting up people for the sole purpose of sex. It's something else to be told I don't deal in love.

"Our clients, due to their status, have a very unique set of challenges when it comes to dating. Not all of them can walk into a bar and talk to a stranger," I say.

He inclines his head. "That can be difficult, yes. But for more people than just the so-called elite."

"You're right. A difficulty with dating isn't unique to the people who hire us," I say, smiling wide again. Whatever he might say, I'll crack him. I'll just have to work a bit harder. "But we always pre-vet clients before accepting them. The level of personal interaction between myself or Vivienne with each client means that the matchmaking is a far smoother process. There's no need to spend three weeks dating someone to later learn you're incompatible on some fundamental level."

"You've turned a messy, human process into something logical?"

"In some ways, yes. But we don't control it. We're just facilitators. The real magic happens when our clients leave this office, ready to meet with someone who's just as ready as they are to find a life partner."

He gazes back at me. "I see."

"Is it all right if I begin with some introductory questions?

Just to get to know you better and round out your client profile."

"Go ahead," he says. Still with that half-scowl, half-amused look on his face. Like he can't believe he's actually here, sitting in this chair, about to do this.

I pick up a notepad and lean back in my chair, crossing my legs. Always better to have the first meeting face-to-face, to connect with a client. The computer comes later.

"Remind me," I say, "how old are you?"

"Thirty-three."

"Terrific." I note it down. "Now, I understand your reticence about us as a company, but I assure you, you're in good hands. We'll be transparent about the entire process."

"I appreciate that."

"Are you looking for a male or female partner?"

There's a smile on his face. "I'm interested in women."

"Excellent."

"Will you praise me after each answer?"

"Only if you'd like me to." I lower the notepad. "Actually, how do you feel about praise? Is it a vital part of a relationship, or just good to have?"

"Knowing that," he says, skepticism lacing every word, "will help me find a life partner?"

"Well, it will help me learn more about what kind of person you are. How you see relationships in general. Let me ask you this instead: what's your ideal long-term relationship?"

"I'm not sure I believe in long-term relationships."

I put the notepad back on my desk. This one has been burned indeed. He should have walked in stamped with a giant red caution sticker. "And why is that?"

"True love is a fairy tale," he says. "Nothing lasts in life, and certainly not love."

There's a quick succession of knocks on my office door. I don't have the time to reply before it's opened, my elegant aunt on the other side. Her face turns into a serviceable smile as soon as she sees the two of us.

"I'm sorry to have kept you waiting," she says, breathing fast. "I'll be happy to meet with you in my office now. Summer, would you mind getting Mr. Winter and myself a cup of coffee?"

My heart stops as I look from her to the man in front of me, the one who never gave me his name. The one who didn't say a word when I made my assumptions.

He rises from his seat and buttons his suit jacket in one smooth gesture. "A pleasure meeting you, Miss Davis," he says. "It was very enlightening."

———

Read on in Saved by the Boss.

OTHER BOOKS BY OLIVIA
LISTED IN READING ORDER

New York Billionaires Series

Think Outside the Boss
Tristan and Freddie

Saved by the Boss
Anthony and Summer

Say Yes to the Boss
Victor and Cecilia

A Ticking Time Boss
Carter and Audrey

Seattle Billionaires Series

Billion Dollar Enemy
Cole and Skye

Billion Dollar Beast
Nick and Blair

Billion Dollar Catch
Ethan and Bella

Billion Dollar Fiancé
Liam and Maddie

Brothers of Paradise Series

Rogue
Lily and Hayden

Ice Cold Boss
Faye and Henry

Red Hot Rebel
Ivy and Rhys

Small Town Hero
Jamie and Parker

Standalones

Arrogant Boss
Julian and Emily

Look But Don't Touch
Grant and Ada

The Billionaire Scrooge Next Door
Adam and Holly

ABOUT OLIVIA

Olivia loves billionaire heroes despite never having met one in person. Taking matters into her own hands, she creates them on the page instead. Stern, charming, cold or brooding, so far she's never met a (fictional) billionaire she didn't like.

Her favorite things include wide-shouldered heroes, late-night conversations, too-expensive wine and romances that lift you up.

Smart and sexy romance—those are her lead themes!

Join her newsletter for updates and bonus content.
www.oliviahayle.com.
Connect with Olivia

- facebook.com/authoroliviahayle
- instagram.com/oliviahayle
- goodreads.com/oliviahayle
- amazon.com/author/oliviahayle
- bookbub.com/profile/olivia-hayle

Lightning Source UK Ltd.
Milton Keynes UK
UKHW011943170223
417143UK00006B/210